A WEDDING IN WILD HARBOR

GRACE WORTHINGTON

GET A FREE SWEET ROMCOM

The Dating Hypothesis is sweet romcom novella available free when you join Grace Worthington's newsletter at graceworthington.com

CHAPTER ONE

LIAM

L iam Henry eyed the carefully wrapped gift on the coffee table.

Please don't let it be another book on dating.

"What's the occasion?" he asked his mother hesitantly.

"No reason," she said, nudging the gift toward him.

He picked it up and slid it into his bag. "Thanks. But I really need to get on the road."

"Why don't you open it before you go?" she urged.

Lately, she'd been dropping hints about dating every time he stopped by. As much as he loved his mother, he couldn't handle her interfering in his dating life. Or in this case, his lack of one. With a careful swipe, he loosened one end of the paper and slid out a glossy book with a happy couple on the front.

"The Successful Man's Guide to Dating and Love." He nodded once. "Looks . . . *interesting.*"

He didn't want to hurt his mother's feelings, but these hints were getting out of hand. "I appreciate the thought. But my life is good without dating."

"Good, but not great," she pointed out.

"My life is great. Almost perfect, in fact. I'm even buying another property today."

"You don't need another building," she lamented. "You need a girlfriend."

"That's the last thing I need," he muttered under his breath.

Why ruin his almost perfect life with a messy relationship? He'd seen the hurt love caused before and would never take that chance again.

"Love is a distraction," he added, sliding the book into his bag. "It doesn't fit with my life right now." He'd worked hard to achieve the life he'd always wanted. He'd decorated his condo in Chicago with modern lines and gleaming surfaces, while his wardrobe consisted of immaculate designer suits, pressed and delivered to his door every Friday like clockwork.

"What kind of life do you want?"

"A perfect one," he whispered as he adjusted his stiff collar under his suit coat and kissed his mother's head before he left. "One that doesn't involve pain."

Because *almost* perfect wasn't good enough. Not for Liam Henry.

To that end, he had two principles around which he'd carefully constructed his life:

1. Avoid love.
2. Only take calculated risks.

Something—or someone—would have to shake up his life completely to change his mind. If he was the author of his own future, he'd already written the perfect ending: he would be the king of his solitary castle, collecting pawns in his own private game of chess.

Today's agenda: Finalizing his acquisition of Books Forever, a struggling store in Wild Harbor that had been hemorrhaging money ever since the online giants had scooped up their book sales. He took pride in buying another building, out to demolish all his competitors in a real-life game of Monopoly. It wasn't ruthless; it was just business as usual.

As the sun reflected off the pavement, Liam sailed down the highway in his Alfa Romeo, the sunroof open and classical music blaring. Granted, he was one of the few guys who listened to soaring violin concertos at obnoxiously loud levels. But that was what he loved about his life. He could listen to whatever he wanted. He'd been taught the great composers from his mother, who had given him his first piano lessons. From then on, the music had stuck, even if the piano playing hadn't.

"Play 'Summer' from *The Four Seasons* by Antonio Vivaldi," he instructed the AI device in his car. Even on this mostly cloudless day, there was one dark cloud in the distance, an ominous sign he tried to ignore.

"I can make it before the rain hits."

He sank his shoulder blades into the immaculate black leather seats. No one rode in this car except for his mother— and occasionally his niece when he transported her to boarding school. But he always enforced strict rules: No eating or drinking in the car. They knew that underneath, he had a soft spot for his family, even if he came across occasionally as a grumpy dictator.

As the violins soared inside the darkened shell of his car, he leaned back, the smooth leather headrest cradling his head. Instead of the usual diesel-soaked, traffic-clogged Chicago streets, the highway to Wild Harbor was a clear ribbon of dazzling pavement, the heat quivering over it like a violin string.

As the orchestra descended into a minor key, a message flashed on his phone. Only his mother ever texted him. He kept his cell phone number private, another distraction he'd lobbed onto the chopping block of his life.

Jane Henry: Please think about what I told you today. Your future is very important to me.

And so are my plans, he thought to himself, adjusting his mirrored sunglasses. He wouldn't bother replying to her constant hounding. In time, she'd see he couldn't risk his future on love. Now that he was acquiring another building, the next step was finding a lakefront property. Chicago to Wild Harbor, Michigan was an easy drive on the weekends and would give him all the time in the world to figure out what was missing in his life.

All the time and none of the distractions.

Jane Henry: And no texting while driving either! It's dangerous.

Liam flicked the message off the screen. All of life was a calculated risk, even texting while driving.

When he looked up, he realized his car had crossed the center line slightly and was careening into the oncoming lane, head-to-head with an approaching car.

He quickly jerked his vehicle back into his lane, while the oncoming driver veered away at the last second, overcorrecting toward the highway's shoulder.

He heaved a sigh of relief. *That could have been bad.*

Behind him, a squeal of tires caught his attention as he glanced in his mirror. The car that he'd almost hit head-on had lost control on the gravel shoulder, its backend fishtailing before veering off the road into a cornfield. Dust and smoke billowed into the air as the car came to rest over flattened corn stalks.

Liam slammed on his brakes, his eyes glued to the accident.

Other than a few unfortunate corn stalks, it looked like everyone was unharmed. He waited on the deserted highway, trying to calculate his risk now.

Should he go back and face an angry driver? Or get to his appointment on time? Stopping now meant that he'd be late to his meeting with a local realtor, assigned to show him available beach properties in the area.

Go back, he could hear his mother call.

He hissed through his teeth. His mother's voice was like an angel on his shoulder, a nagging do-gooder who gave him a conscience whether or not he wanted one. It was the one thing his mother had passed along, her constant reminders to do the right thing circling through his mind even when she was away.

"You win," he muttered. "But only this time."

His foot slowly released the brake pedal as he forced the car into a hard U-turn, headed toward a destiny he only hoped wouldn't ruin his day.

As he pulled near the shoulder of the road, he eyed the woman he'd run off the road. Long auburn hair fell over her shoulders, her striking face frozen in a look of intense concentration as she attempted to back her car out of the muddy field. The car tires spun helplessly as she stepped on the gas, the same way winter tires slipped in heavy snow. Liam slowly exited his car as her engine revved, splattering mud over her fender.

"Excuse me," he yelled, competing with the motor's hum.

The woman didn't notice him. The more she accelerated, the more the tires sank into the mud, creating two duplicate craters. Without realizing her predicament, she continued to throw her car in reverse and pressed the gas pedal harder, making more mud and noise than actual progress.

"Excuse me, ma'am!" he shouted, right before she attempted to rock the car backward, deepening the muddy divots.

Some farmer was going to have a fit when he saw the damage she was doing to his field.

"You're stuck!" Liam approached the car at the same moment she floored the pedal.

"That's a terrible—" he yelled as a spray of mud flew into the air and landed on the lapel of his suit coat. "Idea."

His four-figure designer suit was splattered with mud.

"Hey!" he bellowed, his temper snapping like a brittle twig.

The engine suddenly died and the driver hopped out of the car.

"I had no idea you were there!" the girl exclaimed.

Liam didn't acknowledge her; he was too busy wiping mud off with a monogrammed handkerchief. As he swiped away the dirt, the woman approached, holding a package of wet wipes.

"Did I do that?" She winced at his ruined shirt. "I'm so sorry. Nothing a wet wipe can't fix." She shoved a limp wipe his way.

He didn't want a cheap wet wipe touching his suit, not after she'd caused this mess.

"No, thank you," he said, trying to hide his irritation.

"Please, I'd like to help," she said, plucking a wad of wet wipes from the container and dabbing the arm of the jacket.

"Really, I'm fine. I'll take it to my cleaners." He stepped away and tore his gaze from his mud-splattered coat.

Until now, he'd been too immersed in his stained suit. As he glanced up, he finally observed the tall auburn-haired woman standing in front of him. Not bad looking, although certainly not *his* type. She wore a tank top with some kind of long hippie skirt, the bohemian style all the girls had worn back in college.

He'd thought it was cute back then, but that had been before he made his first million and discovered that the women he rubbed shoulders with wore Ralph Lauren instead of off-brand hippie skirts. His tastes had changed, and everything in his life was a testament to that.

"I'm really very sorry." She bit her lip, her eyes darting over his suit. "If it hadn't been for some driver who veered into my lane . . ." She shook her head, disgusted. "I can pay for your dry cleaning."

Judging by her well-worn sandals, she didn't look like she could afford the bill.

Liam shrank back. Apparently, she hadn't connected the dots between her accident and his car. When she did, she probably wouldn't look at him as a kind stranger stopping to assist a helpless driver.

"There's no need. I can take care of it." Then he crossed around to her car. "Mind if I try?"

"Be my guest," she said, tossing him the keys. "It would save me a towing bill."

He crawled into her pale-blue VW bug, scanning the interior. A garish plastic container with a gas station logo perched in her cupholder. Crumbs peppered the floor, and a giant basket of blueberries had toppled upside down, leaving tiny globes scattered across the floor like marbles. "What a nightmare," he muttered under his breath.

He glanced in the rearview mirror. She stood behind him, the sun glinting off her hair like scarlet ribbons, curling down her shoulders. The light coming off her was almost radiant, momentarily distracting him before he threw the car into reverse.

The familiar squeal from the mud-soaked tires signaled defeat. He crawled out of her tiny vehicle, stepping carefully away from the muddy divots, noticing he'd made no more progress than she had. The best he could offer was the number for a tow truck.

"You're not going to get this car out without a tow truck."

Her face sank. "Really?" She checked her watch. "That could take an hour or more, and I'm supposed to be at work by nine. I was already short on time when I left the farm. That was before I realized I left behind my wildflower bouquet. I was headed back to the farm when someone almost crashed into me."

She leaned into her car, snagging blueberries off the floor, trying to contain the mess. Why bother picking them when there were ample containers at the store?

A circular pendant dangled from her neck, swinging like a pendulum, drawing his eye to her long neck and the smooth outline of her shoulders. He averted his eyes and focused on the muddy car. Even if she wasn't his type, that didn't mean he was blind. He was a man who appreciated beauty.

"If you'd like, I'm headed into Wild Harbor. I can give you a lift."

She straightened her body and leaned her elbow on the door, considering his offer. "What if you helped me push it out?"

He shook his head and laughed. "That's impossible."

Her eyes flitted over his suit as she circled the car. "Are you worried you'll get dirty?"

"Of course not," he shot back. "I'm not trying to be Mr. Negative here, but your car is stuck, thanks to those huge mud holes."

Her lips tightened as she propped one hand on the curve of her hip. "Well, I had little choice, given that I either was going to hit someone or end up in the cornfield."

Her gaze flitted to his car, and a crease formed between her eyes. "Did you say you're headed into town?"

"Yeah, why?" he asked, suddenly feeling damp around his collar. The morning sun battered his neck, and a prickle of sweat crawled down his spine.

"Your car looks like the one that almost hit me." She crossed her arms and tilted her head, her eyes shooting daggers at him. "Are you the driver who veered into my lane?"

He pulled at his collar, trying to air out the stickiness. Cold, hard truth was always better than a flimsy excuse. "I went over the center line for a second. Nothing that should have made you crash into a cornfield. Only you were responsible for that."

Her mouth gaped for a second as indignation flashed across her face. "Are you blaming me?"

"Why, yes, I am," he said. "You lost control of your car."

He needed to remove himself from this situation as quickly as possible. For once, he'd tried to play the nice guy. The last thing he wanted was her blame.

He turned on his heel and headed toward his car. "Are you going with me or not?" he barked over his shoulder.

"Wow, are you kidding me?" An incredulous laugh sputtered from her lips. "You've got some nerve."

The gravel crunched under his feet as he turned toward her. "In case you didn't know it, that wasn't nerve. I was being nice."

She crossed her arms. "Nice would include an apology for running me off the road."

"An apology?" he gasped. If she'd been a careful driver, she could have swerved and avoided losing control, just like he had. Based on the way she screwed up her lips in response, his first instinct was to leave her standing on the shoulder. But walking away felt smarmy, the type of reaction he'd expect from some of the country club guys he occasionally golfed with. Money had made them callous. As much as this chick grated against him, he couldn't just leave her here. The angel on his shoulder applauded.

"How much money do you want?" he asked, pulling out his wallet.

She frowned. "I'm not looking for charity."

"It's for a tow truck. Let me pay, and we'll call it even." He tried to shove a couple hundred bucks at her. Money usually worked as an easy compromise.

"Just forget it." She pushed his fistful of cash back, then spun on her heel and headed toward her car as it started to rain. The single, dark cloud he'd seen earlier had descended on them.

"Why won't you accept this?" he yelled, heading after her as the rain fell faster. It was rare for someone to outright reject his money.

Ignoring his question, she climbed into the driver's seat and pulled it into reverse, the same failed method she'd tried before.

"Try pushing the car!" she instructed.

"Are you crazy? It's raining!"

"Just do it!" she yelled out the window.

He strained hard against the vehicle as her car tires kicked up more mud onto his suit pants.

Great. Of course, he didn't have any spare clothes with him. He'd fix that with his next trip.

He pounded on her window. "Let me talk to you for a second."

"No!" she yelled back and then stepped on the gas so hard that mud shot across his face.

He jumped out of the way as something in his back wrenched painfully. He blinked a few times before realizing that flecks of dirt peppered his lids. Running a hand across his face, he fought to regain control of the flaming frustration coursing through his blood. He'd had enough from this woman. His anger rose like a noxious cloud.

She lowered her window just enough that he could see her cheeks flaming. "Oops." Then she handed a cloth out the small crack of window. "Wet wipe?"

He muttered in a low voice, "I do *not* want a wet wipe here." Then he turned to go.

"*Nor there.* I do not want a wet wipe *anywhere,*" she chanted in a low, singsong voice just loud enough for him to overhear. A stifled laugh followed.

Was she turning his response into a Dr. Seuss quote?

"Are you laughing at me?" he asked, spinning around to her, even though his back was throbbing. He could take her anger, but not her mocking.

"I was trying to lighten the mood." She was clamping down

on her smile, trying to hide her amusement, the tension in her face completely gone.

He pointed at the wipes. "These are used to clean babies, not men." He plucked the wet wipe from her fingertips and started wiping his face anyway. "But I have no other options." He'd already been humiliated, and his handkerchief was completely soiled.

He crumpled the wet wipe in his fist. "I'm late for my appointment," he added, striding to his car. "Do you want a ride or not? This is my last offer."

He didn't care whether she followed him or if her car was stuck in the muddy cornfield for a week. All he wanted was to change his clothes, ice his throbbing back, and sign his papers for the new building. In other words, return to his tidy life, one that did not involve Dr. Seuss quotes or wet wipes.

"Wait!" she yelled, grabbing a few things out of her car. "I call shotgun!"

He stood at the door, one hand propped on the shiny handle. "But you're my only passenger."

Even though it was still raining, she paused on the opposite side, a mischievous curl forming at the edge of her lips. "I thought about asking to drive, but I figured, given my driving record today, you wouldn't let me."

His eyes flitted over the oversized plastic cup in her hand.

"Precisely," he said as he clicked open the door. "Now get in."

CHAPTER TWO

"What brings you to Wild Harbor this morning?" Cassidy asked. Ever since she'd climbed in with her Big Gulp cup, the tension between them was like a taut violin string.

"Business," he stated flatly. His eyes remained glued to the road, like he'd turned into Mr. Safety now that he'd sent her careening into a cornfield.

Judging by the interior of his car, this man was a freak of nature. Every square inch of the vehicle gleamed, and his floor mats didn't show a single speck of dirt—until she arrived with her mud-drenched shoes. Even Martha Stewart couldn't compete with this guy's obsession with perfection.

As he sped down the highway, he kept giving her a side eye every time she sipped her orange soda. *What's wrong with orange soda?*

"You're in business how?" Her voice fluttered. Getting a response from this guy was worse than dealing with customer complaints.

"Property development," he said. Perhaps he thought she wasn't smart enough to follow a conversation about business, but given how rude he'd been to her earlier, she couldn't rule out that he was just a snob.

She sipped her fizzy drink while he gave her another annoyed side eye. "I don't allow food or drinks in the car. Especially orange ones."

What am I, seven?

"Oh, sorry." She rammed her enormous cup into his center holder. "Luckily, I just finished it." A fancy thermal travel mug sat in the other cup holder. "No drinks in the car, huh?"

He pulled his gaze away from the road to see what she was talking about. "Except for my morning coffee."

"Oh, interesting," she said, turning to peer out the window. "Do as I say, not as I do."

He would be the type.

"If you think I'm acting inconsistently, then you are wrong," he said firmly, without taking his eyes off the road. "I always use this special cup with a locking lid. Expensive, but guaranteed not to leak. Whereas those cups"—he nodded toward her monstrous container—"are notorious for faulty lids."

What kind of guy talked down to women like they were toddlers with leaky sippy cups? Apparently, the same jerks who drove you off the road. No wonder he was a bachelor—at least she assumed so, given that his left ring finger was bare. No woman in her right mind would date a guy who barked orders at her.

She noticed he still had flecks of mud sprinkled across his hairline, and a half-laugh escaped her lips.

"What's so funny?" he asked, frowning.

"Nothing," she said, clamping her mouth shut. She didn't need to give him another reason not to like her.

"Something made you laugh."

She quickly changed the subject. "Don't you think it's odd

that I'm letting you drive me into town and I don't even know your name? You could be a murderer."

He wasn't amused by her statement. "I'm *not* a murderer," he replied in that emotionless tone again. "I'm Liam." He sounded like a belligerent kid forced to stand in front of his classmates and introduce himself against his will.

"Don't be so enthusiastic, Liam," she said. "It might make you more fun."

"What was wrong with it?" he asked, deep creases forming between his brows.

He seemed to miss her sarcasm, like those artificial intelligence devices that could understand words, but not context. Her sunny disposition usually cracked open even the grumpiest souls, but not today.

"How many people introduce themselves as *not a murderer?*" she said. "It's a first for me."

"How many people have asked me that? It's a first for me, too."

"Asking you for a ride or if you're a murderer?" she countered with a smirk.

She'd meant it as a joke, but he considered the answer.

"I can't remember the last time I picked up a stranger."

He made it sound as if she were a stray cat with fleas that he'd found on the side of the highway.

"Well, I wouldn't be needing a ride except—"

"You lost control," he finished for her, his knuckles tightening over the steering wheel.

"What was I supposed to do? Let you hit me?"

"A quick adjustment and I was back in my lane. Unlike you."

She gave him a dirty look.

He pointed at the fancy dashboard in front of him. "This vehicle has incredible safety features. Do you want to know what they are?"

She shook her head. All she knew was that when a car was veering toward her, getting out of the way was priority.

"Trust the vehicle," he repeated, like it was an obvious safety lesson.

"Even cars like this get into accidents," she replied, feeling discomfort crawling up her spine. "We can never eliminate driver error."

"It can be with me."

She shifted her body toward him. "You're seriously saying you don't make mistakes?"

"Not in this car. Its job is to keep me from having an accident. It's part of the reason I always buy new."

Guys who were this self-assured had the same effect on her as nails screeching down a chalkboard. She wished she had called an Uber.

"If it's so safe, do you trust me to drive?"

"You?" His eyes flicked her way before they shifted back to the road.

"If your car is so advanced, you don't need to worry about my driving. Trust the vehicle, right?"

He'd never guess her superpower was hiding her feelings under pressure. This was her test for him. If he really believed his car was safe, it wouldn't concern him to hand over the keys.

He slowed to a stop on the shoulder, his eyes darting nervously between her and the steering wheel. "Ever since I tried to push your car out of that stupid field, my back has been screaming in pain. I'll let you drive, but under two conditions." He looked like he was handing his newborn baby over to a stranger. "Even though it stopped raining, you still have to drive safely. And *slowly*."

"Okay, boss." She hopped out. "Whatever you say."

"In case you missed it before, my name's Liam," he said. "Not *boss*." He climbed into the passenger seat, and she could have sworn he let out a low groan. It took some effort to offer her his *precious,* like Gollum's ring. He wiped his hands on his lap before folding them awkwardly between his legs. A fleck of sweat formed on his brow. "Do you want me to show you where everything is?"

She slid her hands across the steering wheel as if she were stroking silk. "Don't worry, I'll figure it out," she said lurching ahead, a trail of mud spraying behind them

His head whipped back as the car bumped onto the pavement.

"Now let's see what this baby can do," she said, glancing at the speedometer.

"Excuse me?" His voice pitched higher.

She pressed the gas pedal and the car smoothly accelerated. *Forty-five, fifty, fifty-five, sixty . . .*

"Good acceleration. Tight steering. Not a bad ride." She glanced at him. "You're not nervous, are you?" she teased.

"No, not at all," he said, trying to act unruffled. Judging by the way his hands had curled into fists, she knew he was faking.

"You didn't tell me your name," he said, attempting to change the subject.

"Cassidy Woods."

She sensed Liam was asking out of obligation rather than friendliness, afraid she'd wreck his car otherwise. This was his version of trying not to provoke her while she was in control of his baby.

"You live in Wild Harbor?" he asked.

"My entire life." When a gentle curve approached, she didn't slow down. The car sailed around it effortlessly. She'd never admit it, but driving this was like the first bite of ice cream on a hot summer day. *Addictive.*

"Family here?" he asked, eyes still glued to the road, his right hand tightening around the door grip.

She could tell he was trying. Maybe her subtext had finally gotten through to his thick robot skull after all.

"Two sisters and a brother. My parents live on the lake next to my sister."

He lifted his eyebrows. "Any chance they're selling?"

"They'll never sell. It was my parents' dream to live there. Why? Are you looking?"

"I might be. I'm meeting with a realtor in Wild Harbor today. A two-bedroom home with beach access. Someplace where there are no crowds, and preferably no neighbors."

"So a property on Mars?" The last thing their small town needed was a rich grump who swore off people. "You're almost guaranteed not to meet anyone there."

His mouth screwed up into that *I refuse to respond to your humor* look. "I'm an introvert. And my mother needs her privacy."

"Your mother?" Cassidy raised her eyebrows. She'd thought he was the type who would never acknowledge his mother because he was an android assembled in a highly evolved factory. If he was looking for shock value, this was the trick he'd saved to measure her reaction.

"You sound surprised," he said.

"I am surprised. I thought you were looking for a bachelor's weekend getaway."

"Most of the time," he stated. "But I need a place she can use. And she doesn't bring drinks in my car either."

Cassidy rolled her eyes. Here she thought he had a heart under that designer suit. If he wasn't so good looking, she'd secretly call him the Grinch.

"Good luck finding your dream house," she said, slowing her speed as they entered the town. "I'll park here and walk the rest of the way."

"I don't mind if you want to drive to your work. No reason to walk." He eyed her scuffed sandals, an old pair that were well loved and well worn. A far cry from the type of sandals he was used to expecting on women.

"I want to," she insisted, adjusting her non-driving foot under her skirt so he wouldn't notice the half-broken strap she'd taped on.

As soon as she pulled onto Main Street, people openly gawked at Liam's car. There were a few wealthy estates in Wild Harbor, but most were normal families with occasional crumbs on the floor. Cars like his attracted attention in a way that made her uncomfortable.

"Now that the rain has stopped, it's a beautiful day for a stroll," she offered as an excuse. The last thing she needed was rumors flying around about her and a mysterious stranger in an Alfa Romeo.

"Park here," he said, pointing to a spot marked *no parking.*

"You can't park here."

"You're not staying," he said. Apparently, where Liam Henry was concerned, rules were for other people.

"As soon as you leave, I'm out of here. And I'm not worried about parking tickets."

"Thanks for the ride," she said, looking at him one last time before he left.

"You're the one who drove." His gaze settled on her for a few seconds too long as one corner of his mouth curved, hinting at a smile.

The grump had a sense of humor after all.

"For once, you're right," she said and something flamed in his eyes.

Liam Henry enjoyed being right. Her words lit something behind his dark lashes.

She needed to leave before they got a ticket or he turned back into the Grinch, whichever came first.

"One more thing," he said, climbing back into the driver's seat and lowering the window. He slid on his spotless aviator sunglasses that had probably cost more than her entire outfit combined.

18

This was it—the apology she'd wanted, finally showing some remorse for the way he'd driven her off the road. Maybe he wasn't such a grump after all.

He snatched her Big Gulp cup from the holder and held it out to her. "Do you mind throwing this away?"

She paused, her hopes collapsing like a tower of blocks. "Whatever you say, *boss.*" She knew he hated the nickname.

"You won't give it up, will you?" he replied, offering her an undeterred grin that only irritated her more.

"Nope," she chirped as she grabbed the cup and tossed it toward a public trash can. Despite its size, the plastic cup sailed into the trash like the final shot in a basketball final.

Liam raised his brows. "Lucky shot," he muttered, pulling away from the curb, his aviators flashing in the sun.

"Or not," she countered.

After the day she'd had, she could use some luck.

CHAPTER THREE

LIAM

EARLIER THAT DAY

"It's only a quick trip to Wild Harbor." Liam kissed his mother on the forehead as she lay on a chaise lounge in her three-season room. She wasn't looking well today. Her face had taken on a grayish pallor, the same color of faded newspaper, the direct result of her cancer treatments.

"It's a surprise," he admitted, kneeling by her chair. "And I can't tell you yet. It's the reason why I need to run to Wild Harbor."

"Oh, I hate when you say you have a secret." She leaned her head back on the chaise languidly, but there was still a spark in her eyes.

Even though she'd been fighting cancer for a year, she still fixed her hair and put on a hint of makeup. Even without it, nothing could diminish her beauty, not even cancer.

"Until it's finalized, I don't want to get your hopes up. But I think the news will please you."

Once the deal was settled, he would share the news, then they could celebrate. She could dream about weekends on the lake, the wind in her hair, the sun flushing life into her cheeks. Right now, too much was still uncertain.

His mother shrugged and sipped her iced tea. "You work too much, Liam. I hardly see you."

Liam tightened his grip around the chair back in front of him. "I do my best."

He was attempting to be a dutiful son, caring for his widowed mother. It was the best he could do.

He stepped into the kitchen and finished spreading some chicken salad on a croissant. He wanted to make sure she ate something while he was gone, even if the chemo dulled her appetite.

With some effort, she slowly rose from the chaise. "I didn't mean it the way it came out. I'm worried about you. But if you barely have time to see me, how in the world are you ever going to meet someone?"

So *that* was on her mind again. No matter how hard he tried to convince her, she didn't understand that he wasn't interested in love right now.

"I'm not worried about meeting anyone," he reminded her. "I'm worried about taking care of *you*." He gave his mother a pointed look as he set her sandwich in the fridge. If her appetite was the same as yesterday, he'd find it untouched when he arrived home.

"As your mother, I'm worried about you." Jane pulled out her cell phone with a sheepish grin. "My friend told me that all the eligible bachelors are on this app." She touched her screen and then turned the phone.

Liam's picture was framed in a circular profile with a brief description underneath.

"What is that, Mom?" he asked, taking the phone from her hands.

He read the caption: *Successful businessman who likes lists and organization, as well as long walks on the beach. Searching for a serious relationship with a beautiful woman.*

His stomach clenched as he glanced at his mom, who wore a tiny, mischievous smirk.

"Long walks on the beach? Since when do I like that?" He couldn't believe his mother would write such a ridiculous caption.

"You need a romantic byline. Something that makes you intriguing."

"Is this a dating app?"

"I know you're opposed to the idea," she argued.

"I'm not just opposed, I said I'd *never* go on one of those apps. An enormous waste of time. I don't want to date desperate women."

"But that's the thing," his mother said. "You don't have time to date anyone. This would simplify that process. You'd have choices. No time wasted on girls who don't meet your *high standards.*"

The way she said it was like nails down a chalkboard. She knew he had his list of what he wanted in a woman. Even though she'd laughed at it, calling his standards unrealistic, he still kept it tucked away in his desk drawer.

"Absolutely not. This profile needs to be deleted."

"See this girl." She held out the phone so he couldn't look away. "She looks nice and even sent a message with a kissing emoji."

Liam rolled his eyes. "No."

"Just take one look." Jane shoved the phone in his face.

He skimmed the profile of a girl whose picture appeared to be on a cruise ship.

"So you want me to choose a girl who looks good in a bikini?

Is that the type of girl I should bring home?" Even he was shocked that his mother would stoop so low.

"Not necessarily. But you actually have lots of interest. As weird as it seems, I feel proud that so many women want to date you."

"You realize that people don't post *actual* pictures. They use filtered photos that don't even look like them. It's like blindly throwing darts at a target."

"But you have options," Jane persisted. "So many women have swiped on your picture."

His mother pulled up a page with dozens of profile pictures.

"Does it seem odd that you're the one pushing me to do this? Shouldn't it be the other way around?" He knew his mother wanted him to find someone to marry, but he'd never guess that she'd create a dating profile behind his back.

"Liam, I might be from a different generation, but this is how people meet each other these days. I want you to find happiness, the way I had it with your dad."

"Not this way," he told her. If he was going to meet someone —and he wasn't planning on it right now—then he'd have to vet her first. Make sure she met his standards. Call him old-fashioned, but he didn't want to find a wife on a dating app. To be honest, he didn't even *want* a wife right now. Dating took a huge amount of time, and he was too busy caring for his mom to think about the complexities of a relationship.

Jane sat down on a barstool, suddenly weary. "Like it or not, I won't always be here for you."

"Don't say that. You're going to beat this. You're a Henry, and the Henrys always win." He kissed his mother's forehead. It still smelled like the cold cream she put on every evening before bed.

"Your father had the same outlook, and he's been gone three years." Jane squeezed her son's hand. "I don't know how I'm going to convince you."

"You're not, Mom. Nobody is. Remember my life principles?" He grabbed an apple and tossed it in the air, catching it in his other hand. As much as he wanted to please his mom, her goal to play matchmaker was becoming a wedge in their relationship. In his current state, he had everything he wanted in life. A successful business, satisfying hobbies, and a wonderful mother. What more did he need?

Definitely not the complications of a relationship.

As he opened the door, Jane reached out and stopped him. "Promise me you'll be open to the idea of dating. I want you to find someone who will make you as happy as your father made me. This is my last wish for you before I'm gone." Jane gripped his arm. "I'm concerned that you'll end up—"

"Alone?" He filled in the blank before she could finish. "Mom, I don't mind being alone."

Her face soured. "That's what I'm afraid of. You'll end up a grumpy old bachelor who yells at the neighbor children to stay off his property."

Liam smiled. "What's so wrong with that?"

"You're just like your father. He was a bit of a grump until we met. But I saw something under that tough exterior that other girls didn't. Love changed him. Getting married, becoming a dad—all that softened him. Before he died, he told me being a father was his proudest achievement. If we hadn't met, I'm afraid he would have become a much different person."

"Are you saying I'm an old grump?"

She smiled. "Not old. But a grump? Sometimes."

"Then it's a good thing I'm not dating anyone." He gave her a kiss on the forehead as he walked toward his car.

"But that's why you need a date."

"Not today, Mother," he called over his shoulder as he climbed into his Alfa Romeo.

A relationship would be a disruption to his life. A distraction. Messy and complicated.

"Just think about it. For me?" she asked.

"Mother, *please,*" he said in that tone, reminding her he'd had enough. "Today, I have enough on my plate." He slammed his door.

As his mother's figure faded in his rearview mirror, he wrestled with a nagging feeling of guilt.

This is my last wish for you.

He wanted his mother to be at peace about his future and hers. So why did she have to place a final request on him, something he didn't even want for himself?

His predictable life couldn't coexist with his mother's wishes. He liked his clean car and his neatly pressed suits, his polished shoes and perfectly manicured yard.

If there was one thing Liam Henry didn't like, it was change. Because change was risky. A gamble, at best. Most of the time, the odds were against you.

The only person he needed to convince of this was his mother. Underneath, she could be just as persistently stubborn as him. But this time, she needed to see the truth.

Liam Henry turned on his classical music and sped down the highway.

Today was not the day to take a risk on love.

CHAPTER FOUR

CASSIDY

C assidy stood in the window of the bookshop, carefully arranging books on a white bookshelf. It was August now, and soon the hordes of tourists would be gone, the familiar foot traffic wiped out with the first crisp chill of fall.

They'd still have the faithful locals who frequented Books Forever. Thelma and Edna, an inseparable pair of older ladies, were some of their most loyal buyers, attending her monthly book club meetings whether or not they'd read the book. The ladies were an eccentric pair of chatty grannies, reminiscing more than they stayed on topic, but Cassidy loved their candor and the way they'd bring chocolates because *every meeting needs snacks.*

It was the reason she loved working at Books Forever. Even if the summer was chaotic, the fall always promised a languid pace, locals dropping by on their lunch hour or on a rainy afternoon, searching for some inspiration. Cassidy understood it. She found her respite in books, especially as a child when she'd carried the weight of a diagnosis that she wanted to keep secret.

Epilepsy was like a scarlet letter that branded her as broken. When she was eight, she'd made a mistake in telling a neighbor boy who ran up to her at recess the next week and started convulsing and shaking before breaking into peals of laughter. After that, she avoided him at all costs, visiting the bookstore after school instead of joining the pack of neighbor kids who roamed from one backyard to the next. The bookstore was the only place she was whole, and she'd become a bookish soul who escaped in the pages of a novel.

Even though her seizures were under control with medication now, that snapshot still haunted her and became the driving force behind her bookstore program for kids who needed reading help or—like her—an escape from their real or imaginary bullies.

Just then, Mrs. Pomfrey entered the shop, and Cassidy's dog, Daisy, bounded over to greet her, mouth open, tongue lolling, paws flailing, a look of pure joy in every fiber of her body. Daisy was their store mascot and official greeter, and Ellen Pomfrey spoiled her like she was her own.

Ellen hunched down, her voice switching into that singsong voice people used for puppies and babies. "You're always so happy to see me," Ellen cooed, giving the golden retriever a brief scratch behind the ears. "Probably even more than my husband."

"I'm sure your husband is glad to see you too. He just doesn't lick your face to show it," Cassidy added.

"*Thankfully,*" Ellen said.

Even though a few residents thought it odd that they had a bookstore dog, the Pomfreys never bended to public opinion. Ellen and Arnold were close to retirement, and Cassidy sensed the slow tearing away from the store they'd built, as if they were mentally preparing themselves for life after the bookshop.

Arnold had opened the store twenty-five years ago, when the sleepy beach town was just being discovered by Chicago residents looking for a quick weekend getaway.

Back then, they hadn't known that online booksellers would take over in the future. But they persisted through the years, and somehow made a life from selling people books that, according to Ellen, helped them escape the monotony of life.

"Did the new shipment of Jodi Picoult books arrive?" Mrs. Pomfrey asked, adjusting her brown bob behind her ears.

Cass shook her head. "Shipping issues. Again."

"Three buyers told Arnold that if it's not here in a week, they're ordering it from somewhere else. No wonder he stopped at the donut shop this morning." It was no secret that Arnold Pomfrey craved sweets like an addiction, but his wife had been pushing salads at him ever since he'd received a poor health report from the doctor.

"I thought his doctor banned him from donuts," Cassidy added, sliding a book with an idyllic ocean scene onto the shelf.

"He's been under a bit of stress with the store finances," Ellen added, waving her hand in the air. "Not sleeping again."

The store had been underperforming for years, which was a nice way of saying losing money like water through a sieve. Although the Pomfreys had dedicated their lives to it, Ellen and Arnold had dropped hints that they were ready to have more freedom. For decades they'd worked weekends, especially during the summers when the weather was as luscious as hot peach pie and the tourists sagged into the store with weary but hopeful faces, searching for a respite from the heat and their lives.

"My offer still stands," Cass reminded her. "Let me work weekends. Take some time off."

Ellen clucked her tongue. "Arnold won't pull himself away until he's sold the place."

Cassidy dragged her finger along the spine of a book, her dream shimmering like the gold-flecked letters lining the book's edge. She'd held the tiny spark of a dream in her fingertips for so long, too many nights spent imagining what she'd do with the bookstore if it were hers. But the harsh reality loomed in front of her like Kilimanjaro. Ever since her dad's stroke, her parents couldn't support her. She was still trying to finish her college degree while saddled with student loans, rent, and car payments. After that, there was no money left to put down on a bookstore, and no bank in their right mind would loan her the cash.

Just like with her epilepsy, she was too much of a liability. Even her ex-boyfriend had told her that when he'd broken their engagement. *It's a risk,* he'd said. *One I can't take.*

Except this time, it was her lack of money. If only she could talk the Pomfreys into waiting a few years, maybe then she'd have a tiny down payment, enough to secure some loans.

"There's something I've been meaning to talk to you about." Mrs. Pomfrey's worried tone sliced through the long pause like a dull knife. "You'll finish college after this semester, and I'm sure you'll want to find a job that pays better."

"I'm not planning on leaving, unless you're kicking me out," she assured Ellen. "I'm hoping to expand the after-school program for kids and bring in more customers that way." The truth was, she loved working at Books Forever, and it didn't matter how little the Pomfreys paid her, she'd probably toil here for free. The feel of the books in her hands as she stroked the smooth cover, that sensation of cracking open the spine for the first time, the fresh scent of newly printed paper without a single bent edge. But most of all, it was the satisfaction of helping people find books that sparked delight—that gave her a joy beyond words. The right story could make your problems evaporate like rain on a sunny sidewalk.

Just then, Arnold came rushing into the store, greeting Cassidy with his usual, "Good morning, darling."

Calling his female customers *darling* endeared him to the silver-haired ladies and gave everyone the false impression that he didn't have a care in the world. *Darling* was the word utterly happy men used. But behind closed doors, he ran his hands through his hair, fretting about monthly finances while his wife shrugged and said, "Maybe next month will be better."

But next month was never better. It was often worse.

"What do you think of the display case?" Cassidy asked, sweeping her hand toward the window display.

"Marvelous, as always," he praised before joining his wife at the checkout counter. Ellen's gaze skated over to her husband, and their eyes met for a second, a flicker of understanding between them.

He cleared his throat. "Do you have a minute?" Arnold asked, his face growing serious.

"Sure. What is it?" Cassidy carried a stack of books toward the counter.

Arnold sifted through an avalanche of papers, like he'd lost something important.

"Shouldn't we wait until the papers have been signed?" Ellen whispered.

"What papers?" Cassidy asked, suddenly overwhelmed with the sensation right before a wave pummels you.

"Our mantra has always been *no secrets*," Arnold said, his voice quavering like the pluck of a single guitar string. "And you should be the first to know." He swallowed hard, and his Adam's apple bobbed in his throat. "We're selling this place."

Cassidy's vision shrank to black, only spots remaining behind a falling curtain of dreams. This conversation wasn't supposed to happen yet. They couldn't retire and leave Books Forever in a stranger's hands. Only she could keep the heart of this place beating, knowing the customers and their book preferences, memorizing every child's name so she could introduce them to her favorite authors, making magic in the children's section with her twinkly lights and plush beanbags.

"Oh," she said so quietly she could barely hear her voice. "Did you put it on the market?" Maybe there was hope she could change their mind, postpone the inevitable death of another small-town brick-and-mortar store.

"It's not on the market," Ellen corrected. "A company stepped forward and made us an offer on the building we couldn't refuse. We were already thinking that we'd like to retire, and with Arnold's high blood pressure, it just made sense. We are losing money hand over fist. If we wait a few more years, who knows what will happen to Arnold's health? We can't afford to lose any more of our retirement funds."

Ellen's face sagged with the admission.

"You've been using your retirement funds on the store?" Cassidy almost dropped the books she was holding.

"Don't worry about us, darling," Arnold assured her, relieved that the truth was finally out. "They gave us more than we'd planned to sell it for."

"Who bought it?" Cassidy asked.

"An out-of-town development company," Arnold explained. "They're undecided about what they will use it for next."

"They won't keep Books Forever open?" Cassidy's chest heaved, the weight of loss forming hairline cracks inside her rib cage.

"We don't actually know." Arnold looked at his wife for help. "Someone is coming to analyze our records from the last few years. We're hoping the charm of the place will sway them to keep it open."

If the financial losses didn't make up their mind right then.

Cassidy's stomach twisted. If there was one thing she feared, it was that someone would close her beloved bookstore forever.

"Wow, this is huge." Cassidy forced a smile. "Congratulations, I guess. You know how much I love this place." Cassidy turned away, stacking more books on shelves, tamping down all her emotions into a tiny box.

Arnold circled the counter and wrapped one arm around her shoulder.

"I know you love this bookstore as much as we do. But the writing is on the wall. All the small bookstores are closing down. They can't compete. Despite its name, Books Forever can't really last forever."

Cassidy focused on the books, avoiding Arnold's gaze.

What would she do if she couldn't work here? Her future was a long stretch of endless ocean. She'd treaded water for so long, only now realizing the life raft she'd banked on was only a mirage.

"Could I meet one of the company reps?" Cassidy asked. "Show him how much potential this place has?"

"Most certainly," Ellen responded. "We want them to meet you, since you're as qualified as us to run this place."

Arnold squeezed her shoulder. "Once they see how much everyone loves you, they'll find you a place."

Arnold's faith bolstered her spirits now, but for how long? He'd known her since she was a girl camping out in the children's section in midwinter, her gloved hands struggling to turn the pages.

Arnold grabbed a few dollars from his pocket. "Why don't you head to the coffee shop and get yourself one of those drinks you like? Matcha something?" Arnold still couldn't pronounce *latte* right despite Cassidy's desperate attempts to correct him. He always pronounced it *late,* and Cassidy had given up reminding him.

"I have money. You pay me to work here, remember?"

He smiled. "Today, the drinks are on me." He closed her fingers around the money and led her to the door. He was in a strange mood, slightly elated, but also a little pushy, like he wanted her to leave. "Pick up some stamps and packing tape from the post office too. Perhaps a few boxes? No rush. If you think of anything else, take all the time you need."

As she headed toward The French Press coffee shop, she noticed Liam's black Alfa Romeo across the street. Next to all the family sedans and dusty pickups, it might as well have a neon sign over it.

Just then, Liam exited the realtor's office, pulling his sunglasses from his pocket, his gaze sweeping the street. Cassidy quickly turned her back, pretending not to see him, and hurried toward the shop.

She didn't want to run into Liam Henry right now. He would ask about her car, and she'd have to admit they'd declined her debit card. *Twice.*

"Hey!" Liam called out.

Pretend you don't hear him. With her gaze glued to the coffee shop, she quickened her stride.

A shrill whistle pierced her ears. "Excuse me!" Liam bellowed. He'd not only followed her, but was now whistling to her like a dog.

She could make up an excuse. *I'm so busy! So much on my mind!* She rushed forward, grabbing the handle, her escape to freedom at her fingertips.

Suddenly, a hand reached over her shoulder and pushed the door shut.

She spun around. His body was so close to hers, she could see the peppered stubble on his jaw.

"So we meet again," she muttered. Why did he have the worst timing?

Liam pulled down his sunglasses and peered over the frames. "Didn't you hear me whistle?"

"Didn't you know it's rude to whistle at a woman?"

He hung back. "I thought you couldn't hear me."

She shook her head. "Wrong answer. You could have used my name."

"You could have acknowledged me."

If she'd left a few minutes earlier, they would have missed each other. It was just her luck that they'd crossed paths at the same time, like those rom-com movies where the romantic leads keep running into each other no matter how hard they try not to.

"Unless . . ." He yanked off his sunglasses, running the end of the earpiece across his lips. It disarmed her in the worst way. "You were avoiding me."

She wouldn't give him the satisfaction of the correct answer.

"No one can avoid you in that car." She tipped her chin toward his vehicle.

It was a jab, but Liam's mouth quirked like he was pleased.

"How was your meeting with the realtor?" she asked.

"No luck. If you hear of any beach houses on the market, could you let me know?"

"Preferably one involving zero interactions with humans?" she asked. "I'm sure your realtor will know before I do. Now, if you'll excuse me, I need a drink." She spun on her heel and let the rush of air-conditioning slam into her as she entered the coffee shop.

She didn't bother looking back, but she could feel his gaze as she stood at the counter, staring at the carefully drawn chalkboard menu.

"Matcha latte," she told Max, the barista who owned the shop.

"Who was that?" Max glanced at the stranger over her shoulder.

Cassidy shrugged. "Some guy from Chicago looking for a beach house."

"Another one?" Max said. "How do you know him?"

"You won't believe this, but we almost had a collision on the highway. I'm okay, but my car's stuck in a cornfield. He drove me into town."

He raised his eyebrows. "I take it you two hit it off, then?"

"Hardly," she snort-laughed, playing with the ragged cuticle on her nail, a nasty habit she'd tried repeatedly to break.

Max kept a straight face as he assembled her drink, part

barista, part informal counselor, never offering more advice than needed.

"I have a strange feeling I can't shake," she said, looking wistfully out the window. Liam was gone, but his car remained in the same spot.

"A bad feeling?" Max slid her drink across the counter.

"Not *bad*. I feel like I've seen him before, but I don't know where."

"Maybe he looks like someone you know."

"Right." She nodded, wishing she could stamp out that weird feeling of déjà vu, like a rogue spark from a sparkler.

She sipped the frothy tea as she continued out the door, her mind spinning across the index of people in her mind, a blur of faces that didn't resemble anyone like Liam.

After heading to the post office, she made her way to the bookstore and noticed someone had taped a handwritten *Temporarily Closed* sign to it.

She pushed on the door, but it wouldn't budge. *Locked.* Arnold and Ellen hadn't mentioned anything about shutting down early. She glanced at her phone for a message before knocking on the door.

Suddenly, Ellen's face appeared in the window, a brief flash of unease drifting across her features.

The lock clicked open. "What are you doing back so soon?" Ellen stood in the doorway, blocking Cassidy from entering.

"What's going on? Why did you close the door?"

"Oh." Ellen fingered the collar of her shirt and glanced over her shoulder. "A visitor stopped by. We shut down the store while we are meeting with him."

That was odd. They'd never closed the store for a visitor before. In the background, Daisy mournfully peered from her kennel, which they only used with dog-averse customers.

"I'll stay out of the way," Cassidy said. "I can shelve new inventory while the store is closed."

Ellen didn't move, her body blocking the entrance, but her jaw twitched, as if she were wrestling with some inner conflict.

Arnold appeared at her shoulder. "It's okay to let her in." He gently pulled his wife back. "He said he's eager to meet our only employee."

As Cassidy stepped inside, she suddenly felt like a stranger in her own store.

"The buyer came by today," Arnold explained, looking sorry. "He asked us to close the store, and since you were gone, we locked up."

Cassidy looked around. "Is the buyer here now?"

Before Arnold could answer, a man entered from the back room. Even from across the stacks of books, Cassidy recognized the immaculate (though now mud-spattered) suit, chiseled jaw, and piercing blue eyes. *Liam Henry.*

He'd mentioned buying businesses, but it never occurred that it would be *her* business.

"What are you doing here?" Liam asked, a familiar frown settling into his brow.

"I could ask you the same thing," she said, matching his expression.

"I'm the new owner of this building," he said as if it were obvious. "You're not the . . ." The answer dawned on him before she could respond.

"This is Cassidy Woods," Ellen interrupted, her voice pitching higher with tension. "Have you met before?"

"Yes," they blurted out together, facing off from across the room like two people caught in a surprise duel.

"Under different circumstances," Liam added. "Her car was stuck."

"He almost ran me off the road," she countered.

"I didn't run you off. You *swerved,* then lost control," he corrected.

"Oh, dear," Ellen said, biting her lip and turning to her husband. "We didn't imagine you'd meet beforehand."

"By accident," Liam said.

"No pun intended," Cassidy added.

She turned to the Pomfreys, the slow tide of anxiety rising inside her. "Is this a done deal?"

Ellen glanced at her husband, who slowly nodded.

"I see," she said, overwhelming emotions swelling and crashing beneath her calm exterior. She wasn't sure whether she felt angry or sad, and like most things, discovered anger and sadness felt much the same, nearly indistinguishable when dumped into a soupy mix.

"But I thought a property development company was buying it," she said.

"It is," Liam responded succinctly. "Mine."

He stepped toward her with the same confident swagger. Maybe he didn't realize the effect he was having on her, but the smirk on his face demanded attention, simultaneously driving her mad and piquing her interest.

She closed her emotions like the swipe of a blind. "You're kidding, right?"

"Do I look like I'm kidding?" He didn't look amused. She wasn't sure there was one funny bone in that man's body. "The question is why do *you* care so much?"

"Because I work at Books Forever."

"Worked," he corrected, his eyes sliding over the shelves of books. "I'm considering a new business. That's not to say I won't rehire you. I just don't make promises I can't keep."

The air drained from her lungs, and she could barely squeak out a response. "Wait. Are you closing Books Forever?"

"I haven't finalized my plans yet. I'm looking over the Pomfreys' financial records now. If you'll excuse me . . ." He returned to the office in the back storeroom while she turned to Ellen and Arnold.

Ellen fidgeted nervously with an endcap display while Arnold's shoulders slumped in defeat. Although they felt like they had no choice, this wasn't what they'd wanted for Books Forever either.

Turning to Ellen, Cassidy lowered her voice so Liam couldn't hear. "You don't have to go through with this. If this isn't what you want, you still have time."

Ellen avoided Cassidy's glare, tidying books instead. "Please don't make this harder than it already is."

"It's never too late," she pleaded. "We can find a way."

"Cassidy." Arnold said it like a long sigh.

She turned toward him. "I can work more. Drop out of college for a semester and come up with plans to boost the store. I've been wanting to ramp up the after-school reading program. It doesn't have to end this way."

"I'm not letting you drop out your last semester," Arnold responded. "And the after-school program is the only thing that's doing well right now. It would take a massive influx of money to prop up this sinking ship, and we don't have it." He shook his head sadly. "We've been considering this for years. We don't have the fight in us that we used to."

She didn't care if Liam heard what she had to say. This was worth the risk. Everything good was worth fighting for. "Why not sell it to someone local? Someone who wants to keep it like it is."

"Who's going to buy a bookshop that isn't making money?" he asked as if he already knew the answer.

"Me," she blurted out. No *just kidding* or *I didn't mean to say that!* She was laying it all out.

Arnold's eyebrows shot up in surprise. "How is that even possible? You're surviving on college loans and ramen noodles."

"I don't know," she said breathlessly, her heart pattering like a rainstorm on a tin roof. "I thought you'd dismiss my dream. Call it absurd." She didn't have the money or credit to get a loan. Her savings account was laughable. This was *absurd.*

Who was insane enough to run a bookshop when people craved the ease of online shopping? Apparently, *she was.*

Cassidy still ardently believed people loved bookshops, like she did. Even though Books Forever wasn't one of the large chain stores, Cassidy carefully curated their stock. When customers walked in, their desire was to help each person find the perfect book. It was never about the money. Only the love of stories. Eventually, everyone needed an escape from the monotony of their lives.

"Why didn't you tell us?" Arnold said.

"Would it have made any difference?" his wife asked. "We need to sell now. Not in five years."

Suddenly, Liam's face poked around the door. "The lawyer said everything's complete. If you'd like to look anything over, now is the time."

Arnold turned to Cassidy. "I'm sorry, darling. It's too late to buy Books Forever. We already signed over the building."

"What?" she said.

He lowered his voice as Liam waited. "If we back out now, he'll get his lawyers involved for a breach of contract." Arnold's face sagged.

Cassidy looked from Ellen to Arnold. "But I thought he was still looking over the financials."

Ellen adjusted another book on the shelf, but her hands were shaking so badly that an entire row of books toppled to the floor. She swept over to pick them up, leaving Arnold with the dirty work of confessing what she couldn't say.

"We signed the offer before you returned. It's why we closed the shop temporarily. We knew he was stopping in today, then he texted last minute to say he was finishing with his realtor and his lawyer could join us virtually. That's why I sent you away. We didn't want you to stop us from making this decision."

Arnold's watery gray eyes were heavy with the weight of hard decisions, as if he knew all that he was giving up.

"You kept it from me?" Cassidy asked, suddenly feeling betrayed. All this time, she thought the Pomfreys would include her in the process of selling, like she was an equal, part of the Books Forever family.

But this confirmed it. She had never been an equal. Only an employee with an outlandish dream.

"I'd do anything for this place," she whispered.

Liam stood in the doorway, clicking a pen, a satisfied expression on his face. "It's not a matter of *if* you could have bought the bookstore. It's a question of whether you could've beaten me. And I'm fairly confident you couldn't have bid higher than what I've already offered." He sank his hands in his pockets, giving a triumphant look that told her she might as well surrender.

Judging by what she knew about Liam Henry, he was probably right. There was no way she could compete with a man like him.

"I see," she said, trying not to reveal the sinking feeling in her stomach. "How much longer?"

"I'm not sure yet. A month, maybe two. Until the bookstore officially closes, you'll have a job. Then we can start the hiring process for the new business, and you're welcome to apply."

Working for him seemed like a betrayal, especially if he was planning to shutter the bookstore.

But could she leave the heavy wood bookshelves with their promised delights? Her eyes flitted over the oak beams in the ceiling, the antique chairs tucked into corners, inviting readers to sit awhile. The children's section had been her space, with its twinkle lights draped across the ceiling and reading tents so children could disappear with a book.

"First, you ran me off the road, and now, you're firing me."

His jaw clenched, then released. "No, I'm giving you notice, so you can apply for another job. Some would call this kindness."

The fact that he saw this as some sort of charity—giving her a future firing date—just confirmed what she suspected. He cared more about the bottom line than saving a local business.

"If you think this is kindness, Mr. Henry, then you're doing it wrong. Books Forever is a staple of our community. People in Wild Harbor have kept it in business for twenty-five years, and that's because they care about the future of this town."

He stepped forward to challenge her. "If they cared so much, then why is the store losing money now? Have you answered that question?"

She swallowed hard. "I have my guess."

None of them could figure out exactly why the store was losing money. The world they lived in had changed drastically in twenty-five years, and every delivery truck rumbling along Main Street reminded them of that.

"Guesses don't make it in the business world," he said. "Give me some hard facts, and we can talk about the future of Books Forever."

"Facts don't always predict the future," she said. "But I'm planning on taking my after-school program with me even if I'm not working here anymore."

A hint of surprise swept across his face before he pulled his expression back. For one moment, she'd found a chink in his armor. He didn't like to lose, but he didn't try to woo her back either.

"If that's what you want." Then he turned back to the Pomfreys. "Do you have a minute to talk through the details?"

Ellen froze in place, while Arnold gave her an apologetic look before following Liam to the office.

She stumbled to the checkout counter and pulled a book from under the shelf: her beloved copy of *Pride and Prejudice*, a book she'd read at least once a year since she was sixteen. Other than her dog, this was all she had to take with her, one story representing a lifetime of love for books.

Though her work at Books Forever was over, she had a new resolve rising in her chest. Even if he shut her down, she'd fight back against closing the doors of Books Forever, no matter what Liam Henry said.

CHAPTER FIVE

LIAM

"She'll be back," Liam said without looking at the Pomfreys. He sat at their desk, pen in hand, official papers fanned out in front of him. They looked like lost puppies who didn't know what to do. For twenty-five years, this had been their office, their desk, their lives, but now it was his.

"You let her go," Ellen stammered.

"I gave her a choice," he reminded her, making a list on a yellow Post-it note from the desk. "She chose to leave."

"But we didn't even say goodbye." Ellen's voice trembled like a singer with a fast vibrato.

"It's not like you won't see her. It's a small town," he said. They'd see her at every community event, at every town Christmas tree lighting, and on the beach. Ample opportunities. And he'd make sure he avoided all of those.

To be fair, Liam hadn't wanted things to go badly with the only bookstore employee. But he hadn't expected meeting anyone today, and he definitely hadn't thought it would be *her*, the crazy woman in the cornfield who'd splattered mud across his face.

"How soon can we get rid of the books?" Liam asked without looking at the devastated couple. "Two weeks?"

"We can't close the store without some additional time and help," Ellen explained, wringing her fingers like she was twisting a wet towel. "Arnold and I can't pack these books. Can't we keep the store open longer?"

He'd glanced over their financial records for the last five years. It had been a steep downward slide toward fewer profits and more losses. A money pit.

"I don't have time to waste. If I start with a fresh business, it'll stir the town's interest. This bookstore seems tired. And it's reflected in your sales."

"People are excited about Cassidy's after-school reading program. It's the one thing that attracts new customers. We need time to notify the parents."

He folded his fingers. "A children's reading program is not a moneymaker."

The Pomfreys glanced at each other. "It will crush Cassidy that we're closing so quickly."

"Cassidy left. She can take her program with her," he said without making eye contact.

"If we'd known you weren't giving Cassidy a chance, I'm not sure we would've sold so quickly."

"Well, you did, and the deal is done," he said, glancing over the papers.

He hadn't anticipated that the day would descend into mud-slinging chaos, looking more like a toddler's finger-painting project than a business transaction. So far he'd almost had an accident, hurt his back, dirtied his suit, and had lost one employee. Worst of all, his mother had signed him up for a dating app.

He dragged his hand through his hair. If there was one skill he'd learned from his dad, it was strong-arming for control. Forging ahead, despite resistance. It's the reason he'd been so successful in business.

"As far as your store closing, hire extra help," he stated swiftly. "Surely you have people who've worked here before."

Arnold and Ellen glanced at each other before Arnold spoke up. "Cassidy is the only one who has worked here for years. When her dad had his stroke, they could no longer afford to help her with school expenses. It's how she's paid for her college education. That's why it's taken her longer to get through school. Before that, it was just Ellen and me. We're a mom-and-pop shop. Never needed to hire."

Liam stared at them. "Not even for the holidays?"

Arnold shook his head. "Ellen and I put in extra hours as needed. When Cassidy started, she covered the extra holiday hours. It was such an enormous relief."

Liam sighed. "Isn't there anyone you can think of?"

"Anyone?" Arnold asked again.

Had the old man not heard him the first time? "Yes, someone who can get the job done. I want to close the store as quickly as possible. Remove the books next week."

"Oh, I wasn't thinking that soon." Arnold's gaze slid to his wife. "I forgot to mention something."

"Which is?" Liam gathered his papers into a neat pile, making sure the edges were even. The Pomfreys were holding him up, and he needed to get back to business.

"The wife and I have a vacation planned for the next two weeks," Arnold explained. "Cassidy was going to cover while we were gone."

Liam stared at the couple. "You're telling me this now? Leaving when you have a store to clean out?"

"It happened so fast. We never dreamed our vacation would conflict."

"You should have said that before your only employee

walked out." Liam tried not to show his irritation. "Could you change your vacation? You only have a few more weeks until you retire. Then you'll have all the time in the world to take a vacation."

Ellen did more hand-wringing. "We're supposed to go on a cruise."

"See if you can postpone it," he suggested, pushing the papers into a manilla folder.

"No changes or cancellations," she said. "Or we lose the trip." Ellen squeezed her hands so tight, the knuckles were white.

"If you can find someone to run the store, we'll delay packing until you return. I need one person."

"But we don't have time to train anyone new before we go," Arnold explained.

Liam was getting exasperated by these people. No wonder their store had failed. For every problem, they seemed helpless to offer a solution.

"Then what do you propose?" he asked, trying to compromise.

"You need to beg Cassidy to come back," Arnold said.

"Not possible," he muttered. He'd not only started off on the wrong foot with her, he'd burned down the whole bridge.

"I don't know if I can convince her without your help." Arnold shook his head. "Not after what happened."

"Well, she isn't returning on my account." His mother had hinted that he came across as a royal grump. Maybe it was true, but he had his reasons. Running multiple businesses wasn't exactly easy. Sometimes you had to show your employees who was boss. "And don't ask me to beg. I don't stoop that low."

"No amount of begging will bring her back," Arnold remarked. "But you might have a chance if you apologized."

"What for?" Sure, he'd offended her by buying the building, but he couldn't apologize for that. It was a done deal.

"She mentioned how you ran her off the road," Arnold said.

"It was an accident," he emphasized. "I avoided hitting her."

"Her car is probably still stuck because she maxed out her credit cards. Did you offer to tow it?"

He grimaced. "She wouldn't take my money."

"That's where you can start," Arnold advised. "Show her she's needed here."

"Wait a minute." Liam stopped. "Why don't you ask her? She likes you."

"She'll say no unless you make it clear she's wanted here. It's the only way."

Despite Arnold's unassuming appearance, the man had a way of bossing people around. Maybe he wasn't the bottom-line, strategic thinker that Liam was, but he'd poked holes in Liam's plan that were valid.

Liam couldn't stay all week and run the store. He had seven-figure deals to negotiate. "If that's what it takes," he said, fishing for his phone in his pocket.

"Not a phone call. Go to her apartment," Arnold advised.

Liam set his jaw. The list of demands was snowballing. "I might have time later this week, depending," Liam said, adding it to his list.

"That's too late. Stop by tomorrow. Then I can go over the restrictions on renovations in this building."

Liam frowned. "What restrictions?"

"Restrictions on historical buildings. You'll want to review those before you make plans with the building contractor."

"This building has an official registry?"

"Yes, a historical designation."

Liam rolled his eyes. "And you're mentioning this to me now?"

"It was in the contract." Arnold pointed at the papers. "Or didn't you read it carefully enough?"

Liam wasn't about to admit he'd missed that part. This would make the renovations for his new business a little more complicated, but it was nothing he couldn't handle. He'd need to rearrange his work schedule this week so he could manage his businesses in Chicago remotely. "Tomorrow, then."

"Also, the Wild Harbor Newspaper will probably stop for an interview tomorrow," Arnold added.

"Wait a minute. How did the newspaper find out?"

"Word travels fast," Arnold said.

"Who leaked the news?" He looked at Arnold.

"Don't look at me. I've been here the entire time," Arnold said. "But haven't you noticed the group of ladies around your car?"

Liam darted to the window and peered down the street. Sure enough, women gathered on the sidewalk next to his pristine vehicle.

"But they don't know who I am." Liam pressed his hands on the glass. "Who told them?"

He spun around and noticed Arnold was missing his familiar sidekick. Ellen had slipped away during their conversation about rehiring Cassidy. He glanced back and pinpointed Ellen, chatting away.

He pressed his knuckles to the windowsill and leaned his forehead against the cool glass.

Arnold's voice erupted behind him. "I've been married for over forty years. A man knows what his wife is up to without even being told."

Another reason not to get married.

He needed to build some community support, not start damaging rumors which could ruin his next business venture.

Returning to Chicago today was not an option. He'd book a night at a local hotel and then track down Cassidy.

He needed her help if he wanted the community to buy into his next business. A beloved local could help him win support, but how would he convince her?

His phone buzzed, and his mother's name appeared on the

screen. With her health situation, he always answered the phone. Even though he usually let his phone go to voice mail, his time with his mom was limited. There were no guarantees how many weeks were left.

"Everything okay, Mom?" Somewhere in the back of the store, he could hear Arnold moving boxes.

"I'm fine. I wondered if you thought any more about what I asked you."

His mother was tireless in her attempts to find him a wife.

"Not yet." His mother wouldn't understand the details he was trying to iron out, like a wrinkled pair of trousers. "Have you shut down my account on the dating app?"

"You're getting a flood of interest," she said, her voice brightening, like it was enough to convince him. "Only problem is, I don't know how to take your name off the app."

"I'll do it when I return." Which might take a few days. Not ideal. "For now, ignore all messages. Be blunt. Tell them I'm not interested."

"I can't do that. One of them might be your future wife!"

"Not if I have anything to say about it," he grumbled.

"Give it a chance," she begged.

"No," he growled.

"Even Abby agrees you need a date."

"You told Abby?"

"She's the one who helped me set up the account!" Jane said.

Even though he had custody of his eight-year-old niece, they weren't exactly close. Ever since his brother had died, she'd attended a nearby boarding school and only visited him and Jane on the weekends. Jane had been the one to step in as parental figure since Abby's mom was out of the picture. Liam merely provided the financial and legal support.

The only reason he did it was for his brother. A car accident claimed his life the same year as their father's heart attack. Liam had learned to block it out, to close off everything that might hurt him or his mother.

"I can't believe you involved an eight-year-old in my dating life," he said.

"She suggested the line about the long walks on the beach. She said you took her on one."

"Only *once*." Right after his brother had died, when he hadn't known what to do with an eight-year-old girl. Most days, he still didn't.

"Please don't respond to anyone on there. Understand?"

"Yes," she mumbled. "Although there's something else I haven't told you."

"If it's related to dating, I can't talk now. We'll deal with it when I get home, which might not be for another day. I need to stay overnight."

He checked out on Ellen, who was gathering more bystanders by the minute.

"I can send you screenshots of some pretty girls!"

"Mother." He gritted his teeth. He knew exactly what his mother was doing. Couldn't she understand that after all their grief, he wouldn't expose himself to the same devastation? His sole focus was on protecting himself from loss. Personal heartbreak was avoidable if you built your fortress big enough.

"I need to go," he said, trying to soften his tone.

"I just want to see you happy," she urged.

"I *am* happy," he reminded her.

"Eventually, you won't have me around," Jane said, her voice brittle. "It's only a matter of time."

"You shouldn't say that," he warned. "You'll get better."

"Liam," she pleaded.

"I *promise*," he said. "We'll throw all our money at your cancer until you're well again."

His mother was silent as Liam perused a few self-help books, his eyes skimming over the various ways to fix relationships or manage grief, topics he didn't want to touch.

"Just consider what I'm asking."

He tightened his lips. "Of course," he said, trying to end the conversation so he could plan for the store's closing. "See you tomorrow."

He slid his phone into his pocket and found Arnold in the storage room trying to organize boxes. "Where's the best place to get a room for tonight? Any local hotel chains?"

"The best place is The Red Poppy Inn."

"One of those bed-and-breakfast places where everyone is super chatty?" He much preferred a hotel where business guests went about their business with little to no contact. It was easier that way.

"Depends who's staying there." He shrugged. "But it's the only decent place."

It would have to do for one night. "What's Cassidy's number in case she's not home?"

"She'll be home." Arnold leaned toward Liam as if he were giving away a secret. "That girl has no life."

Liam wondered why Cassidy was stuck at home when she'd given him such a hard time about not wanting neighbors.

"Wish me luck," Liam said, hoping for a last word of advice. "I'm going to need it."

CHAPTER SIX

LIAM

As Liam pulled up to a wedding shop, he double-checked the location on his maps app. "This can't be right," he muttered.

It was the same address Arnold had given him for Cassidy. He glanced at the old brick storefront again, its display window decked out in lavish displays of lace and satin dresses, the kind that would make his niece squeal.

He plucked a wildflower bouquet from the backseat, and noticed the building had a small second-floor apartment, accessible only by a shared entrance with the shop.

Before heading up the steps, two women at the store glanced at him before exchanging pointed looks. Perhaps Cassidy rarely had guests in her home, and if she did, it usually wasn't men like him.

No turning back now.

At the top of the stairs, a dog howled as he approached the door. He was certain it was the same dog from the bookstore who'd slobbered all over his suit before the Pomfreys caged her.

She'd either jump all over him with sloppy kisses or threaten him with a low growl.

Just then, the door swung open and Cassidy stood on the other side, dressed in a tank top and cutoff jean shorts that showed off her legs. He immediately flicked his eyes to her face and hid the bouquet behind his back.

Surprise flitted across her face before a familiar frown settled between her eyes.

"Cassidy?" he said, as if he'd forgotten her name. Of course, he hadn't forgotten. But the jean shorts had temporarily left his mind blank.

"Liam. How did you know?" She stopped, the answer registering. "Arnold gave you my address, didn't he?"

"I'm surprised you opened your door," he shouted over the loud barking.

"The ladies downstairs notified me. My free security guards." She tipped her head toward the dog. "Along with Daisy."

From the sound of her deep rumbling growl, she wanted to rip Liam's head off.

Blocking her apartment, she refused to swing the door wide enough to allow him to glimpse inside.

"May I come in?" he asked, then hesitated. "If Daisy will allow it."

Her eyes narrowed as she considered his request. "She might. How tough are you around an overly friendly retriever who might lick you to death?"

"I can handle it," Liam said. "Since I'm wearing the same mud-splattered suit, it won't matter if she drools on it."

Her eyes flicked across his jacket, then her lips curled. "I wondered about that."

"I'm finishing a few things before I return to Chicago. You were first on the list. Have you gotten your car yet?"

She pulled a loose strand over her ear. "I'm waiting to hear from the tow truck driver."

"I can assist with that," he offered. Arnold had made it clear that she needed help, and he wasn't about to let her decline his offer.

"You really don't have to, but thank you," she added before trying to shut him out.

He wasn't used to people refusing him, especially women. But her face was a closed door, locked up so tight, he'd have to discover what lay beneath. As the door swung closed, he jammed his foot in the way, pinching his toes.

"At least give me a chance to prove something," he said through the crack, his foot aching painfully. He could barely make out a sliver of her arm. "For the Pomfreys' sake. And because you forgot this."

He held out the bouquet she'd left at the farm, hoping this peace offering would sway her.

Her eye appeared in the crack, flitting over the flowers. "*Only* for the Pomfreys," she replied, the door squeaking open.

As he entered her apartment, he'd forgotten about Daisy until a huge yellow creature with a lolling tongue knocked into him, nearly tackling him.

"Wow, she's a friendly one," he choked out as Daisy gave him a slobbery kiss on the lips.

"She was just cleaning herself two seconds ago," she said with a mischievous grin.

Daisy's tongue had probably been in places he didn't want to think about. He pulled the dog off of him.

Daisy resisted and then circled the couch in a game of tag.

"Daisy apparently hasn't learned her manners." He wiped the dog drool off his face.

"She gets so excited when people come over, which, honestly, isn't very often. But at the bookstore, she's the chillest dog around."

"Except when it comes to me," he said.

Cassidy was now chasing Daisy around the couch while the

pooch successfully eluded her. She lunged toward her collar, but with every attempt, Daisy bolted away. Finally, she swung her legs over the couch and attempted a shortcut, causing Daisy to dart sideways, avoiding her just in time.

Liam placed a fist over his mouth to hide an amused smile.

Cassidy dodged and weaved like a clownish circus act. Even Daisy seemed to think it was a game, darting behind the chair before skittering across the room, nails pattering the floor like spilled tacks. Daisy leapt grandly onto the couch and sat down with a triumphant doggy smile to boast her success.

"Daisy!" Cassidy bellowed, frustrated by the dog's apparent amusement.

Liam gave a tiny snort. It was like watching a game of cat and mouse, only more amusing.

"What are you laughing at?" she asked, frowning.

"The dog won," he claimed. "I've never seen a pet so happy to outsmart a human."

"That's the thing with Daisy. She thinks she *is* human."

Daisy's tongue lolled out the side of her mouth as she panted, her marble eyes glued on Cassidy's every move.

Cassidy's minuscule apartment wasn't big enough for such a large pet. The kitchen, living room, and dining room were all one space, but Daisy used every piece of furniture to her advantage.

Cassidy gave one last attempt to lunge for Daisy's collar as she leapt off the couch.

Liam stepped forward, sensing that Daisy's behavior was a sign that she wanted to spend time with him.

"Do you mind if I try?" Liam asked. "I've been around dogs my whole life. Perhaps she doesn't want you to put her away while I'm here."

"Be my guest," Cassidy said, flopping onto the couch and eyeing Liam suspiciously.

Daisy had settled under the dining room table. Liam

squatted down at Daisy's eye level and reached out his hand for her to sniff. "Come here, Daisy," Liam invited.

Daisy immediately bolted from her hideout, brushing past Liam's hand and knocking him backwards onto the floor, where she gave him another dog-welcoming kiss.

"Daisy!" Cassidy cried, tugging at the dog's collar.

When Liam opened his eyes, a wet animal nose sniffed his face with the sour notes of dog breath.

As Liam stood, the dog sat on her haunches with a pathetic expression of repentance.

"Let me try again."

Cassidy paused, still holding on to Daisy's collar as she tried to wriggle loose. "Are you sure?"

"One more try," he promised. "I'll win Daisy over yet."

Daisy gave a low bark as if to confirm his statement.

"If you say so," Cassidy said, before slowly releasing Daisy's collar. Daisy hesitated for a split second before leaping toward him.

But this time, Liam was ready. He motioned for Daisy to stop. "Sit, Daisy." The dog immediately halted, tilted her head curiously, then leaned on her backside.

Remarkably, Daisy wasn't as wild as she appeared. She only needed a firm hand and follow-through. She waited for Liam to give her a command to release, but Liam froze.

"See? Nothing to it." Liam shrugged.

"Usually the only person Daisy listens to is me, and that's hit or miss," Cassidy said.

For once, he'd earned her respect, even if it had come at the cost of his pride.

"Some dogs need an alpha in their life," Liam said, with his hand still in the *sit* command. "If they sense you're not the alpha, they'll run the show until an alpha puts them in their place."

"Why am I not surprised you're the alpha male to put Daisy

in her place?" A smile curled on the edge of her mouth. "Now what are you going to do? Leave her there forever?"

Liam walked to the couch and gave a low whistle. "Come here, girl." Daisy bounded toward him, awaiting his next command.

"Now, lie down." He pointed to the floor, where Daisy flopped next to his feet.

Liam scratched Daisy's head. "See? Nothing to it." Daisy lazily rolled onto her side, inviting Liam to rub her belly.

"Except for the requirement that you rub her belly." Cassidy settled on the couch, her eyebrows raised. "Such an attention hog."

"I'm sure you're not here to make friends with my dog," she said.

He suddenly remembered Arnold's instructions.

"Right," he said, switching back into boss mode. The ruckus with the dog had forced him to let his guard down, something he didn't do often.

"About the car . . ." he said, searching for the right words. He was usually swift and efficient with his apologies, but something about sitting next to her was causing him to crumble. His confidence, his focus, even the precise words, all of them falling through his fingers like sand.

She crossed her arms. "The accident?"

"Yes, that and . . ." He folded his hands, hoping he appeared as harmless as her now-docile dog. "Well, I should have been more considerate when you landed in the cornfield."

"Yes, you should have," she agreed, not letting him off the hook for his rude behavior.

"And the sale of the building. No one was supposed to know until the Pomfreys had talked with you. They wanted to share it privately. Except you ruined their plan."

"You make it sound like it was my fault," she challenged. "I felt tricked, and then you had the audacity to force me out."

"I wasn't trying to force you out . . ."

She gave him a look, and her posture stiffened like a brick wall.

He'd made the mistake of arguing with her before. He needed to back off as the alpha until he could convince her to return to the store.

"I can see why you took it that way," he said carefully. "I would have felt the same."

She raised her eyebrows. "Really? I didn't imagine you had any feelings," she said with a pinched face.

"I'm sorry about how things turned out. The accident, the store. All of it. That's why I'm here. I'm wondering—no, not wondering, *asking*—if you could give it another chance?"

She frowned. "The store is closing."

"Eventually, yes, when the Pomfreys return. But we need your help until then," he said.

"So you're offering me a temporary position?"

"You could keep your after-school program going. Say a proper goodbye to the patrons of the store."

She considered this. "What do I get?"

"A pay raise, for starters."

"I'm not in it for the money, though I'll take it." She glanced down at her folded hands like she was afraid of suggesting a compromise. "How about keeping the store open longer than the original plan?"

He considered her request. "How long? Originally, I was thinking the store would remain open for two weeks to sell the inventory."

"Two weeks? That's it?" Her surprised laugh erupted like his suggestion was a joke.

He wasn't, and apparently, she wasn't either.

"You need at least a month," she told him. "Maybe two."

"I don't like to prolong the inevitable, but I'll consider an extension with your help. That would please the Pomfreys. Ellen was upset over the way things were left."

Cassidy's face softened. "She was?" It was obvious she and Ellen had a friendship that went beyond the bounds of typical boss–employee relationships.

"I don't ask you to do it for me. But I think it would make the Pomfreys feel better if you kept working."

She hesitated. "I'll think about it," she fiddled with the hem of her shirt. "With conditions."

She started for the fridge and pulled out a half-gallon of juice, tipping the jug into her mouth.

As he stared at her, she held out the jug for him. "Juice?"

He shook his head.

"Sorry," she said sheepishly. "I live alone, so usually there is no one watching."

"I live alone too, but I don't drink from the bottle. When my brother or I tried that as kids and our mom caught us, we got in major trouble. I can't un-train myself now."

For a moment, they just stared at each other and he felt the heat rise under his suit coat. What was it with this girl? She was getting under his skin, making him feel things he normally could suppress.

"So a full month on the store," he said. "Is it a deal?"

"Only if you'll allow me to keep my after-school literacy program too."

"Of course, it's *your* program," he said. He never intended to take that away. "You'll just have to find a new location."

"But if I can raise extra support for the program, would you consider keeping the store open longer?"

"That seems unlikely. The store is in pretty awful shape financially," he said, trying to let her down easy.

"But you're saying you *could* be convinced." She leaned forward on the back of the couch, her arms straddling it.

"Perhaps," he said. "But unlikely."

"But what if?" she tried again.

"If, by some miracle, the store is profitable, then we'll talk."

Her eyes widened like she was about to explode with laughter, her joy as palpable as a child anticipating her birthday party.

She put a hand on his arm, the heat of her fingers sending electricity through him. "If you're saying there's a chance that Books Forever could survive, then I'll come in tomorrow." He knew that in her excitement, the touch was mere accident.

"Deal," he said, pulling away from her before standing. It had been a long time since a woman had touched him. He cleared his throat, hoping it would focus his thoughts. This new plan would delay the opening of his next business and cost him more than he wanted, but he could live with it. After this week, it was unlikely their paths would cross. The Pomfreys could help oversee the closing of the store, and he'd probably never run into her again.

"One last thing . . ." he said.

She turned, a confused look on her face.

"There's still the issue of your car. If you're going to work at the bookstore, you'll need a vehicle." He handed her an envelope with money. "For the tow truck. It's the least I can do."

She took the money. This time, she didn't refuse.

CHAPTER SEVEN

CASSIDY

"I know I've seen him before," Cassidy told Aspen as she slid on an oven mitt and gently coerced a tin of muffins from the oven.

The muffins filled the kitchen with the enticing scent of cinnamon and brown sugar, something that was bound to attract guests from their rooms. She often spent her free time helping Aspen at her lakeside inn and filling in as hostess when Aspen had an out-of-town photo shoot. She supplemented her bookstore income that way, which barely gave her enough to live on, after she paid for school expenses. Now that she was going to lose her job at the bookstore, it would be her only income.

"But I can't remember where," she added, turning the muffin pan over so they spilled across the counter. That was the funny thing about memory: the sheer *unpredictability*. When you aren't trying to remember something, that's when the memories emerged, like a plant heavy with blossoms.

So it was no surprise that Cassidy couldn't place where she'd seen Liam Henry's face before.

"Maybe the newspaper?" Aspen suggested, tucking the muffins into a yellow towel inside a beautiful basket. "Or social media? Have you googled him online?"

Cassidy was hesitant to admit it, fearing she'd look like a stalker. "I did. And I couldn't find out that much. His dad made headlines with his controversial business dealings—especially since he was known for firing executives after he acquired their companies. Liam keeps a low profile, except I found him on a dating app."

Aspen turned around. "You're on a dating app?"

"More out of curiosity than anything," Cassidy explained. "I haven't looked at it in probably seven or eight months. But his description was nothing like the man I met today. On the app, he seemed so . . ." She searched for the right word. Dare she admit it? "*Nice.* The person I met this week was mostly the opposite. A total grump, until he met Daisy."

"Daisy has that effect on people," Aspen laughed, setting out sachets of tea and antique teacups. "Even if he is closing the bookstore, the town will only support his new business if he becomes one of us. Nobody is going to rally around some blowhard. He has to get his hands dirty in the community and show he cares for something more than money."

Cassidy agreed, but by the time he proved that, the bookstore would be long gone. "What am I going to do if I can't work at the bookstore?"

Aspen grabbed her suitcase, signaling it was time to leave for her trip.

She shrugged. "Convince him to keep Books Forever alive. If anyone could do it, you could. See you in a few days."

Like that, Aspen was gone, and Cassidy had the inn to herself. For tonight, there were only three men staying overnight from an auto racing team who'd be at the racetrack most of the evening. It seemed unlikely that another visitor would arrive since it was a Monday. Nobody came on Mondays. She might as well settle in with a good book and a cup of tea.

That was when she heard a car roar into the driveway. Before she could even reach it, someone was already pounding on the door.

She froze instantly at the sight of the man outside. Liam Henry blinked back at her.

"What are you doing here?" she asked.

"This is where I stayed last week," he said. "I have another meeting in the morning with the contractor and my realtor. I arranged it with Aspen." His glance skirted across the room. "Where is she?"

"I work part-time at the inn, filling in for Aspen when she's away." Aspen must have forgotten to tell her—unless she hadn't wanted to because of Cassidy's rant about Liam. "She's engaged to my brother, Matt, and they have a double wedding planned with my sister and her fiancé."

He raised his eyebrows. "It sounds like a Hallmark movie, where everyone is related."

"Not really," Cassidy said. "But you can't hide like you can in the big city."

"And also why you got roped into working here." He glanced at the exterior. "It's a nice place. At least you'll have a job when the bookstore closes."

The smile fell from her face. *Not if I have anything to do with it.* "Does it make you feel better about tossing me on the street?"

"Contrary to what you might believe, I don't throw people on the street. I walk them there," he said with a smirk.

"That's not even funny." She resisted the urge to cancel his reservation even though she was tempted.

"I was joking. Don't you have a sense of humor?" he asked, trying to step around her.

She blocked his way. "Not with things I care about. I take those very seriously. I'm not a pushover."

His face shifted, softening around the corners. "I never said you were."

He paused, trying to assess whether she'd let him in, which gave her a squeeze of pleasure. It was nice to hold some power over him, even if it was only for mere seconds.

"Now that we have that straight, let's check you in." She invited him to follow her to an antique desk where Aspen kept the reservations. She handed him an old-fashioned reservation slip on a clipboard. "I'll also need to see picture I.D. and a credit card."

As she glanced over his driver's license, she noticed he was thirty. Six years older than her. That put him at the same age as her sister Lily. He laid his phone on the desk and a photo appeared on the screen of him in a tux alongside an elegant older lady.

"What a nice photo," she remarked. "Who is the woman in the picture?"

"My mother. We were at a fundraising gala last year when she was well. At least, we thought she was." A shadow flickered across his face.

"Is she okay?" A familiar sense of déjà vu climbed through Cassidy's mind like an invasive vine.

"She will be. Cancer doesn't stop her. She's as feisty as ever."

The way he tilted his head and the curl of his lips reminded Cassidy of a billboard she'd seen on her drive to Grand Rapids. She had passed it last week when the Pomfreys had asked her to attend a booksellers' convention in the city. In bold text beside the man's face, a question was plastered next to a phone number: *Would you like to go out with me? Make my mother's wish come true before she dies.*

Typically, she ignored billboards, but the absurdity of advertising for a date had caught her attention. Who would plaster their face on a billboard for a girlfriend?

That's when it hit her. The photo on Liam's phone was the same face on the billboard, minus his mother. Someone had cropped the picture and used it to advertise for a date.

Heat shot through her chest at the realization. Should she ask him, or pretend she was oblivious? What if someone had swiped his picture and was using it for advertising? Liam might not have a clue that he'd been a victim of identity theft.

Liam Henry would never willingly plaster a dating request on a billboard. After all, a rich, good-looking guy like him didn't need to advertise. If he wasn't seeing anyone, it was his *own* choice. Even if he had the personality of an ogre, enough desperate women abounded in the world who couldn't care less.

She scraped the memory from her mind, trying to filter the hazy details. It was a desperate, sentimental plea that was so unlike the man standing in front of her. Since he didn't care about closing her beloved bookstore, how could he have anything but a heart of stone?

She bit her lip and gave Liam a side eye, weighing her options. Should she ask him or not?

He suddenly jerked his head toward her. "Why are you staring at me like that?"

She slid her gaze away and pretended to shuffle some papers on the desk.

"Uh, no reason," she squeaked as the heat prickled in her neck. She fingered the collar of her shirt, loosening its constricting hold.

"That picture looks so familiar." She nodded toward his screen.

"Oh, really?" he said, signing the bottom of the reservation slip. He slid it toward her. "That's too long."

"Excuse me?" she asked.

"Your form asked too many questions. I'm only staying one night."

"It's so we can get to know you," she said. "That's what we do here."

Although the inn wasn't a luxury resort, it was tidy and homey with a lovely view of the lake from the back patio.

"I've stayed at five-star resorts that want to know less. It verges on a violation of privacy."

"If you're so private, why is there a billboard with your picture on it?"

"Excuse me?" He frowned.

"On the highway. I knew I had seen you somewhere. It wasn't until I saw the picture on your phone. It's the same one, cropped to exclude your mother."

"What was the billboard advertising?" He eyed her suspiciously.

She hesitated, afraid to answer. "It was advertising a date with you."

His mouth twitched before he responded. "I think you must have me mistaken for someone else. I would never advertise for a date." His forehead creased into a deep furrow.

Cassidy glanced back at the picture. "I'm ninety-nine percent sure it was this shot."

"How? I'm the only person who has that picture." He paused as his cheeks colored. "You said the billboard was advertising a date with me?"

"Yep, with a number to text," she answered.

"Excuse me for a moment." He stepped to the other side of the room and quickly pulled up a number. "Hello, Mother? Please tell me you didn't buy a billboard to find me a date."

He paused, his back turned to her. She couldn't hear his mother's response, but he lowered his chin to his chest and rubbed his neck.

"I want it taken down *immediately*," he articulated. "I can't wait until the billboard contract is up. I want it removed. *Now.*"

He ended the call and stared at something outside the window. "Well, that explains why you saw my picture," he said. "My mother was behind it."

He flopped into a chair, his mind far away. "She's afraid she'll die before I find someone. But I enjoy living alone." He looked at her. "Do you think everyone in town recognizes me from the billboard?"

For once, he seemed desperate for her to agree with him. She almost felt sorry for him.

"Not everyone," she said. "The billboard is an hour away."

"Close enough," he muttered.

"On the bright side, I bet you get lots of inquiries."

"I'm not interested," he growled.

He seemed to do that a lot when he was unhappy.

"Why does it matter?" she said. "Your mother only wants what's best for you."

He rolled his eyes. "You sound like her. I need a stalling tactic, something that will stop her attempts at setting me up, like a fake girlfriend."

"Good luck with that," Cassidy said flatly. It didn't surprise her that Liam would suggest the idea.

A group of men descended the stairs, their gruff voices echoing off the walls. She had forgotten about the auto racing team leaving for the race tonight.

"Hey, Cassidy," one of them said. "We're heading to the race."

"Good luck tonight," she said, smiling.

Trevor was a sandy-haired, baby-faced flirt, not looking a day older than his twenty-two years. With his clean-shaven jaw and single dimple, it didn't surprise Cassidy that hordes of admirers followed him on social media. When they'd met earlier, he'd stolen one of her chocolate chip cookies with a smile that made her stomach flip.

"Coming to the racetrack tonight?" Trevor asked, his boyish grin waking something inside her, making her feel like a giddy teenager.

"I should probably stay here," she said as the heat rose into her chest. She averted her eyes, hoping he couldn't see the effect he was having on her. She didn't show her emotions easily, but guys like Trevor made her heart trip.

"If I win, I'd love to take a victory lap with you in my car." He was grinning from ear to ear.

From across the room, she could feel Liam's eyes on her.

"Maybe next time," she said, avoiding Liam's gaze. He probably hated staying over with these guys. Unlike famous NASCAR drivers, these men were backcountry racers, just getting started while working a full-time job. They weren't rich and certainly weren't entitled.

"The invitation is always open," Trevor said as the men hustled out the door.

As soon as the door shut, Liam grunted. "Victory lap, my foot," he muttered. "He'd like to score a victory with *you*."

"He'd get slapped across the face if he tried," she said. "I'm not that type of girl."

"He clearly likes you," he stated without emotion. "His attempts to flirt with you were sickening."

"I know *that*," she said. "And I'm not interested either, if you're wondering."

"Then why did you smile at him?" he asked.

"I was trying to act friendly," she said, moving away from Liam to chase the cat off the couch. "Maybe you should take lessons."

"I *am* friendly," he replied.

"Seriously?" she laughed. "There's a reason your mother has to find you a girlfriend."

"I don't want a girlfriend. It's my mother who won't accept that."

"Why would she go behind your back?"

"It's complicated," he said, grabbing his suitcase and pulling it toward the steps.

For once, she could sense he didn't like this conversation.

A knock came at the door as he tried to escape to his room.

She opened the door, and a vaguely familiar face stood on the other side.

"Hello," said the woman, gently removing her sunhat. "I was wondering if my son is here."

Cassidy tried to match her face with one of the race car drivers. "I'm sorry, but who is your son?"

"Mother?" Liam said, brushing by Cassidy. "What are you doing here?"

"When you called, I was already on my way." She tapped him on the shoulder, a gleam in her eye. "Surprise!"

"Why didn't you tell me?"

"I decided after you left. Since you're considering a lake home, I need to see this town." She strode past him, her flowered kimono jacket flowing like a cape.

"You can't stay here," Liam insisted.

"Why ever not?" she said, turning in a circle, scanning the interior of the inn. "This place reminds me of an inn where I stayed as a child. It's darling."

She perused the crowded bookshelves before sinking into a loveseat, where she fanned herself with her hat.

Liam frowned. "Mother, do you need something? A drink?" He fussed over her like she was an invalid.

Cassidy thought she could hardly look better. A pink glow swept across her cheeks. Her peppered gray bob was neatly pulled back into a becoming ponytail.

She gave Liam an affectionate smile. "I'm fine." She waved him away.

Cassidy could hardly believe how Liam had transformed. The hard shell of his grumpy exterior had faded, revealing a man who was not only tender underneath, but someone who actually cared.

He turned to Cassidy, concern etched between his brows. "Can you get my mom checked in?"

As she returned with the forms and a key, she handed them to the elegant woman on the couch who wore a welcoming smile.

"I'm Cassidy," she said.

"It's so nice to meet you. I'm Jane Henry. Your inn is simply wonderful."

"Oh, it's not mine," Cassidy said, glancing at the shiplap walls and old wood floors. "My future sister-in-law's."

"Wedding plans in your future?" She lifted an eyebrow.

"Aspen is marrying my brother," she replied. "I'm not engaged."

"Your parents must be so pleased," Jane said, a soft smile spreading across her lips. "I can only hope for the same with my only remaining son." She reached up and grabbed Liam's hand. Knowing how angry he had been about the billboard, she expected him to pull away.

Instead, he squeezed his mother's hand before shooting her a look. "You know my feelings about this."

"Liam is against dating anyone," Jane told Cassidy. "Even though the billboard I bought for him has worked remarkably well." She pulled out her phone. "Look at all the text messages I've received." She pushed the phone his way.

He pushed it back. "Anyone who responds to a billboard dating inquiry is not my type."

Her smile faded. "Until you're dating someone, I'm not taking it down."

"If it makes you happy, I'll *buy* you a billboard with my face on it."

"That's not the same," she insisted. Her gaze slid to where Cassidy had stopped to straighten books on a shelf behind him.

Jane looked at her curiously. "Cassidy, I'm sorry you're witnessing our disagreement. It seems we're at an impasse. I only want to see my son happy, like when I met my husband. I bet a beautiful girl like you doesn't have any problems getting a date."

Cassidy turned, avoiding Liam's glare. He'd moved closer to her, and her elbow brushed his arm.

"Actually, I'm not dating anyone seriously," she admitted.

Liam's gaze caught hers, something darkening in his eyes. "Which is why I asked if she wanted to go to the racetrack tonight." He paused. "With me." He didn't pull away, but she could see his desperate plea for agreement.

Cassidy froze, her fingers gripping the top of the wingback chair.

"Is this true?" Jane questioned, a smile curling across her lips.

A weird guttural sound escaped Cassidy's lips as she tried to remember how to speak. She didn't want to date Liam. He was the guy closing the bookstore. *Her* bookstore. She didn't care how handsome he was.

"I was invited to the race tonight," Cassidy said. Never mind that it was Trevor who'd invited her. The gorgeous race car driver with the flirty smile.

"How did this happen?" Jane asked, baffled. The pleasure on her face was unmistakable.

"We met at my new property." Liam beamed. It was the same inspired look that new fathers have when they introduce their babies. Except for Liam, his baby was a building.

That's when the idea occurred to Cassidy. If he wanted to make a bargain, she could play this game, too.

"Did you know he bought the building where I work?" Cassidy asked.

Jane shook her head. "I can hardly keep up with his new properties these days. He's always buying *something*."

How convenient that Jane didn't know that Liam planned to close the bookstore.

Cassidy drew toward Liam, shrinking the distance between them. She was about to drop the bomb of the century on Liam Henry.

"He's a hero for doing it," Cassidy said, brushing so close she could smell his cologne.

"I am?" Liam raised his eyebrows, the perfect setup for her surprise.

"Especially since he agreed to do everything possible to save the bookstore." She glanced at him, sending an obvious message. *Agree to this and I won't tell your mom the truth.* "That's really what did it," she added. "His promise to revitalize the store."

Liam's face fell as Cassidy gave him a triumphant smile.

She knew how to drive a bargain just as hard as he did. And she was about to prove it.

CHAPTER EIGHT

LIAM

His stomach dropped as soon as Cassidy mentioned the bookstore he was shutting down. Liam wasn't trying to bargain; he was only desperate to persuade his mother to stop playing matchmaker. Taking Cassidy to the racetrack had seemed like a simple solution.

Until now.

"You're saving the bookstore?" Jane asked, an expression of dappled wonder crossing her face.

"I haven't arranged anything yet," he replied vaguely, knowing he had zero intention of doing such a thing. Why did anyone need to keep a bookstore open when online retailers could deliver the same merchandise in two days? His high-tech-gym idea had far more potential for Wild Harbor.

Cassidy remained firmly planted beside him. "Over the next month, he's going to throw all his expertise into making this a profitable shop."

"Really?" Jane asked. "He's usually the guy who shutters businesses, just like his father. He can smell a dying animal from a mile away."

Cassidy's mouth twitched. "He won't shut down the bookstore yet. It's one thing we agreed on before he asked me out." Cassidy's gaze caught his, and a mischievous glimmer sparked behind her eyes.

Jane's face tilted toward his. "I've never heard you talk about racing before."

"I haven't," he blurted. "But since there's a racetrack outside of town, I figured it's a good idea to try something new."

He'd never watched racing for more than a few minutes on TV. His tiny twisted truth was now spiraling into a giant tangled web of deception.

"Cassidy, may I speak to you alone?" he asked firmly, not trying to cover up the underlying demand.

"Sure," she said as he dragged her by the elbow toward the dining room.

Liam spun around to face Cassidy. "What are you doing?" he hissed under his breath. "I have no intentions of keeping the bookstore open for longer than needed. I thought I made that clear."

"You did," Cassidy said. "And then you changed the rules. You put me in an extremely uncomfortable situation."

"I was going to explain eventually," he said. "I'm trying to convince her to take down the billboard. That's all. I have no expectations that you'll date me."

Cassidy crossed her arms. "That's wrong."

"I'm telling her the truth later," he said, bristling. Cassidy was making him feel worse by the minute.

"It doesn't matter," Cassidy said. "You're pressuring me into an awkward position. For your mother's sake, I didn't out you, but I refuse to let you use me as a convenient excuse. If you're expecting me to go along with your little pretend date, then I expect something in return."

"I'm not keeping a dying business open," he insisted. "I don't need a date that bad."

As the words tumbled out, he realized his mistake. He hadn't meant it as a personal insult, but judging from the look on her face, she had taken it that way.

"Then I'm sure your mother will understand when I explain everything to her."

She started for the living room, but he grabbed her arm before she could leave. A current looped between them as she glanced at his hand. He wondered if she felt it too.

"Don't," he told her, letting go of her wrist. "Hear me out first. My reasons for not dating are complicated. They would only hurt my mother's feelings," he confessed. "Trust me on this."

"I'm not sure I can," Cassidy said, her expression wavering.

"Try me," he said, his voice low.

Cassidy paused, considering his words. "If you're involving me in this, then I expect something in return. And that something is the bookstore." She propped one hand on her hip. Despite appearing like a docile woman, there was a tiger buried underneath.

"I'm not willing to negotiate," he shot back. "Keeping the bookstore open longer than needed is foolish."

"Like going along with your little scheme," she said, inching toward him.

Jane's heels clicked toward them.

"Cassidy," he pleaded in a low growl.

She crossed her arms, her face resolute.

Jane appeared in the doorway. "Liam, do you mind if I rest a while? I'm tired after making the drive from Chicago."

This was his way out of their date. "I can keep you company tonight." With effort, his eyes swung over to Cassidy. "Unfortunately, we'll have to postpone our date."

"Oh, goodness. Absolutely not." Jane waved her hand in the

air. "I'm not planning on going anywhere except this gorgeous patio." She peeked out the door where a row of comfortable lounge chairs faced the lake. "You two kids have fun. I'll be perfectly happy here and head to bed when I'm tired."

"I couldn't leave you alone," he quickly sidestepped. "How about we go out for a nice dinner, and then I'll show you the town?"

Jane shook her head. "I'm too exhausted to go out. You can tell me about the race when you return, if I'm not already asleep in my room." She patted his arm. "I won't wait up." Jane left them to claim one of the lounge chairs outside.

As soon as the door closed, Liam felt the heat of Cassidy's angry gaze on his back. He edged around, trying to figure out what he could do to pacify her. "Before you blame me—"

"If you think I'm going to the race with you, think again," Cassidy interrupted from across the room. "I have a guest to take care of this evening."

"Mother will most likely be snoring by the time the race is over," he said. "Now, about that proposition." He needed to think fast. Offer her something she couldn't resist.

"The bookstore?" she suggested, interested in his compromise.

"I already negotiated a month until closing." If she was playing a game, he could play it too.

"What if the plan was to revitalize it?" She raised her eyebrows. "Would you try?"

"Perhaps. But not indefinitely. I can't prop up a failing store any more than a doctor can revive a dead man. I'm not a miracle worker."

"You have a lot of money, though," she said.

"You can't throw money at a problem and expect a problem to fix itself. Contrary to popular belief, money doesn't solve everything."

"But you have business expertise. So much more than the Pomfreys." For once, she looked hopeful, like he held the answers to her problem. The Pomfreys had learned everything by trial and error, which counted for something, but in their case, it hadn't been enough. They didn't have an MBA or the experience of working under successful business mentors. Liam had all that and more.

"But if there's no longer a market for books in this town, I can't reestablish that. No one can."

She hesitated, chewing her lip in that cute, perplexed way. "I believe you can."

Her faith in him was exhilarating, but he didn't want to give her false hope. "Then you have more hope than me."

He already had done his market research for a high-tech gym powered by the latest equipment. Wild Harbor lacked *any* gym, and he predicted that health-conscious people would buy into it. That seemed like a far better prospect than revitalizing a failing bookstore.

But convincing her of that? He wasn't sure how, unless he showed her how impossible it was to save the bookstore. She needed proof.

"How about a compromise?" he offered. "I can't promise that the bookstore will be profitable. But I can try to give it one month. After that, I'll decide based on numbers. If it's not making enough to pay for itself, we'll have a closing period of two weeks, just like we originally agreed to."

"One month?" She flopped onto a dining room chair. "How is that even possible?"

"I'm not asking for the store to turn a profit. Merely cover costs—a break-even proposition," he said. "In exchange for a few dates—as friends—for my mother's sake."

She bit down on a fingernail, considering his request. "For how long?"

"Until my mother takes that ridiculous billboard down. Or thirty days. Whichever comes first."

"One month is not long enough to turn around the store," she said. "I need more time."

Instead of closing the business, he had given her an additional month of trying to make it profitable. What more could he offer? "Six weeks," he said.

"Two months," she said. "No less."

"Two months?" he exclaimed. "The store will bleed money."

"But your mother will be happy," she said, her eyes drifting to where Jane dozed on a sunny chaise lounge. "Your only options are dating me or one of the dating pool applicants. Your choice."

She had him in a corner. "I'm only doing this for my mother," he said. "No more extensions."

"Me too," Cassidy said. "I can see how much Jane wants this. I'm not going to disappoint her."

Until now, Liam had assumed Cassidy wanted to play the martyr, willing to die on the metaphorical hill of saving local bookstores. But now his assumptions about her were changing. If she would make this sacrifice for his mom, perhaps there was more to her than he'd first believed.

"Two months, then. But you start now," he insisted. "Even though I can't stand racing."

"Me neither," she admitted with a guilty grin. "But I couldn't tell Trevor that."

"From now on, we'll arrange dates when it's convenient for you," he said, looking at the calendar on his phone. "And mutually beneficial to me."

"That sounds so romantic," she said flatly.

"Romance was never part of the agreement," he said.

"That's obvious," she said. "You probably think counting your money is romantic."

"Not really," he challenged. "But I'm quite romantic. I could sweep a woman off her feet if I really wanted to."

A doubtful laugh escaped her lips. "I'd like to see you try."

"Is that a challenge?" he countered, narrowing his gaze.

She glanced away. "You don't seem like the romantic type."

"Then you underestimate me." He accepted her challenge and was determined to win her over. No matter what it took.

"Really?" Her uncertainty dared him to prove her wrong. "Then can I ask you a question?" she said, finally meeting his gaze. "If you need a date, why not ask a girl who *actually* wants to date you?"

"Too complicated," he said, rolling up his sleeves. "You have no emotional investment in the relationship. When two months are over, I won't have to worry about your feelings. It is—how can I say it?—a convenient choice."

Cassidy's mouth tightened as she glanced at the floor. "*Convenient.* I see."

"When it's over, I'll make up some excuse about why we broke up," he said, as if that solved everything. For now, it would have to.

He'd explain that she was too needy. Not his type. After his money. His mother would understand.

Cassidy's face softened. "I'd hate to disappoint her."

For the first time, he glimpsed something tender under her usual show of strength. In the short time he'd known her, Cassidy had attempted to keep her emotions under control, her face a placid wall. But if someone observed her carefully, genuine emotions were there, under the surface.

"She will understand in time. I need to prove to her that a relationship is not the key to my happiness, even if it was for her."

"Why not tell her that now?"

"My mother doesn't have long to live. And I'm willing to make her happy. Even if it's only temporary."

"I'm doing this for her," Cassidy said, crossing to the door. "I don't agree with giving her false hope. That's the worst kind of hope to have. Trust me, I know."

What had she gone through that made her admit that? How had she been hurt, and who had done it? Even though he hardly knew her, a protective instinct rose in his chest.

That's what he was good at. Fighting for the people he cared about.

All he was trying to do was fulfill his mother's last wish. Give her peace that he'd be okay without her, even though he hated that thought.

Hope had nothing to do with it.

Cassidy turned to him one last time. "You've got two months."

LIAM SHIFTED UNCOMFORTABLY on the hot metal bench that seared his thighs, grateful he wasn't wearing shorts. He'd shed his suitcoat, opting for a dress shirt and pants, but he was still grossly overdressed for the event. Most men sported T-shirts or tank tops; they'd probably never even seen an Armani suit.

"Do you have a favorite driver?" he asked, staring at the racing program.

"Except for the racers staying at the inn, I'm clueless," she remarked.

Cassidy had been unusually subdued ever since they'd left the inn, making the silence between them even more awkward. He was still uncomfortable with the idea of dating a woman whose job he was about to axe in two months.

But he kept circling back to his reasons: The store would remain open and that would satisfy his mother. A win-win situation, right? Temporary victories on both counts, but still wins.

Even so, the situation pricked his conscience. It was only a matter of time before someone lost this game, and he was afraid that someone would be him.

Cassidy had changed into her cutoff jean shorts, and he wrestled with the same distraction as last time. Now he was forced to stare at his phone rather than her, which only solidified his reputation with her as a jerk.

"I'm hungry for a funnel cake." Cassidy turned toward the snack bar, squinting to read the menu. "They're messy, but worth it." She glanced at his outfit. "You might need to drop your clothes at the dry cleaners afterward."

"I already plan to." He gave her a look. "I don't do laundry."

"Must be nice," she said, stretching out her sun-kissed legs.

Those shorts again. He averted his eyes to his phone.

"So if laundry isn't a problem, do you want to split one?" she asked.

"I'm not hungry for fried food." He wished they'd reserved a table at a decent restaurant. Some place where he could enjoy a gourmet meal along with air-conditioning. The racetrack was almost unbearably stifling.

"Well, what do you like to eat?"

"I like steak, medium rare, with a little blood."

"Ew." She grimaced. "Of course they won't have *that.*"

"I know," he said, holding back a smile. "But you asked what I was hungry for." He hadn't meant to appall her, but her look of disgust amused him. "Since this isn't really a date, I'm not worried about offending you."

"Offend away," she invited. "I can take it. Especially since we're *not* dating." She held her fingers up as air quotes to make a point. "Maybe Phil can just give you a quarter pound of raw hamburger on a bun. It's not steak, but it's the closest they've got." She tugged on his sleeve to follow her.

His eyes skirted over her hand like it was a magnet. "I'm sure they won't." His empty stomach rumbled.

"Come with me." She pulled on his forearm again, her touch

spiking his pulse. "You never know what surprise might happen here." Then she let him go, the disappointment settling into him like a dull ache. Why was his body reacting this way? He normally had no problem resisting attractive women. But Cassidy was different.

He followed her to the snack bar, where a glowing sign listed a menu of mostly fried and greasy foods. A smoky grill sizzled in the back, and the scent of burgers filled the air.

A man in a worn apron approached, giving Cassidy a welcoming smile. "Surprised to see you here," he said. "Since you're not really a racing fan."

"I'm usually working in the evenings," she said. "But a girl needs to get out every once in a while. You got any steak in the back?"

"No steak. Mostly hamburgers and hot dogs." Phil was a large man who looked like he ate too much of his own food. "Don't tell anyone, but I might have enough for a Philly cheesesteak."

Cassidy nodded. "We'll take it, along with a funnel cake."

Phil disappeared to the back to find meat for the grill. Cassidy drifted to a shady spot under the snack bar awning while they waited.

"You didn't ask me whether I wanted a sandwich," he said, surprised.

"You think Phil would offer this to just anyone?" she asked. "Consider it your lucky day."

Lucky day. Today had been anything *but* that. Still, the way his stomach rumbled, he had little choice.

Cassidy peered over his shoulder at a crowd of men on the racetrack.

"Do you see him yet?" he asked, turning his focus to his phone.

"Who?" she said, pretending she hadn't been straining to glimpse the small-town heartthrob.

"Trevor," Liam responded. Why did this bother him? Maybe it was because Trevor looked like he'd been cast in a race car movie, the type of role defined as a *handsome male lead with a six-pack and a winning smile.*

Trevor didn't have to take off his shirt to prove it, but the guy looked chiseled from stone.

"Now that we're here, you don't have to stick around," he said, trying not to care that she would likely choose Trevor over him. "You came with me. That was the only requirement."

"Requirement? You make it sound like a job description," she said.

This *was* a job description, not an actual date. Not that he remembered what a real date was like. Ever since his dad had died, he'd been too busy working to even consider a relationship. It was safer that way. He needed all his time and attention for his mother.

"I wouldn't want to get in the way of you staring at Trevor," he said, giving her a side eye.

She pulled her gaze away from the racetrack. "I'm *not* staring."

"Hello, Cassidy," an older gentleman said.

Her face lit up as she turned to the man with a warm smile. "Joshua! I'm surprised to see you here."

"Haven't attended in years."

She gave Liam a look that warned him to be nice. "Joshua, this is Liam Henry."

Liam offered his hand. "Good to meet you." When he glanced down, he could see a scar etched deep on the man's wrist.

"You're not from around here," Joshua remarked. "Small towns take some getting used to."

Liam shifted uncomfortably. Was it really that obvious? "I'm from Chicago. Hoping to buy a place on the beach." He gave Cassidy a look that said *Good enough?*

Joshua looked curiously between Cassidy and Liam. "If you ever need any old stuff, I have a salvage shop. Lots of nice antiques." He pulled a business card from his wallet.

Liam took the card, even though he wasn't into discarded junk.

"Stop by with your mom," Joshua said.

"How do you know my mom?" Liam asked.

"Everyone has a mom." Joshua smiled before heading on.

"Strange man," Liam muttered under his breath as he watched Joshua leave.

"You could act a little more friendly," Cassidy said.

"That *was* my version of friendly," Liam reminded her.

She shook her head. "It was obvious you didn't want to talk."

"First, I'm not a man of many words," he said. "Second, small talk is a waste of time."

"Do you measure *everything* by how it benefits you?"

He hadn't thought about it that way, but she was right. "I don't even know that guy. But I don't waste my time unless someone is worth it. You should do the same. Especially if you want to date that guy." He nodded toward the racetrack where Trevor was sliding on a helmet.

Trevor glanced toward the crowd and waved when he saw Cassidy.

"I don't want to date him." She gave a sheepish wave back. Her cheeks flamed pink as she turned away from the racetrack.

"Sure looks like you do," he said, swiping a finger across her cheek. She might not show her emotions easily, but he was beginning to read her through small nuances, the faint glow in her cheeks, an upturned corner of her mouth. Even if she denied it, there was something she liked about that race car driver. No doubt she'd pick Trevor over him, which stung a little since he was used to girls falling all over themselves. But Cassidy was different, immune to him, perhaps even repulsed.

Why would she choose some backwoods, no-name kid who drove fast cars?

"One Philly cheesesteak coming right up," Phil said, holding a huge sandwich loaded with smoking meat. "And a funnel cake." He might regret eating that later when he had heartburn, but he was so hungry right now, he didn't even care.

Liam pulled out his phone to pay.

"Cash only," Phil said, ringing up their order on what looked like a cash register from the 1980s.

"I don't carry cash," Liam said. He probably hadn't used paper money in over a year.

Cassidy pulled out a twenty. "I'll get it." She handed Phil a bill.

"You didn't need to do that," Liam quickly responded, embarrassed that she was paying for him, especially when he had the money and she was soon to be out of a job.

"Do you want the money via PayPal, Venmo, Apple pay?" he asked, searching for his cash apps.

"Don't bother. You were the one who said this wasn't a date." She lobbed his words at him before grabbing the cardboard container, which was spilling over with a humongous bun and melted cheese.

"I want to pay," he insisted.

"Get over yourself, Liam." She shoved the funnel cake and a handful of napkins at his chest before wandering back to her seat.

While they were gone, the row had ballooned with spectators, leaving little space for two people. Cassidy slid onto the bench and attempted to scoot over so Liam could sandwich himself between her and an older lady in an oversized straw hat.

The lady's gargantuan hat forced Liam to slide closer to Cassidy, their legs briefly touching as they tried to balance the sandwich and funnel cake on their laps.

The older lady glanced between them. "Cassidy, are you trying to sneak past me without so much as a hello?"

"Thelma, I could never sneak past you." Cassidy handed Liam the sandwich so he could wrangle it into two halves with a plastic knife as she nibbled on the funnel cake. "This is Liam Henry," she added. "A guest at the inn."

Thelma looked him over the same way a shopper might study a pot roast before dropping it into their grocery cart. "You're not from around here, are you?"

"I'm not." Was it that obvious he was an out-of-towner?

"A businessman from Chicago," Cassidy answered, stealing a cheesy piece of beef from the container before Liam could finish cutting. "I'm introducing him to Wild Harbor."

"That's good," Thelma answered with a mischievous smile. "I thought you were on a date."

Liam didn't know what to make of these people. They seemed to enjoy talking about him as if he weren't there.

Thelma rotated her body to get a better look at him, her hat shading her wrinkled face. "You seem familiar. Do I know you from somewhere?"

Liam focused on his plastic knife, hoping she wouldn't figure it out. *The billboard.* "We've never met before," he said, watching his knife bend pathetically as he sawed at the bread.

"I've seen your face before," Thelma replied. "Have you been on TV?"

This woman couldn't take a hint.

He finally gave up on the knife and tore the sandwich in two, handing Cassidy her half before biting into the hot beef. If his mouth was full, she'd leave him alone.

"I swear I recognize you!" Thelma said.

"Not from TV," Cassidy replied. "And because I know you're going to ask, he's not my date either."

Thelma raised one eyebrow skeptically. "Honey, if I were

thirty years younger, I would claim him as my date even if he wasn't."

Thelma leaned toward Liam and nodded at Cassidy. "You gotta admit she has great legs."

Liam sputtered and choked on his sandwich as Cassidy's mouth fell open.

"Thelma!"

Thelma cackled and smacked her leg.

The sweat prickled around Liam's collar and not because he was wedged between these two women.

Cassidy was having an effect on him, and the last thing he wanted was for her to notice.

Just then, Trevor jogged to the fence to meet his fans. Several older women giggled while two high schoolers asked for selfies. One lady showed off her T-shirt with his face plastered on it. Trevor's expression swelled with a pride that made Liam's stomach turn. Anyone could drive fast.

Trevor's gaze shifted to where Cassidy was seated, and a huge smile spread across his face. "Hey, you made it!" he yelled.

"Stick around afterward for that ride I promised," Trevor said, winking at Cassidy.

"Sounds fun, but I'm not sure I can." She glanced awkwardly at Liam, an unspoken tension between them. Even though he'd made it clear they weren't on a date, it would create an awkward situation if she returned to the inn with Trevor and not him.

Liam cleared his throat, but Trevor ignored him, pretending he didn't exist. "Then how about a dessert or drink afterward? Brewster's is open late," he said, trying to woo her with that ridiculously toothy smile that made women weak in the knees. The man missed his calling in a toothpaste commercial.

"Not tonight," Cassidy replied, attempting to let him down easy.

A stranger in front of Cassidy swiveled toward her. "Come on, lady. Don't leave a nice guy hanging like that."

"I'll go out with you," another girl volunteered.

"See? They're lining up for me." Trevor was a girl magnet, and he knew it.

"Well," she said sheepishly. "I'm not, um . . ." Cassidy stumbled over her words, the pressure of his charm wearing her down.

Liam finally stood up. "She's not going out with you, because she's on a date with me."

Until now, Trevor hadn't even noticed him, just another faceless guy in the crowd. But Trevor's expression shifted, like someone had slapped him. The crowd turned toward Liam, the stranger who'd staked his claim on Cassidy.

Now everyone in town knew about their supposed relationship.

"Sorry, man," Trevor said, backing off. "I didn't know she came with you."

"Maybe you should ask next time," Liam said, sitting down like a boxer who'd just won the first round.

Cassidy turned to glare at Liam. "What are you doing?" she whispered.

"Standing up for you," he replied, as if it were obvious.

"Thanks, but I don't need your help," she replied, clearly annoyed.

"I thought you wanted him to leave you alone."

"If I did, I wouldn't ask *you*," she huffed before biting into her sandwich. Usually, he didn't care if he angered people. But this time, it bothered him that he'd actually made an effort for her. Instead of thanking him, she'd brushed him off.

He looked at his program, trying to focus on anything but her.

He leaned over to Thelma. "Is Jose Rodriguez any good? I'm trying to pick a winner."

"Rodriguez isn't bad, but Trevor is the favorite." She smirked. "Of course, you probably don't like him much now. Why did you tell me you weren't on a date?"

"It's complicated," he said, brushing her off. "But I'm cheering for Rodriguez."

"The underdog?" Cassidy asked. He thought she hadn't been listening to the conversation.

"Always the underdog," he said as the flag waved and the engines roared to life.

The cars gained speed, and the crowd cheered as Trevor pulled to the front.

A racer named Lee Henderson pulled in to second place, while Rodriguez held third. A trail of cars put the pressure on from behind.

As the cars passed the grandstand, Cassidy stood and cupped her hands around her mouth. "Come on, Trevor!"

For someone who normally tamped down her emotions in public, she wasn't afraid to let loose during a competition.

Liam joined her, whistling loudly. "Let's go, Rodriguez."

Cassidy glared at him. "Do you even know that guy?"

"Of course not," he said. "I'm cheering for anyone besides Trevor."

She gave him a dirty look before scouring the speeding cars for Trevor's place.

He still held the lead as the cars circled the track several more times. When Rodriguez attempted to make a swift break around him, Trevor blocked him from passing.

If Trevor could hold back his competition, he'd secure a win, no problem. Watching his quick maneuvering made Liam burn that he couldn't impress Cassidy by giving Trevor a run for first place.

Cassidy cheered louder with every lap, giving Liam little hope that Trevor would lose his lead. Now that the drivers were on their final lap, the entire crowd rose to their feet, cheering for Trevor, anticipating his all-but-assured first-place finish.

Suddenly, Henderson snuck to the outside lane, but Trevor quickly shifted to block him, leaving just enough space on the inside for Rodriguez to slip through.

As soon as Liam saw it, he whispered, "Come on, come on."

Rodriguez accelerated like fire in the brief space Trevor had left him, pulling evenly into a tied first place with Trevor.

As Trevor attempted to take back his lead, he swerved to cut off Rodriguez, and ended up snagging his bumper, causing both cars to lose control on the last lap.

"Oh, no!" Cassidy yelled, as both Trevor's and Rodriguez's cars spun out, smashing against the wall, and crashing to a stop. The other race cars avoided the crash, leaving Lee Henderson claiming first place.

People in the stands groaned from the unexpected results as the checkered flag waved in triumph.

But Cassidy's attention was glued to Trevor's car as he and Rodriguez exited their wrecked vehicles safely.

She breathed a sigh of relief. "Thank goodness," she whispered, almost as an afterthought. There would be no victory lap tonight.

Thelma leaned toward Liam. "Good thing you're not a betting man. Your driver lost."

"As long as Trevor didn't win."

Cassidy scowled. "Seriously? The guy could have been killed and you're happy about his loss?" She scrambled over his legs, trying to exit the row.

"Where are you going? I didn't mean it like that." But it was too late.

She descended the stadium steps and jogged alongside the fence to find Trevor.

So maybe he was a little jealous. He didn't want the guy to

end up seriously hurt, but he couldn't seem to stop himself from feeling a small thrill of pride when he'd lost.

Thelma stood to leave. "You know I'm not a betting woman," she said. "But if I were, I'd bet on you over him."

"Thanks," he muttered. "Not everyone feels that way." His gaze skirted back to Cassidy before he noticed that he'd dropped cheese sauce on his pants.

"You're kidding me," he groaned as he wiped at the spot.

CHAPTER NINE

CASSIDY

A s Cassidy hurried around the kitchen preparing food for the inn's guests, she had one goal in mind: avoid Liam after their disastrous date. She didn't want to hear any snide comments about Trevor, who was fine after the accident except for a few cuts and bruises.

Breathing a sigh of relief, she arranged the muffins on a silver tray so she could head into the bookstore for work. Most of the guests had left early, and the only ones remaining were Liam and his mother.

And she wanted to avoid Liam at all costs.

Because every time he was around, she had this mixture of emotions. Something like sandpaper on skin, followed by a wildly opposite reaction resembling chemistry. As much as she wanted to smash it to pieces, her attraction to him only seemed to swell. That was, if he didn't make her crazy angry.

Staying away was what she needed to do. No matter what.

"Leaving already?" a male voice asked.

Busted. Her stomach jumped at the sound of Liam's voice.

"Heading to the bookstore," she said, trying to calm her wild heartbeat. "You're welcome to help yourself to breakfast."

"That's too bad. My mother wanted to talk to you this morning," he said with a curious expression.

"What about?" she asked. "And why are you looking at me like you expect me to cooperate?"

He shrugged. "I don't expect anything after that billboard is down."

"That's not my problem," she said, straightening the napkins.

"Then consider yourself lucky," he said, pouring himself a cup of coffee.

Just then, Jane came downstairs, wearing a long, clingy ocean-blue dress, her bob perfectly turned under.

"I was hoping you were still here, Cassidy," she said, her eyes bright. "Liam said the race was exciting. Although I'm very sorry to hear about the accident."

"They're both fine," she said. "But I'm surprised Liam mentioned it." She raised her eyebrows at him.

"I'm not one to attend races," Jane said. "Too much for this old heart." She patted her chest. "But I would love to attend next week's garden party in town. I met Agnes yesterday, and she invited me. I'm not sure I can convince Liam to go, though."

Cassidy glanced at Liam, who had suspiciously made his way to the tray of muffins, pretending not to hear their conversation.

Well, this was awkward. Cassidy hadn't planned on attending the Bellavues' garden party. To be honest, it wasn't her thing. Sitting around sipping punch while admiring the Bellavues' rose garden wasn't something she had time for, not since her father had had a stroke last year. Although he was finally walking again, he still wasn't back to normal. That left Cassidy to take care of things when her mom needed help.

Now that her siblings were both involved in committed relationships, Cassidy was left assisting her parents the most. She didn't mind, but between her two jobs and school, she had little time for gallivanting to garden parties.

"Well, that is kind, but I can't take time off. Liam has big plans for the bookstore."

"You could take the day off," he said. "The bookstore will be fine."

"But I can't. We need the bookstore to make money," she reminded him. She only had two months.

Jane fingered a chocolate croissant and placed it on her plate. "I was hoping to get to know you better. Since you're the first woman my son has dated in years."

Cassidy tried to hide her surprise. How was it possible a man like Liam Henry hadn't dated anyone recently? It wasn't because he lacked anything. More than likely, he couldn't find anyone up to his standards.

"Abby would love to meet you," Jane said.

Liam sat at the dining room table, trying to avoid eye contact with either his mother or Cassidy.

"I don't think that's a good idea," he said. "Abby is eight. Why would she want to attend a garden party?"

"Who is Abby?" Cassidy asked. She couldn't imagine Liam being a dad. He seemed way too self-absorbed.

"Abby is my granddaughter. My son Luke's only child," Jane clarified. "After he died in a car accident, the court appointed Liam as guardian."

Liam cut in. "I mainly act as her legal guardian while she attends boarding school." His face was calm, like he was negotiating a business deal instead of his orphaned niece.

"But what about her mom?" Cassidy asked.

Liam flinched. "She left when Abby was two. She wanted her freedom and a divorce. Unfortunately, she didn't want custody of Abby. So my brother raised her, with Mom's help. But when my brother passed, I ended up with custody. She attends a private boarding school most of the year and spends holidays and some weekends with us."

Jane's face brightened. "How about taking her to the garden party? She might want to meet new friends."

Liam looked wary. "I don't want to get her hopes up. The bookstore acquisition is going to take all my time for the next month. I'm not attending any parties." He carefully formed his words, trying not to make promises he couldn't keep.

"But she's too secluded at school," Jane mentioned. "All the other girls leave for weekends and have fun things to look forward to. But not Abby."

Liam bristled in his seat. "School is a good place for Abby. It gives her the stability she needs. With your cancer treatments and my schedule, school is the best option for her. She's happy there."

Jane picked at the croissant on her plate. "It's not a business decision, Liam. She's family."

Cassidy didn't have to be a rocket scientist to see that Jane desperately wanted to spend more time with her granddaughter. But with her cancer treatments, she didn't have the energy to raise a child.

"I'll go with you to the party," Cassidy interrupted. "I'd like to meet Abby. I'll even give her a tour of Wild Harbor and all the fun kid places. If Agnes's garden party is a bore, I'll bribe her with Lily's chocolate shop afterward."

Before Liam could respond, Jane's eyes lit up. "That sounds perfect." She turned to her son. "I don't care what you say, Liam, Abby will love visiting."

"I'm concerned she'll have expectations," he said.

Cassidy wasn't sure whether he was referring to living in Wild Harbor or making Abby believe that Cassidy was Liam's girlfriend. Either way, Cassidy didn't care. After everything Abby had been through, she wanted to treat her like a princess.

"I won't tell her about the beach house or you two," Jane

promised. "We'll say that Cassidy is my new friend, and she'll be none the wiser."

Liam frowned, displeased with this plan. "As long as you keep it a secret," he said, giving them a warning glance.

AFTER LIAM and Jane headed back to Chicago, Cassidy's life returned to normal, for at least the time being. With the Pomfreys on vacation, Cassidy ran the store with Liam texting from Chicago for regular updates.

Liam: How are things going at the store?
Cassidy: The usual. One kid ripped pages out of a book today. Another spilled his sippy cup on *The Complete Works of Shakespeare*, which is completely ruined. Shakespeare would be appalled. :)
Liam: He's not the only one. Why are the *Complete Works* in the children's section?
Cassidy: They aren't. The kid snuck into the Classics section and climbed the bookshelves while his mother was reading the latest Colleen Hoover romance.
Liam: I hope they bought something.
Cassidy: The Fraziers can't afford to buy anything. They can barely pay for groceries.
Liam: No wonder this store isn't making money.
Cassidy: But this is their happy place! With free air-conditioning! A bonus! You ought to see their children's faces when I hand out suckers.
Liam: Won't that make the books sticky?
Cassidy: We've only lost a few.
Liam: Like two?
Cassidy: Like two dozen.
Liam: New company policy: no more suckers.

Cassidy: You're no fun. How am I supposed to motivate my after-school reading club?

Liam: I don't know. Stickers?

Cassidy: Those also ruin books.

Liam: No stickers! Positive reinforcement?

Cassidy: You're so boring.

Liam: Some boring people are good at making money.

Cassidy: But still boring.

Liam: Ouch. How is the marketing plan going?

Cassidy: What marketing plan?

Liam: I was afraid you'd say that.

Cassidy: I've been trying to salvage sticky books. Chocolate milk is not a becoming addition to Shakespeare.

Liam: Shakespeare is dead. And the bookstore will be too if we don't get more paying customers. You only have two months.

Cassidy: No pressure, right?

As Cassidy sent the last message, her stomach clenched. How in the world could she get the town to rally behind this dusty old bookshop? People always remarked that the store was unique. *One of the last small-town bookstores left in America.* But that only meant they liked the store in theory, like a historical artifact. Not as something useful to their lives.

No one buys books from a bookshop anymore, one lady told her.

Even with Liam's money, it was like trying to save the Titanic. *Impossible.*

Although it should have been a relief not to see Liam, she was completely distracted by him. How he took care of Abby. The way his face softened when he talked to his mother. The flash of jealousy when she mentioned Trevor.

Her initial impression was that he was a stuck-up, rich snob, but the more she uncovered his past, the more she realized he had another side. *A loving one.*

Under that stuffed shirt and grumpy exterior, he actually cared. He just didn't want anyone to know it. Especially not her.

After a week of designing marketing plans and then erasing them completely, she finally put the plan aside and stuck the pencil behind her ear, like a frazzled school teacher.

How would she explain to Liam that a week had passed and still she had nothing to show for it? She felt like a frustrated author with writer's block. The growing pressure to save the bookstore was actually creating a total mental block. She took a deep breath as she sat at Mr. Pomfrey's old desk.

The only thing she could do was focus on the two things that mattered. The customers and her after-school reading program. It was her favorite part of the job, and the kids she helped made it more than worth it, even if it wasn't bringing in big bucks. She'd sell Liam on the idea. Maybe even get his niece involved on the weekends.

Cassidy nervously fixed her hair in the glass window of the office door before she gathered her notebook and laptop and headed to meet Abby and Jane for the garden party. Grabbing her phone, she noticed a message.

Liam: Do you mind if I attend the garden party?
Cassidy: Is this the same Liam Henry who adamantly refused to attend a week ago? Or has an alien taken over Liam's body and is now pretending to act as Mr. Henry?
Liam: Guilty as charged.
Cassidy: You're an alien?
Liam: No. I changed my mind. Isn't that allowed?
Cassidy: Not when you're Liam Henry. What's the reason?
Liam: No reason.
Cassidy: I don't believe you. You do everything for a reason.
Liam: I want to see you.

Cassidy almost dropped her phone. Her hands shook as her

thumbs hovered over the screen. Of course, he didn't mean anything by it. That was the thing with phone messages. It was hard to tell subtext.

She started her reply. Then erased it. Then retyped. Then erased.

Was he kidding? He could have meant anything by it. Or nothing. Take your pick.

She dropped her phone into her purse and headed home to change clothes for the party.

Like it or not, she'd face Liam Henry today.

When one o'clock came round, the smooth purr of his car in front of the wedding shop caused her heart to jump.

Cassidy waited inside with the owner attempting to distract herself with the latest shipment of pretty bridal gowns.

"So, who is this mystery man?" Mila asked as she straightened the lace train on a mannequin. Her gaze drifted outside to Liam as he opened the car door for Jane.

"My new boss," Cassidy said casually.

Mila lifted onto her tiptoes. "I see he doesn't have a ring." Mila smiled. "That's convenient."

Cassidy bit her lip. If she was going to pretend to date Liam, that meant she couldn't tell Mila the truth. Or anyone.

A young girl with a cascade of long blonde curls rushed into the shop.

"These dresses are so beautiful!" she exclaimed, zigzagging past racks of sparkling gowns.

"Don't touch anything," Liam called out.

The atmosphere shifted and crackled as soon as Liam walked into the store. He wore a summer suit and a light blue dress shirt that brought out his eyes. As their gazes locked, the heat climbed her back beneath her sundress.

Abby dutifully clasped her hands behind her back. "I won't, Uncle Liam."

The way he barked orders at Abby reminded her of Captain Von Trapp. It wouldn't surprise her if he even had a special whistle.

"Please excuse Abby," he apologized to Mila. "She still adores princesses and gowns. When she heard we were stopping at a wedding shop, she was over the moon."

Cassidy tore her eyes from Liam and turned to Abby with what she hoped passed for a warm smile.

"Hi, I'm Cassidy, but you can call me Cass."

"Uncle Liam doesn't call you that," she said.

Her eyes flicked over to Liam. "Well, it's the name I only let special people use."

"You mean Uncle Liam isn't special?" she asked.

"He is, but not as special as you," she said.

"You're a lot prettier than I thought. And nicer. I didn't think Uncle Liam would pick someone like you."

"Now, Abby," Jane corrected before giving her a pointed look.

"He usually complains about every girl," Abby confessed. "He's a lot pickier than I am!"

Mila and Cassidy laughed, but Liam clamped his lips together. For the first time, Cassidy thought he looked embarrassed.

"Normally, he brushes women off," Abby revealed as she circled a rack of dresses. "I can't believe he's dating you."

Liam checked his watch. "We need to go. I don't want to arrive late."

Saved by her fake boyfriend. She gave Mila an apologetic smile and held out her hand for Abby.

"I'm happy to take your mom and Abby," Cassidy offered. "You don't have to attend."

She wanted to offer him a way out, in case he regretted the text he sent earlier.

"I said I was going," Liam insisted.

"He wants to go with you, of course!" Abby exclaimed before dragging Cassidy behind.

He certainly had fooled his niece, and worst of all, she'd have to pretend all afternoon that they were dating for Jane and Abby's sake.

She followed him to his car and lowered her voice as Abby and Jane climbed in. "It's really not a problem for you to stay behind."

He looked at her with the same ocean-blue eyes that haunted her as she lay in bed at night.

"I thought I made it clear in my text," he said without emotion.

But that was the problem. His text hadn't been clear at all.

Was this part of the dating agreement? Or was there something more?

When they arrived, Abby was the first one out of the car. She scrambled over to the entrance of the garden before Liam barked out, "Wait, Abby!"

She spun on her heel. "What now?"

"Be on your best behavior," he reminded her.

"I promise," she said.

"Why don't you stay with Grandmother?" He nodded toward Jane.

"Aw, do I have to? I want to hang out with Cassidy."

Her eyes pleaded for Cassidy to say yes.

"How about I take both of you ladies through the garden?" Cassidy said. "I don't mind."

That would give them space, and neither would have to pretend.

Liam looked relieved. "That's perfect. I need to talk to Agnes."

As Liam drifted inside to find the hostess, Jane admired the scarlet climbing roses and purple clematis.

"Coming here makes me feel like a princess!" Abby exclaimed. "Like this could be a secret garden. Or the place where the prince falls in love with me." She skipped ahead on the garden path, rounding a curve too quickly, where she nearly slammed into Edna, an elegant older lady who acted as the town's mother hen. She nearly dropped her Pekingese dog, Peaches.

"Oh, dear. Who are you?" Edna exclaimed, looking at the girl.

"I'm Abby."

"She's with me," Cassidy said. "This is her grandmother, Jane."

"Oh hello, Jane and Abby." Edna held out her hand, her fingers covered in large rings and gemstones. "I'm Edna."

Jane admired a large turquoise stone on Edna's ring finger. "How beautiful. It's a pleasure to meet you, Edna. Cassidy is showing us around."

As soon as Abby noticed Peaches, she drew closer. "May I hold your dog?"

"Of course, dear," she said, placing Peaches in Abby's arms.

"Uncle Liam won't let me have a dog," she said, frowning. "I think he puts me in a boarding school so I can't have one."

"Well, you can take care of Peaches at the party," Edna offered. "She'd love a walk around the garden."

"Really?" Abby said, setting the dog on the stone path and giving her leash a tiny pull. "Come on, Peaches," Abby invited, then the dog bolted ahead and yanked Abby along.

"I'd better help Abby," Cassidy said, leaving the two older women behind.

As Peaches found a bush to sniff, Cassidy caught up with Abby.

"That was nice of Edna to let you babysit her dog," Cassidy said.

"Maybe I can dog sit when we move here," Abby said.

"So your uncle told you?" Cassidy asked.

"Uncle Liam mentioned that he bought the bookstore and is looking for a lake house. Soon, I'll visit all the time."

"I'd love that," Cassidy said, smiling at Abby. She had the same eyes as Liam.

"Do you really like my uncle?" Abby asked. "I think you should marry him." The hope in her expression was unmistakable.

Cassidy tried to let her down gently. "We've only known each other for a short time."

"Oh, that doesn't matter! People fall in love all the time the first time they meet. Haven't you read about all the princesses?"

"I have, but this isn't a fairy tale. I hardly even know your uncle," Cassidy responded gently. Even if it was true, this conversation was making her feel like a complete fraud. If Abby knew the truth, she'd probably hate her.

"That doesn't matter. If it's love at first sight, then it's *meant to be*." She said it with a lilt in her voice, like she was trying to wish it into existence. "Besides, my uncle *needs* a woman."

"Abby . . ." Cassidy could no longer stand it. She wanted to be honest with Abby before her hopes skyrocketed any more. It would only make it that much more painful if she had to dash her hopes later.

At that moment, Abby accidentally let go of Peaches's leash, and the small dog took off down a garden path.

"Peaches, come back!" Abby yelled, racing after her.

Cassidy followed, running through garden beds of red bee balm and yellow coneflowers, prickly rose bushes and lush hydrangea. Peaches dodged and weaved under bushes, evading their attempts at catching her. Every time Cassidy reached for her, Peaches darted down another path, taking corners at lightning speed.

"You head down that path," she pointed for Abby. "I'll take this one. We'll cut her off."

As they separated, Cassidy ran down a private garden path, giving up hope that they'd ever catch Peaches.

As she rounded a corner lined with a tall compact hedge of well-manicured bushes, Liam's voice drifted from the other side. Although Cassidy couldn't see who was with him, he was addressing someone in a low voice.

"I'm not interested in dating. Or marriage, either," Liam said. "I have too many businesses to run."

Cassidy's mouth fell open as she leaned closer to the bushes to see what other secrets he would share. The hedge was so dense, she couldn't see him, but eavesdropping was no problem.

"What kind of woman would you want to date?" another male voice asked. "Besides someone who looks like a supermodel."

A few men laughed. She couldn't tell if Liam was one of them, but he obviously wasn't alone.

"She would have to be superior in looks, brains, even business. Someone who is my equal in every way," Liam remarked. "Otherwise, she isn't good enough."

Cassidy almost choked on his words. His arrogance was astounding.

"You mean, you want the perfect woman?" another man asked. More chuckles rumbled around the group.

"Don't we all?" Liam said.

The men agreed and glasses clinked together in solidarity.

Cassidy wanted to vomit in her own mouth. She couldn't stand this boys' club mentality.

"The problem is," Liam went on, "my mother and I have different standards for who I date."

"What kind of girl does your mom want?" another man asked.

"A nice girl from a small town."

"Nothing wrong with that!" a third man replied.

That's right, she wanted to scream in agreement, but at that moment, Peaches whipped around a bush, with Abby on her heels.

"Help, Cassidy!" Abby yelled. "Get Peaches!"

Cassidy lunged toward the dog and scooped her up before she could scramble away.

Liam rounded the bushes to see what was going on. "How long have you been there?"

"Long enough," Cassidy said with a razor-sharp edge in her voice. Although she wouldn't confront him here in front of a crowd, she made certain her underlying tone was clear.

"Edna's dog got loose. We were trying to help," Abby said.

His niece held the dog in her arms, hugging it gently.

"Please take the dog back to its owner," Liam told Abby.

Abby and the men wandered away, leaving Cassidy alone with Liam.

Cassidy crossed her arms and started to walk away before Liam stopped her. Though she was good at keeping her feelings hidden, her silence was just as deadly.

"What's wrong?" he asked.

She couldn't believe he didn't know. Her fingers flicked a faded bloom off a stem. Deadheading was so satisfying when people irritated her. "You can learn a lot about what someone thinks of you when they don't know you're listening."

He looked confused. "I didn't say anything about you."

"You implied I'm beneath you." She tossed the dead flower to the ground. "I can't measure up to you in brains, looks, or business. So why are you pretending to date me if I'm so inadequate?"

"That's not what I said," he countered.

"You said your standards are different from your mom's. As if that were a bad thing."

"It's the way things are. My parents were complete opposites. It doesn't mean they despised their differences."

"Well, it sounds like you do," she said. "I agreed to this fake dating to keep the bookstore open, but I'm rethinking the deal." She turned on her heel, pushing through bushes to get away from him.

In his mind, she was a convenience, nothing more. He hadn't chosen her because he might consider her an equal match. No wonder she felt like trash.

He followed her, grabbing her wrist. "Please don't go," he said, turning her toward him. Something softened in his gaze. "If I've offended you, then I apologize."

"You *did* offend me," she tossed back.

"Again, I'm sorry." His jaw clenched as if it were difficult to admit. "If you leave now, Abby will be crushed."

The heat of his fingers pulsated through her arm. She hated that even when she couldn't stand him, he still drew her in. "For Abby's sake, I'll stay," she reluctantly agreed, pulling her wrist from his grasp.

She turned to leave, but could feel Liam's gaze on her.

Abby had found her way back to Jane and was seated at one of the garden tables, surrounded by a group of older women dressed in bright flowing blouses and fancy wide-brimmed hats. It felt like most of Wild Harbor's elite was here, their jeweled ears sparkling in the sun.

"Cassidy, we were wondering what happened to you." Jane patted the seat next to her.

Peaches squirmed in Edna's arms, begging to escape.

Abby bit into a crostini topped with blended cream cheese and a sprig of basil. A smudge of cheese dotted the corner of her lips.

"Everything is so fancy!" Abby exclaimed. "I feel like I'm at a queen's house."

She picked up a teacup and held out her pinky while taking a sip. "I bet Uncle Liam approves!" She waved to her uncle from across the garden, where he hung in the back, returning her gesture with a nod and a smile.

As much as he pretended not to care, Abby had clearly cracked open his grinch-like heart.

A microphone crackled as Agnes stepped to the front and cleared her throat. "Welcome to this year's garden party, especially our new guests." She motioned toward the Henrys. "Liam Henry recently bought Books Forever, which has been a staple of our town. I encourage you to buy your books locally and to support programs like Cassidy's after-school reading program for kids."

Cassidy glanced over at Liam, wondering how he'd roped Agnes into becoming the store's cheerleader. When he looked her way, she quietly mouthed the words *thank you.* His mouth quirked in response, the first hint of approval.

Agnes finished her welcome speech and invited Jane and Abby to tour her home. As she watched them leave, Liam made his way toward her, a glass of something cold in his hand.

"Am I allowed to sit here, or are you still mad at me?" he said with an amused grin.

She shrugged. "Since you somehow twisted Agnes's arm to support the store, I'll allow it."

Liam lowered himself into a chair across from Cassidy. "I asked her to mention it a few days ago." No wonder Liam had wanted to attend the garden party. It wasn't because of their dating arrangement. It just made good business sense.

"But why?" As much as she wanted the bookstore to stay open, she didn't think Liam did.

"That was part of the deal, wasn't it? For our *arrangement,*" he stated in a low voice, leaning across the table. She could see the yellow flecks in his irises, a pool of grays and blues surrounding it.

"What about your fancy gym?"

"I made a promise to you. One thing to know about the Henrys, we keep our promises."

His gaze bore through her, making her heart jumpy. She couldn't let this favor change her feelings for him. He'd made it clear how he felt about girls like her. She wasn't up to his standards.

"Thank you," she murmured.

"For what?" he said, taking a sip of his iced tea.

"For doing something nice for me," she said. "And here I thought you were a big grump."

His lips curled into a smile. "I may just prove you right."

CHAPTER TEN

LIAM

"Uncle Liam!" Abby ran across the garden, a crown of braided flowers on her head. "This place is amazing. I want to stay forever!"

He'd spent an entire afternoon at a garden party and was ready to go home, but from the looks of it, Abby wasn't.

"Cass said she'd like to take me to the chocolate shop now," Abby said. "Can I go, please?"

"I'm not sure," he said, his gaze sweeping the crowd. "Where's your grandmother?"

"I already asked her, and she said it was fine. Cass said you probably wouldn't want to go."

"Oh, did she?" he said, tickling her side. "Well, I'll show her."

"Hey!" Abby giggled. "Cassidy, tell Uncle Liam to stop!"

"What's going on?" Cassidy said.

"Uncle Liam won't stop tickling me! And he wants to go to the chocolate shop with us." Abby darted behind Cassidy for protection.

"He does?" Cassidy said.

The way Abby had warmed up to Cassidy was a tremendous relief. For the longest time, he'd wanted someone to take her under her wing.

Liam held his hands up. "I'll stop. *If* you let me come."

Cassidy's eyes widened. "Are you sure?"

"Why is that such a shock?"

Wisps of hair had loosened from her braid and were dancing in the breeze. She was distracting. And beautiful. But he couldn't tell her that. Not here.

"You never do fun things with me," Abby admitted.

"Don't you trust me with Abby?" Cassidy asked.

"I trust you fully," he said. "Can't I have fun for once?"

Abby and Cassidy exchanged looks before Abby blurted out, "I don't know what happened to my uncle, but whoever you are, please give him back."

Liam laughed. "Am I really that dull?"

Abby screwed up her mouth in thought. "Don't take this the wrong way, but yes."

A small snort laugh escaped from Cassidy.

Liam opened his mouth in mock horror. "How rude!" he teased, grabbing his niece and tickling her sides again.

"Hey!" she giggled. "You wanted the truth, right?"

"Not that much!" he said, continuing to tickle her until she begged him to stop.

Jane rushed over, her cheeks glowing with pleasure. "It looks like you've had fun," she said to Liam and Abby. "I've met so many new people today, and they all want to hear about you and Cassidy."

He could feel the heat of Cassidy's embarrassment without even looking at her.

"I hope you didn't say anything," he said, his tone quickly growing serious.

"They're delighted she is dating again!" she said, turning to

Cassidy. "Edna and Thelma told me the story of your broken engagement."

Engaged? Cassidy hadn't mentioned it to him before. Who was the guy?

Cassidy shifted uncomfortably. "I don't like to talk about it."

"I'm so sorry. But it's good it didn't work out. After all, you couldn't date my son if it had."

"Mother," Liam warned.

"What?" She shrugged. "Can't a mother want the best for her son?"

"You're jumping to conclusions," he growled.

"That's what mothers do," she reminded Liam.

"I'm heading to the chocolate shop with Abby now," Cassidy said, pulling Abby by the arm.

"Wait, Cassidy," Liam said, jogging after her.

Cassidy was practically running from the garden party.

"It's a gorgeous day. Let's walk to the shop," she said, her cheeks still heated.

Liam kept pace with Cassidy while Abby skipped ahead.

"I'm sorry about my mom," Liam said.

"It's not her fault. I should have told you."

"You don't have to tell anyone," he insisted. "It's none of their business."

"Try telling Edna and Thelma that. I shouldn't have come today. I knew people would talk about us."

"At least your bookstore might get a rush of clients."

"Mine?" she asked. "The bookstore is yours."

"Technically, yes, but it's your passion project," he said. He admired her ability to stand behind a dream that wasn't just built on money. She actually cared about books and the people who bought them.

"A passion project that you're about to crush in less than two months," she reminded him.

Even if he could fix the lack of sales, the bookstore might soldier on, but for how long?

"I'm not out to destroy the bookstore," he told her. "I can't fix what's not profitable."

"Then what will it take to get more time?" she asked. "The promise of my firstborn child?"

He didn't want to tell her it wasn't possible. Not without him majorly funding the losses.

"No more kids. I've got my hands full with that one," he said, pointing to his niece.

Abby turned, a mischievous smile spreading across her face. "You two look cute together. Have you held hands yet?"

"Absolutely not," Liam said. "And you won't either until you're twenty."

Cassidy raised an eyebrow. "Twenty? Are you going to lock her in a tower too? You know, hand holding is pretty innocent."

"Yeah, it is," Abby agreed. "Which is why you should hold hands. You're dating, right?"

"Abby." Liam's voice was firm. For so long, he'd lived with the belief that no one could measure up and that love only meant hurt. He didn't want to experience what his mother had —the excruciating loss of her dearest love.

"But why wouldn't you want to hold her hand if you're dating?" In Abby's mind, it was the most natural thing in the world.

"How about I'll hold *your* hand," he said to Abby.

"No way. I'm too old for that," she said, clasping her hands behind her back so he couldn't touch her. "But I still think you should hold Cassidy's hand. It's what all the romantic guys do."

"Maybe I'm not a romantic guy," he said with a smile.

Abby sighed dramatically. "That's why everyone calls you *Uncle Grumpy.*"

"Everyone?" he questioned. Eight-year-olds were great at taking one comment and applying it to everyone.

"My friends call you Uncle Grumpy," she admitted. "Whenever you pick me up for the weekend, they say, '*Is Uncle Grumpy coming to get you in his Grumpymobile?*'"

"Seriously?" he asked. "When they grow up and see the price tag on my car, they'll think I'm cool."

He glanced over at Cassidy who wasn't doing a good job of hiding her amusement.

"What?" he asked, shrugging.

"I'm laughing at the fact that eight-year-old girls think your fancy car is a *Grumpymobile.*"

"See?" Abby added. "If you keep acting like a grump, everyone in Wild Harbor will think of you the same way."

"How about we change Uncle Grumpy into a romantic?" Cassidy suggested. Then she grabbed Liam's hand.

"What are you doing?" he asked, trying to wriggle it away. Her hand touching his was like fire. On the one hand, he liked it —even *more than* liked it. But he shouldn't hold her hand—or enjoy the sensation of it—when he wasn't really dating her.

"I'm making your niece's day," she said. "It's your job to teach her how a young man should treat her."

Liam frowned. "She's too young to date."

"But she's right," Abby agreed. "It's *your* job."

He knew that one day she'd probably get married and his responsibilities as guardian would end. But he hadn't realized that boarding school didn't teach dating rules.

He glanced at Cassidy. "First rule. Never grab a guy's hand."

Cassidy rolled her eyes. "Don't listen to your uncle. A girl can grab a guy's hand."

"But not you," he told Abby.

"How rude," she muttered, crossing her arms. "If it's so wrong, then why do you look like you're enjoying it?"

Was it really that obvious? Cassidy's touch was driving him crazy. He hadn't held hands with a woman in so long, he'd forgotten how it felt. Her touch was turning his brain to mush.

He couldn't form one rational response to his niece. All he knew was that he liked it. He just hoped Cassidy couldn't tell.

If they were really dating, then why stop at hand holding? He'd like to run his fingers through her hair or wrap one arm around her waist and pull her toward him before . . .

"Look, the chocolate shop!" Abby shrieked as they turned the corner and the quaint storefront came into view.

He couldn't let his mind go there now. Cassidy was his employee. His fake date. Touching her was causing fireworks to go off in his body, but he couldn't let his mind wander anymore. It was too dangerous given that their arrangement was temporary.

Cassidy quickly dropped his hand as they approached the door. "Let me introduce you to my sister."

"Hey, sis," Lily said from across the shop.

Abby dashed to the display case to gawk at the chocolates. "Wow, these are amazing! Can I have them all?"

"No," Liam said before Cassidy could respond.

"Lily, this is Liam and his niece, Abby."

"The new bookstore owner," Lily said. "Good to meet you both."

Abby turned to her uncle. "Can I have some chocolate?"

"You can pick one," he said.

Abby scowled. "But one isn't enough. Look at these! Chocolate-covered peanuts, turtles, peanut butter cups, truffles."

"How about we put together a small sampler box of chocolates," Lily suggested. "I have some in the back. Do you mind if I take her with me?"

Abby clapped her hands together. "Yes, if it's okay with you?" she asked Liam with a hopeful expression.

"Of course," he said. "Have fun."

Lily led Abby to the back, leaving Liam and Cassidy alone. "Lily left something for us to nibble on." She nodded toward a plate on a nearby café table. "My sister is always trying to feed me chocolates." They sat across from each other and Cassidy pushed the plate toward Liam. "It's all yours."

Usually, he wasn't one for sweets. "I shouldn't."

"You really should. My sister's chocolates will change your life."

He smiled politely. "I don't need my life changed."

"Are you sure?" she asked. "Because I think you do." A mischievous gleam sparked in her eyes. She picked up a chocolate and held it out for him.

"Chocolates are messy."

"Life is messy," she said, holding the treat closer.

"You still don't have me convinced," he said.

"Just eat it."

"No way—"

Before he could even finish, she reached across the table and pushed it into his mouth.

He bit into something gooey that melted in his mouth.

"How is it?" she asked.

He savored the confection, letting the salted caramel and luscious chocolate set off all the endorphins in his brain.

"Besides the fact you almost shoved a piece of food down my throat, it's good."

She crossed her arms in satisfaction. "You're a lot more approachable when you smile."

Normally, he'd reply with a self-deprecating remark to take the attention off of him. But instead, something was splitting open his chest, an unfamiliar glow rising inside him. If his smile pleased her that much, he needed to smile more.

"No more Uncle Grumpy?" he teased. "That's too bad. I thought it would come in handy for Abby's teen years."

"Don't worry. You'll still scare off her potential boyfriends," she said with a smirk. "You have the best serious face of anyone. It would frighten a psychopath."

"But does it scare *you* away?" he asked. He'd posed it as a joke, but underneath, he wanted to know if it was true.

"Always. You're super intimidating when you combine that face with your suit. You belong in the next *Men in Black* sequel."

So he still intimidated her? That wasn't the answer he wanted. If they were going to make this partnership work, he needed to make her trust him.

"What can I do to make you more comfortable?" he said. "So you're not intimidated?"

"You're my boss. How else should it be?" she said.

He couldn't read her face, but she picked at the plate of chocolates, resigned to the situation. So she only saw him as her boss. To be fair, he didn't know what he saw her as anymore. She wasn't his real girlfriend, even if he felt attracted to her. Could he at least convince her to become friends?

"If we're working together while pretending to date, we could make this enjoyable."

She narrowed her eyes. "Liam Henry, are you asking me to be your friend?"

Awkwardness swept over him, like he was back in high school asking out a girl.

"I guess?" he said. "But talking about it is even stranger. I'm a guy. I don't ask people to be my friend."

"Well, I do, so you'll just have to get used to it. Because like it or not, you're stuck with me, until our time is up."

"Stuck? I wouldn't put it that way," he said. Her smile melted him like the inside of a truffle.

"As your friend, can I officially call you Uncle Grumpy? I'm sure that would win brownie points with Abby."

"No, you may not," he insisted.

"If I act like your girlfriend, I should have some ridiculously sappy nickname for you. Like *sweetie pie* or *honey pot*."

He winced. "I hate when girls do that. And I'm sure their boyfriends agree."

"It's all pretend, since we're not actually dating, *sweetie.*" She gave him an evil grin.

"If you do it again, I'll force you to eat this chocolate." He picked up a confection on the plate.

"You wouldn't dare," she challenged. "*Honey.*"

He lunged across the table. She dodged him, scrambling from her seat and circling the table until he cornered her between a potted plant and another table.

He grabbed her arm and pulled her close. He didn't have time to think about the effect it would have on him, but as soon as their bodies brushed, he felt a current of excitement rush through him.

"Don't you . . ." she started, but he was too fast. He popped the chocolate between her teeth as she uttered a muffled *"dare."*

"I'll get you for this," she said, her mouth full of chocolate.

He'd gladly let her.

Just then, Abby bounded from the back room. She froze, her eyes wide as she stared at the pair.

They looked like they'd been caught in an embrace, even though it was nothing of the sort.

Lily brought out a tray of confections, her gaze landing on Cassidy. "Oh, so sorry. We didn't mean to interrupt." She grabbed Abby by the arm and tried to pull her back.

"You didn't interrupt!" Cassidy shouted, stepping away from Liam like she'd seen a spider.

Abby smiled. "Cass, why do you have chocolate smeared on your mouth?"

Cassidy's cheeks flushed as she wiped her mouth with the back of her hand. "We were eating chocolate."

"Oh, really?" Abby said. Even at eight, she didn't believe them at all.

"He forced me to eat it." Cassidy turned to Liam. "Didn't you?" She nudged Liam.

"After you shoved chocolate in my mouth," he accused.

He couldn't remember the last time he'd acted so childishly. His father had instilled a serious approach to life, demonstrating that men hardly ever cracked smiles or acted silly. The only model of fatherhood Liam had ever seen was a man who appeared like a stone wall, entirely impenetrable.

He straightened up. "You won't see me acting that way again," he said to Abby, avoiding Cassidy's glare.

"Like someone who could have fun?" Cassidy asked.

"No, like someone in love," Abby replied as she stole a chocolate off of Lily's tray.

"Hardly," he said. "You wouldn't understand." He pulled out his phone and checked his email.

"I do understand love!" Abby shot back. Her face crumpled as she turned away and stormed into the back room.

He sighed. It was for the best that he crush her hopes now. If he let her believe that a serious relationship with Cassidy was possible, it would only make things worse later when he revealed they were no longer a couple.

Or worse, if they found out about the fake dating arrangement. He cringed thinking about it.

It had seemed like such an easy answer at the time, but now his emotions were caught in a tightly woven knot that he couldn't seem to untangle.

Everyone in his family was rooting for this match. If he was honest with himself, something inside him was too.

CHAPTER ELEVEN

"You can do this," she said to herself in the mirror, pulling back the sides of her hair so it wouldn't fall in her face. "Just try on the dress and pretend you're dating Liam. It will turn out fine."

Ever since Liam Henry had burst into her life, she'd forgotten everything outside of her own confused existence. Even the bridesmaid dress fitting had slipped from her mind. Her siblings' double wedding had originally seemed light years away, but with only a few months to go, it was bearing down on her like a freight train.

Ever since her brother, Matt, had asked Aspen to marry him, her sister Megan had joked that they should have a double wedding since she was also engaged to Finn. The two couples had agreed that a double wedding would have its benefits. They could work together on the plans, split the costs, and have the dream beach wedding they'd always wanted.

Since her remaining two siblings were engaged, Cassidy was the only one who wasn't in a relationship. But now that she had

Liam Henry in her life, could she pretend it was real? Would anyone believe her?

Ever since the chocolate incident, she couldn't stop thinking of Liam. Even though he'd hinted that girls like her weren't up to his standards, her heart was like a hive that had been poked and was swarming with bees.

She felt alive, even though the outcome was hopeless.

As she entered Mila's wedding shop, Megan's voice echoed across the store. "Look who arrived! The girl who's dating her boss and didn't bother to tell me."

Cassidy gave Lily a look. "You told her."

"If I hadn't, you know Edna would have," Lily defended.

"I didn't want everyone involved yet. Not when things are so uncertain," she said.

"Uncertain?" Megan frowned. "You went to the garden party with him."

Megan adjusted the lacy veil on her head. She still had on her work attire: a navy pencil skirt with a deep green blouse that flattered her eyes. She looked ridiculous and adorable all at the same time.

"When were you planning on telling me about your boss?" Megan was like a bulldozer in her approach to everything.

"We're not serious," Cassidy admitted. "His mother pressured him to find a date." She averted her eyes so that she wouldn't have to face her sisters. It was true, even if it wasn't the total story.

Megan propped a hand on her hip. "A grown man doesn't give in to pressure from his mother."

"He does if his mother is fighting cancer," Cassidy said. "But it's awkward because I'm his employee."

She didn't reveal her fake dating scheme. If they knew the truth, they'd insist she didn't need the store. But she didn't want to hold the program any place else. She'd worked hard to create an environment that made kids feel safe.

"Then quit your job," Megan said.

"Books Forever isn't just a job," Cassidy said. "I've invested my life in it."

Megan squeezed her sister's arm. "If you marry him, you'll never have to worry about working at the bookstore again."

Cassidy rolled her eyes before escaping into a dressing room. "Please don't mention the big 'M' again. It's a surefire way to scare a man away," she warned her sisters.

As Cassidy slid her body into the ivory bridesmaid gown with gold flecks that shimmered across every curve, she took a long look at herself in the mirror. The dress highlighted the soft lines of her body. No longer did she look like a young woman in her usual cotton sundress or boho blouse, but someone with money, which was laughable, given her bank account neared zero. She desperately needed more funding to keep the bookstore alive. Because if the store tanked, then so would the afterschool program. The fact that she was gallivanting around town on the arm of a millionaire was a joke.

And when the truth gets out, it's going to be on you.

As much as it hurt, it was true. Once Liam closed the store and broke things off, what would she have left?

Her dream was like a kid's sandcastle on the beach, caving in on itself with the first wave. Tears pooled in her eyes as she stared at herself in the mirror. It wasn't just about the store anymore, was it? When her heart had gotten tangled up in her feelings for Liam, she'd known the outcome before it even began.

Because if her ex, Cameron, had taught her anything, it's that men could pretend they love you and then leave you in a second, even when you believed the feelings were real.

Her chest heaved with a silent sob as she wiped the corners of her eyes.

"Almost ready?" Mila's voice drifted over the top of the door.

"Just about," she said, inhaling so she wouldn't look

distraught, even though her insides were quaking. She needed to enjoy this moment for Megan and Aspen's sake. No matter what Liam thought of her, there was no way he couldn't notice her when she was wearing this.

As she stepped from her dressing room, she was shocked to see Liam and Abby had joined the women. Liam's gaze flicked to Cassidy, and her whole body heated.

"What are you doing here?" she asked.

Liam's eyes slid over her dress, then back to her face. She couldn't read his mind, but it was unusual for him not to respond with a brusque reply. Instead, he quirked his lips.

"I invited him and Abby," Lily confessed. "They should join us now that our families are connected."

"And Abby needs a new dress," Liam added.

Abby dashed over to Cassidy with a huge smile as Liam kept his distance. "Cass, you look like a princess!" Abby exclaimed.

Cassidy's embarrassment quickly faded as she observed Abby's excitement. "You're going to look like a princess too. I can't wait to see your dress."

"Follow me to the back." Mila motioned to Abby. "I want to show you some of the children's dresses." Then she turned to Liam. "You can stay here if you want. I'll bring Abby out to you."

Mila took Abby's hand and led her away while Cassidy hung back, awkwardly clasping her hands. For once, she had nothing to say to Liam, who was trying to look anywhere but at her.

Even her sisters had wandered to the other side of the store, leaving her and Liam alone.

"You look nice," he said stiffly, his eyes darting back to her dress. For the first time, she sensed he was more uncomfortable that her, although she couldn't imagine why. He didn't have to pretend to like her when no one was watching.

"I'm sorry if my family roped you into this."

He shook his head, digging his hands into his pockets. "My mother dropped a hint about it to your mom."

"Jane met my mother? But how?" This was getting out of hand fast. Now she was going to have to explain to her mom why she had kept her relationship with Liam a secret. The lies and deceit were piling up fast.

"After the garden party, she ran into her in town. I never thought my mother would be so bold. She practically invited us to your family's double wedding."

Cassidy closed her eyes for a long second. "I'll be playing damage control the rest of the month."

"Mother is going to expect me to attend the wedding now. And that's past our agreed date on this arrangement." He looked squarely at her to see if she understood. That meant they'd need to pretend to date longer.

"I don't want to put you in an awkward situation, but is it possible to continue dating through the wedding . . . for Abby's sake?" he asked. "She's thrilled about attending the wedding."

For once, he didn't look like a businessman cutting her a deal. He looked like a father asking to make his daughter's wish come true.

"I'll consider it," she said. The thought of hurting either of them was like a lead weight suffocating her. Inevitably, she'd have to tell them the truth, but for now, she couldn't worry about that.

Liam leaned closer. "For the record, I won't let this agreement hurt them—or you."

How it was possible to shield her from what she inevitably knew—that she'd get hurt in the end, no matter what?

His eyes skimmed over her once more. "That dress is very becoming."

Cassidy wrapped her arms across her waist, wishing she could drape a giant blanket over her head. The way he stared at her made a wave of gooseflesh ripple over her arms. She could barely resist the longing in his eyes, even if it was just admiration over a pretty dress.

"Does that mean you approve? I know you have high standards," she said.

A laugh escaped his lips. "More than approve. I'm probably going to beat off all the guys who will fall all over themselves for you."

"I always wanted a bodyguard," she said, relaxing a little. At least she looked dressed up enough to pass as his date. It had been a long time since she'd felt this special, like he'd be proud to attend with her on his arm.

He wrapped one arm around her waist and turned her toward the mirror. "You belong with someone better than me," he said. "I don't deserve you."

Even while wearing the strapless number, she felt warmth soar through her middle. Why would he say that when she didn't live up to his standards?

Between his arm circling her waist and his body close to hers, she couldn't help but swell with heat. If he only knew how he was making her feel.

Abby bolted from the dressing room, sparkling in a cream and gold gown with fluffy tulle exploding from the skirt. Liam dropped his arm and stepped back to admire his niece. The shade was like Cassidy's, but the design was a princess cut with a full skirt, turning her into a miniature storybook princess.

"This one is my favorite!" She twirled like she was playing in dress-up clothes.

"I'm not sure how I feel about you looking so ladylike," he said with a mixture of pride and displeasure.

Her face fell. "I'm only pretending. It's not like I have a real date, like you!"

He wrapped one arm around Abby's shoulder. "I'll be your date any time. And if any future dates break your heart, then I'm going to . . ." His hands curled into fists, imagining some young jerk breaking Abby's heart.

"Teach her how a gentleman should treat her," Cassidy insisted.

"Uncle Liam is going to give him a knuckle sandwich, aren't you?" Abby asked.

"I'd like to," he said, ruffling her hair. "But Cassidy's right."

It was endearing to witness Liam's protective instincts for his niece, but seriously, he couldn't punch all the guys that broke Abby's heart, no matter how much he wanted to. Her ex, Cameron, had made her dad so angry after their breakup, he'd gone out fishing the next day to calm himself down.

Liam glanced at Cassidy. "Your dress fits like they designed it for you." Something sparked in Liam's expression. "It's perfect."

Cassidy pulled at the dress, suddenly feeling the heat well up under the fabric. She couldn't take his gaze or his compliments. Their fake dating arrangement was the best possible plan for saving the store but clearly not for her heart.

She beelined back to her dressing room, calling over her shoulder, "I need to change." Not just her clothes, but her feelings for this man.

As soon as she shed this gown, he'd see she was only a *nice girl from a small town.* The very words he'd used when he'd clearly stated the type of girl he didn't want to date. To make matters worse, she still hadn't revealed the full truth about her epilepsy. She was afraid that he'd think less of her, judging her as incapable.

Abby followed her to the dressing room. "Cassidy, wait!"

She locked herself inside and reached for her zipper, which was at an impossible spot in the middle of her back.

"What is it? I need to take off this dress. I'm sweating like crazy," she said, bending her arm at an awkward angle. The droplets of sweat prickled down her spine.

"Uncle Liam wanted a picture together," she said.

"I can't," Cassidy said. "I'm already changing."

As Abby told Liam, she slumped onto a bench in the room, frustrated with her zipper and herself. Why was Liam having this effect on her? She stood to unzip her gown and grabbed the pull, tugging it down. Halfway down, the zipper snagged on the fabric and stopped. She tried to wriggle out of the dress, but it was too tight. She'd rip a seam if she pulled the dress off without loosening the back more.

She yanked harder, but the zipper refused to budge. There was no way she could fix it without help. If someone could untangle it, she could handle the rest on her own.

"Um, anyone there?" she called from the dressing room. "My zipper is stuck. Can someone help?"

A quiet knock sounded at the door. She swung the door open, hoping to see Mila or Abby. Instead, Liam stood on the other side, hands in his pockets, his mouth hitched into a half-grin. "You need help?"

She pushed her back against the door, trying to hide the half-open zipper. "Uh, no." She waved him away.

His smile grew as if he knew her secret. "That's interesting. Because I could have sworn you were calling for help."

She avoided his gaze. "I have a minor problem."

"I can help."

"You *cannot*."

"Try me," he said.

Her heart skipped a beat under his intense stare.

"My zipper's stuck in the middle of my back," she admitted.

"Are you indecent?" he asked.

"No, of course not," she said.

"Then turn around."

"But don't you think it will be weird?" She winced. "You're my boss."

He ignored her comment. "I can fix it."

He looked as calm as a cucumber. This was so unfair.

She could feel the heat rising to her cheeks as he waited for her to turn. "I'm not letting you unzip my dress."

"Will it show anything inappropriate?" he asked. "I've seen a woman's back before. This is a beach town. Women walk around in their bikinis."

"I know, but . . ." What could it hurt? He'd only see a little skin. As far as she could tell, this was a matter of getting her unstuck. He was doing her a favor.

She slowly circled so her back faced him and hid her face. She was sure it was as bright as a fire truck.

Long seconds stretched by as she waited for the tug of the zipper. Holding her breath, she finally turned her head over her shoulder.

"Well?" she asked, growing impatient. She felt vulnerable with her back to him, unable to see him. How long did it take to look at a zipper?

"I'm examining it," he said.

She stared at the wall. His hands spidered across her spine, every touch sending chills down her arms. She didn't want to react, but his movement was like a current of energy. Live, hot, jolting.

"It's stuck," he said.

"Well, I knew *that*," she said. "The question is whether you can get it unstuck."

He paused, his breath warming her shoulder. The corner of the dressing room mirror caught a half-section of his face, revealing his gaze trailing along on the bare skin of her shoulders.

His fingers traced the seam, folding the zipper backwards, his hands working magic on some problem she couldn't see.

She swallowed hard, before the zipper gently released in a painfully slow line down her back. Her breath hitched. Every time his fingers touched her skin, it was like lighter fluid tossed onto a fire. When he zipped it up, his hands quickly dropped, as if he'd been burned. Maybe he'd felt it too, this wildfire between them. If he had, then he knew the solution as well as she did. *Hands off.*

He cleared his throat, erasing the tension of the moment, signaling his job was complete. "You should be able to unzip it now," he said, his voice slightly pinched.

She turned to thank him, but her voice caught.

He placed his hand on the door, a conflicted expression washing over him. Instead of appearing strong and secure, his eyes held a wild and desperate hunger.

"Thank you," she forced out, wondering if she was as transparent as him, her walls so dissolved he could see right through her.

All she knew was this: if he leaned forward and touched her, she wouldn't stop him.

Maybe that was why he looked so defenseless.

If he could see her unspoken longing, that was a clear warning. This was no longer a game. They were playing with fire. One of them needed to leave before they both got burned.

CHAPTER TWELVE

LIAM

"The store can't stay open," he muttered to himself, practicing the speech he wanted to give to Cassidy when he arrived at the bookstore. He was ready to confess the truth about the store's future as he strolled down the sidewalk, approaching the storefront with its color-coordinated display of book covers, a snapshot of beauty worthy of an Instagram post.

Only three weeks into their arrangement, and he could already see the writing on the wall. It would take a miracle to keep this place alive. Even with more townspeople buying books, the store was unlikely to last past their arranged two-month mark.

And if the store couldn't make it, could they?

A sharp pang twisted his stomach.

Ever since the zipper incident, he couldn't stop thinking of Cass, which would be entirely normal if they were *actually* dating. But they weren't dating, *not really*.

After their agreement was up, he'd face the end of Books

Forever and, possibly, their relationship, whatever that was. He wasn't even sure anymore. But he wanted more than a pretend arrangement.

An older gentleman stepped out the door of the bookshop, broom in hand, and began sweeping the sidewalk.

His face looked familiar, but Liam couldn't place why he was working at the bookstore.

Liam approached him. "Excuse me. What are you doing?"

The man stopped and rested against the broom, a long scar peeking out from under his shirtsleeve. He'd seen it somewhere before.

"Filling in," the man said, his face warming into a gentle grin. "I'm Joshua. We met at the racetrack."

"That's right," Liam said, embarrassed that the old man had remembered him before he had. "And why are you sweeping the walk?"

"Cass always needs an extra hand on the days of her after-school program."

"Of course," he said, realizing he'd totally forgotten about the program she talked about incessantly. He hadn't told her he'd stop in today, but the realtor had called with a few more lake houses to look at, so he thought he'd surprise her.

"Thank you, but now that I'm here, you don't have to do that." He motioned toward the broom.

"Don't mind if I do," Joshua said, brushing the stiff bristles across the cement. "I was wondering what your plans were when you bought the bookstore."

This guy didn't mess around. Whatever game he was playing, he seemed keenly interested in Liam's intentions.

"I'm giving the store a trial run. If it doesn't make it, my plans are to turn it into a high-tech gym, with machines powered by computers that sync to your device to track each person's progress. Imagine that your smart watch could adjust your weights and then devise the ultimate workout for you."

Joshua scratched his head. "Sounds fancy. But what will happen to Cassidy's after-school program?"

He didn't know why Joshua was concerned. "Reading clubs can happen anywhere."

"Not this one," Joshua said, the swishing sound from the broom punctuating the silence. "She's developed something special here. Kids who are behind in their reading make incredible progress with her. Cassidy takes them under her wing and gives them a safe space where no one is going to tease them for being behind. It's a tremendous benefit to our community. And Cassidy's best work."

"Really?"

"She's created something magical here." Joshua's eyes sparked with mystery as he opened the door for Liam.

The store was noticeably vacant, except for Daisy greeting him at the door. He walked to the children's section and stopped. Cassidy had pushed a table to the side and replaced it with furry beanbags and books. Lights twinkled from the ceiling, a warm glow hovering over the space. She'd even set up a tent with battery-operated lanterns for the children. It looked like she'd created a full-scale camping scene in the middle of the store.

Fully absorbed in her setup, she'd crawled into the tent to fix a sagging corner. Only her legs stuck out of the flap door.

"This is quite the view," he remarked, admiring the setup—and her legs. Daisy gave a low woof before flopping onto a beanbag.

She poked her head out. "Liam! What are you doing?"

"I'd like to ask you the same thing," he said.

"Setting up for my kids," she said. "Twice a week for ten kids in the program. Right now, that's all I can handle."

Ten kids. That was it? It wasn't big enough to justify keeping the store open. "That's why we need to talk," he said gently.

"One second," she said, hanging a circular lamp. "I need to

make sure the star lamp is working." She flicked a switch and the lamp rotated, casting stars on the walls like they were in a planetarium.

"Nice effect," he said, turning slowly around. No doubt Abby would love this space. "But do their parents buy books?"

"Whose?"

"The parents who send their kids here."

"Oh, no. They usually drop their kids off and run errands. It makes it easier that way."

That was problem number one. Parents were the spenders, not the kids. No wonder this store wasn't making it.

"We need parents to buy from the store," he explained. "We can't run an after-school program when families aren't even supporting the business."

Cassidy's face fell. "I understand that. But this is a service to the community. It helps kids who might get left behind in school. There might not be an obvious financial advantage, but there is definitely a benefit for the children."

He couldn't win this argument. "It's noble to serve the community, but it doesn't make good business sense. Do you want this store to survive?"

"As long as you don't touch this program," she said firmly.

He hated when that stubborn expression crossed her face. There was no way he could sway her now. "Can you encourage parents to buy books? You don't have to pressure them, but telling them which books their child likes might help."

Her face softened as she drummed her nails on the bookshelf. "I hate that you're right. But I'm willing to talk about it."

She motioned toward a table in the children's section. The chairs were so tiny, his legs couldn't possibly squeeze under the table.

He lowered himself onto the pint-sized chair, his knees almost even with his shoulders. "Is there a reason we're sitting here?"

She glanced at his awkward position and attempted not to laugh. "You look miserable."

"I am miserable," he complained. His backside was already hurting. He grimaced as he tried to maneuver his legs so his laptop could balance precariously on his knees. "Could you look over these marketing ideas?"

She lowered herself into a chair and her leg brushed his, lighting him up like a jolt of electrical energy. Her scent of soft vanilla was torturous as she scooted closer.

He tried to focus on the document, but it was harder with every second. "It's a list of sales, promotions, and local businesses that we can ask to buy books."

"If we discount our books, we won't make much, and the popular titles will sell out," she said. "Unless you're planning on buying more inventory?"

He shook his head. "Too risky at this point. We need to focus on selling what we have. Unless you have some additional ideas."

She leaned closer to his computer. "Why not highlight the ways we're serving the community and send a press release to the paper? I'm sure Megan can put me on their schedule."

"Highlighting your after-school program?"

"And our weekly nursing home program and the Books for Veterans program."

"Wait . . . are these all free programs to the community?"

She nodded. "They've been very successful over the years."

"But are you selling books?"

"Oh, no, usually we donate them," she said. "But folks in the community sometimes donate money to support the programs."

He leaned his elbows on knees and dropped his forehead in his hands. That explained why the store was in financial distress. They were behaving more like a nonprofit that offered free services rather than a storefront. And that required an entirely different business model.

"Cassidy, those are wonderful programs. But unless they're producing income, they aren't helping us. What we need is a big corporation to buy a book for every employee as part of a work reading program. Or a school to purchase every student a book at Christmas."

She wrinkled her nose. "They don't have the money for that."

"And neither do we," he countered. "Which is why we need to change our focus."

"That hasn't been our mission. We're focused on education and outreach, helping groups in our community who struggle to get access to books."

"Then let's monetize that," he said.

She frowned and rose from her chair. "What if I don't want to monetize that? What if I want to help people?"

Why did she have to be so giving? He'd never met anyone who cared less about money than her, while his entire world revolved around it. He snapped his laptop shut. "Then you can say goodbye to Books Forever."

"I'm going to find a way. *Despite* your beliefs." She folded her arms and the strap of her dress slipped down. As he reached to fix it, she stepped back before he could touch her. "We might pretend to date, but otherwise, hands off." She hoisted the strap over her shoulder as she turned and stormed to the back room.

This was why it would never work between them. He was a bottom-line straight shooter who wasn't afraid of cutting people and programs, while she'd give her last dime to help a person in need. Although he admired her generous heart, it was the exact reason the store was in free fall.

At some point, they had to stop offering handouts.

A bell jingled as a customer entered the store with a shy, brown-eyed girl. Cassidy was still in the back, probably fuming after their conversation.

"Can I help you find a book?" he asked. He might as well start selling books now, if she wasn't going to.

Confusion crossed the mother's face. "We're here for the after-school program."

"Mom, look!" The girl pointed at the white lights hanging from the children's section before racing toward the camping scene.

Cassidy greeted her with a smile. "Hannah, it's good to see you! Which reading spot do you want today?"

"The tent!" she exclaimed, crawling through the flap door.

Cassidy followed, like it was normal to shrink yourself and squeeze into a tiny tent.

The mom turned toward Liam. "I take it you're the new owner?"

He nodded. "But Cassidy is the one running the store since the Pomfreys retired."

"Well, I hope you'll keep this program running. It's been extremely helpful for my daughter. She was diagnosed with epilepsy last year and has a reading disability. School has been a major struggle. Knowing Cassidy has the same issues has helped my daughter feel less alone."

He turned suddenly to the woman. "What did you say?"

The woman nodded. "That was the reason she started this program. She was diagnosed about the same age. Didn't she tell you?"

He shook his head, trying not to show his shock. "She never mentioned it."

"If it wasn't for her, I don't know what I'd do." The woman's eyes filled with tears. "Excuse me," she said, her voice quavering, before rushing out of the store.

No wonder Cassidy had defended the program so adamantly. It was personal. But why hadn't she told him? Was she too embarrassed to admit it?

He stopped himself from interrupting the reading time in the tent. An apology seemed lame anyway. The best thing he could do to help her was discover a way to continue the program. But she needed a place to do that. And she needed *this* place.

The bell on the door jingled again, and a man dressed in aviator sunglasses and a hip black jacket entered the store. He wore tight jeans and a pair of expensive sneakers. Blond with a chiseled jaw, he flicked off his glasses and scanned the room.

Daisy gave a low *ruff* and refused to get up. For a dog who liked everyone, that was unusual.

"Can I help you?" Liam asked, approaching the man.

The man frowned as he looked over Liam. "What happened to the Pomfreys? And where is Cass?"

Cass? Cassidy had told Abby that was the name only special people used.

"I'm Liam Henry, the new owner. The Pomfreys recently retired, but Cassidy still works here. She's currently reading to a child."

"Oh, yeah. The after-school program. I forgot." He glanced at his watch before taking a long look at Liam as if he were sizing him up.

"And you are?" Liam asked.

"I'm Cameron." The man leaned his elbow on a bookshelf. He may as well have been posing for a magazine.

"And how do you know Cassidy?"

"We go way back," Cameron said, jutting out his chin before glancing over Liam's shoulders as if he were trying to check out Cassidy.

Liam sensed this guy didn't like him, although he didn't know why.

"We dated," Cameron added, his eyes flicking back to Liam's.

Her ex. The guy she had once been engaged to. Cameron's smug look put Liam on the defensive.

"I'm only in town for a short time. I was hoping to catch her on a break." Cameron straightened his spine, trying to match Liam's height, even though he was several inches shorter. He got the feeling the man was trying to intimidate him. "If she can get off work early."

"She's working until closing. Sorry, but *no*," he said flatly. He wasn't sorry at all.

Cassidy crawled out of the tent, the strap of her sundress dangling off her shoulder, an invitation he did not want Cameron to see. Why did Cassidy have to wear those sundresses that revealed her legs and shoulders anyway? If it was up to him, he'd show Cameron the exit. He didn't want this guy coming around when he wasn't here.

"Cam," she said, her eyes wide. "What are you doing here?'

Cam? Apparently, they were still on nickname terms.

"I was helping my parents with a house project and wanted to see you." Cameron reached out for a hug.

She hesitated for a second before stepping into his arms, then quickly pulled away.

Hannah peeked out of the tent. "Cassidy, are you going to finish the book?"

"In a minute, Hannah," she said, trying to appease her.

"Cass, how are you?" Cameron asked, as if she were the only one in the room. His gaze slid down her shoulder to the slipped strap.

Her hand quickly corrected it. "I'm good. Everything's good," she said vaguely. "Still doing my after-school program."

"I see that," Cameron said, ignoring the girl who was now begging from across the store.

"I want to know what happens and I can't read by myself!" Hannah called.

"In a second, sweetie," she stalled. Liam pretended to straighten some books nearby.

"Cassidy, could you please hurry?" the girl whimpered.

Cameron ignored the girl's pleas. "You'll never guess who's moving back to the area."

The little girl moaned and fell onto a beanbag.

"Who?" Cassidy's brow crumpled.

"Me," Cameron said. "I got a job in the next county over. My parents are struggling with some health issues."

Cassidy forced a smile. "Wow. That is news."

It was obvious Cassidy wasn't excited about Cam's return. And Liam definitely wasn't thrilled about it, either.

"My parents are getting older and need someone around, especially since my dad fell last month."

Hannah called a little louder. "Please, Cassidy!"

"One more minute," she said.

"I'll read your book to you," Liam volunteered.

"You will? Yay!" she squealed. "Get in the tent with me!"

She disappeared inside before he could make an alternate suggestion for a reading spot. There was no way he was going to fit, and he had a suit on, which made the situation even more awkward.

As he attempted an army-man crawl into the tent, his knee stuck in the door, and he could neither move in nor out of the tent without ripping the seam of his pants.

A stifled laugh erupted from the other side. When he peeked out, Cassidy covered her smile.

"Do you have a better suggestion?" he asked.

"You don't fit inside very good," Hannah said, matter-of-factly. "You're too big. Can't you shrink yourself?"

He was stuck halfway in, while one foot dangled outside.

"Impossible," he said. "Maybe we could just read like this." He rolled onto his side.

"Great idea!" she said, squishing him into the side of the tent. Why did kids have no sense of personal space?

Although he could no longer see Cassidy, he could still hear every word of her conversation through the flimsy tent walls.

"I'd love for us to talk sometime," Cameron told Cassidy. "We need to catch up."

"Uh, okay," she said hesitantly.

Just say no, Liam wanted to blurt out as he read *Goldilocks and the Three Bears.*

"How about this week?" Cameron asked. Liam held his breath.

Hannah nudged her elbow into his side. "Why did you stop?"

"I'm sorry," he mumbled, still distracted by the conversation outside.

"I'll check my schedule," Cassidy said.

Liam might have to schedule her for every night this week. Or forever. He'd make sure she had no time to see Cameron.

"Sounds great!" Cameron said. "I'll be in touch."

"Not if I can help it," Liam muttered under his breath.

"That's not what the story says!" Hannah stated in an irritated voice. "It says, *And this porridge is just right.*"

"Hey, I thought you couldn't read," he questioned.

Hannah gave him a sly smile. "A little. But don't tell Cassidy. I don't want her to kick me out."

"She would never do that," he said. Then he lifted his eyebrows. "Would she?"

"Not on purpose. But she can only take ten kids, and I don't want to lose my spot." He could see how desperately Hannah wanted to stay.

"We need to change that," he said.

"We do," she agreed. "But first, finish the book. Or are you still listening to their conversation?"

"What? No!" he whispered. "And who said I was eavesdropping?"

The little girl rolled her eyes. "It is *so* obvious. Why don't you just tell her?"

"I don't know what you're talking about," he said, feigning ignorance.

Hannah cupped her hands around her mouth and whispered in his ear. "You don't like that other guy."

"Well, if you can read minds so easily, let's see if you can finish this book."

He pushed the book her way and peeked out of the tent.

Cameron was gone, but not for long. And when he returned, Liam would need a plan.

CHAPTER THIRTEEN

CASSIDY

Cassidy ran the numbers while her stomach clenched. "Please let there be an error," she mumbled.

Short.

She didn't have enough to cover rent or her last semester of tuition because she'd spent too much on her after-school program. *Again.*

Daisy gave her an unsympathetic look.

"What was I supposed to do?" she replied. "Let my kids down?"

If only pets could offer sympathy. Or chocolate.

She popped another chip into her mouth, scanning her apartment for something to sell. She hadn't cleaned in weeks. Clean clothes were draped across chairs. Unwashed dishes were clumsily stacked in the sink. Not to mention the bra she'd flung over the back of a chair. She was planning on spending the evening alone, and comfort was top priority.

She filled the teakettle and turned the burner on high, anticipating the floral scent of chamomile tea. Looking at the pile of dishes, she grabbed a scrubber pad and decided to work off her stress on the dirty plates.

At least this week's sales at the store had been better than expected, thanks to Liam's surprise visits. Ever since Cam had returned, Liam kept "popping into the store for a second," like he lived next door and not several hours away. He claimed it was to work on the marketing plan. Occasionally, Jane or Abby would come with him, which gave her a nervous, sinking feeling. If they saw her run-down apartment or depleted bank account, they'd assume she was dating Liam for one reason alone: his money. It wouldn't take a rocket scientist to figure out that she wasn't the type of girl Liam Henry would fall for. His comments at the garden party had confirmed that.

Her phone buzzed on the counter as Cameron's name appeared on the screen.

"Hello?" Her voice sounded unusually tight and squeaky.

"Hey, it's me," Cam stated casually, like he was sliding on a comfortable jacket. She had the feeling he wanted to pick up where they had left off: Cass as the loyal girlfriend, always sacrificing, making herself smaller so Cam could be bigger, bolder, *the standout.*

"I was wondering what you're doing tonight," he said with that touch of southern drawl from the years he'd lived down south.

"I'm busy with work," she said flatly. He wouldn't understand that she was struggling under the weight of financial pressures. She couldn't ask for Liam's help. His money was only good until the store closed or their dating arrangement was over, whichever came first.

"Come on, sweetheart, you gotta take a break from your job sometimes," he crooned.

She hated that he still called her *sweetheart.*

"That new boss of yours isn't working you too hard, is he?" he asked.

"No, but the after-school program is in dire need of help."

Why was she explaining this to him? He had never been that interested in her program, even when they were dating.

"Have you applied for any help?" he asked. "There's loads of grant money out there for educational programs."

"Since the program is under the umbrella of the store, we don't qualify."

"True. But that's where I can help," he said. "You need to get your program out and register it as a nonprofit. You don't want that boss of yours to take your program down when he closes the place, do you?"

"No," she said. "But he wouldn't do that."

The water on the stove was now boiling furiously, like the worry that rose in her stomach. The Pomfreys had been extremely casual about their business arrangements. They had always called it *her program,* letting Cassidy take full control of it. But now Liam was the one who technically owned her program.

As she poured herself a cup of hot water, the steam snaked into the air.

"Why don't we meet and I'll walk you through the steps of becoming a nonprofit?" Cam said.

Wasn't this an easy yes?

She blew on her tea before taking a sip, but the water still scalded her tongue.

"What's that going to cost?" she said, trying to pretend she hadn't burned her mouth.

"Free," Cameron said as smoothly as a used car salesman. "Just agree to meet with me."

Her stomach rolled nervously. The last time she'd had dinner with him, he'd broken up with her. Even though they'd dated since their senior year of high school, he'd let it all go in a matter of seconds.

"I met a girl at college," he'd told her back then, letting his drawl sound like a sad country song. "And she's willing to follow me to North Carolina."

She could have accepted his rejection in time, but it was the next statement that had crushed her: *"I can't marry someone who might die of a seizure at any moment."*

She'd opened her mouth, but nothing had come out but a weird throaty, *huh.* "My seizures are mostly under control. I haven't had one in years."

"But what if we had children, and you passed it on to them?" he argued, his brow folding into deep lines.

So that's what he was worried about. Having kids who might not be perfect.

"People with epilepsy have healthy children all the time," she told him.

"But they never figured out *why* you have it." He pointed at the table. "You told me you could have an underlying genetic issue."

"But nobody knows," she argued. "You can't predict the future."

"I realize that."

But did he? Because if so, then this wouldn't be impossible to accept. Death was a given any day.

"But I don't want our kids to struggle in school the way you did. God forbid they have a seizure and die," he said with a wildness in his eyes. "Or I leave you alone, and you have a seizure. Cass, the worry is killing me."

His worry had become an unscalable mountain. Somehow, they'd ended up on two different sides, a future built on what-ifs they couldn't control. Compared to someone healthy, the odds were stacked against her.

Even her parents had accepted that her epilepsy was in God's hands. There was no cure for her condition. No silver bullet. No miracle healing.

But Cameron couldn't seem to reconcile a life with an

epileptic. He wanted perfect. All the cards stacked in his favor. In his mind, she always fell short.

"I'm not blaming you for your epilepsy," he said. "It's not your fault you were born this way."

But it was her fault.

That's why he'd broken up with her. And now he'd had the audacity to return to Wild Harbor and pretend that he'd never rejected her for something she couldn't control.

"You still there?" Cam's voice roused her.

"Yeah, sure," she said, her cup of hot tea abandoned on the counter.

"Great, I'll make reservations somewhere this week."

Wait, she'd just agreed to dinner? Their meeting was strictly business. Nothing more.

"I'd rather not discuss the program or my money situation in public," she said. "Let me make this clear: this is not a date. Do you understand?"

A peculiar smell tinged the air, like something was burning. She sniffed at her teacup. Chamomile steam filled her lungs.

"Loud and clear," he said. "But my intention is to win you back, Cassidy Woods."

She nearly choked on her tea, the hot water burning her nostrils as she sputtered and coughed.

"You okay?" he asked.

"Yeah, I'm fine," she said in a raspy voice. Until now, she'd avoided talking about Liam, afraid Cameron would guess the truth. But what did she have to lose now? "Cameron, I'm dating someone."

The silence on the phone was heavy. "Who is it?"

"I'd rather not say."

"Your new boss?" he asked.

"I'm not telling," she said.

"Then I'll have to show you that I'm the better man."

So, he wanted to win her back. Prove he was the better man.

Good luck with that, Cam. I won't fall for it this time.

A knock sounded at the door.

"I gotta run. Someone's here."

Distracted by her thoughts, she threw open the door. Liam gaped at her from the other side, his gaze tracing over her over-sized, button-down shirt paired with pajama shorts.

"Um," he mumbled, unprepared for her attire. "I can come back later."

She glanced down at her sleep shirt. Luckily she'd thrown on a tank top underneath, so there was no worry about the missing bra, *except that* it was still hanging off the chair in plain sight.

She blocked his view of the undergarment with her body.

"Are you sure I shouldn't come back later?" he said, his dark eyes pinned on hers.

She got the feeling he was trying not to stare at her legs.

"I'm dressed for bed, but I wasn't actually going to bed." She sounded like a teenager trying to justify her poor clothing choices. "Can you hang on a sec?" Before he could answer, she slammed the door. She plucked the bra and tossed it behind the TV where he couldn't see it. Then she hurried to the door, taking a final breath to calm her heart which was slamming into her chest like a jackhammer.

"Sorry. I needed to take care of something." She smiled, trying to pretend she was unfazed.

"I'm not here to make judgments about your pajama choices."

She looked at her clothes. "What's wrong with my pajamas?"

"Nothing," he replied, a slow grin creeping into his lips. "Nothing at all." He sniffed the air. "Did you burn something?"

She spun around. "I can't figure it out either. I only heated water."

He scanned her kitchen and rushed to the stove. A dishrag lying by the burner was smoking.

"Do you have a fire extinguisher?" he shouted.

"No," she said. "I always thought I should buy one of those."

He threw open her drawers and pulled out metal tongs, plucking the flaming dishrag and tossing it into the sink. He turned on the water as the rag sizzled.

"You could have burned down this building," he said.

"I was on the phone with Cam when I made the tea."

He glanced at her, startled by the news. "Cam called you?"

She couldn't reveal their conversation. If he found out, he might think she was bailing on him. "I was talking to him about finances and my future," she said vaguely.

"That's why I came over," he said. "I wanted to hear more of your ideas."

Something had changed since she'd first met him, when his face had been like flint, hard and closed off. Now there was a tenderness in his expression, and she wondered if she was reading into things.

"I thought your plan was to turn it into a fancy gym once our dating agreement is over?"

"When I saw you with Hannah last week, I felt guilty. Those kids deserve a program like yours. I'm trying to figure out how we can make it happen."

Cam's warning circled in her mind. *You don't want that boss to take your program down when he closes the store.*

"This is an unexpected change," she said, plopping down on the couch. "What happened?"

"Ever since the garden party, Abby hasn't stopped talking about you. You've seen how I act with her. I'm more like a dictator than a father figure." He lowered himself onto the couch next to her. "My father was the same way, ordering my brother and me around like we were his servants, not his children. I never learned how to have fun with kids."

"You can start now," Cassidy said. "It helps if you're not wearing a suit." She tugged at the collar of his coat, and he let it slide off. "You'll fit in the tent better this way." She smiled, remembering how he couldn't fold his body inside.

"Hannah's mom told me something the other day," he said, his forehead creased into deep grooves. "She mentioned you have epilepsy."

Her stomach sank. People always treated her differently after they knew. "I haven't had a seizure in over five years. You don't need to worry about it happening when I'm alone in the store," she defended. "And my learning disability doesn't get in the way of my work either."

"I'm not worried about the store. You're more than capable." His eyes lifted to hers. "I'm worried about you."

She swallowed hard. "Me?"

"Why didn't you tell me that's why you started this program? It's the reason this bookstore matters so much, isn't it?"

"In school, kids made fun of me because I struggled to read. They didn't understand that epilepsy has affected me in ways we'll never understand. The few times I had a seizure at school, the teasing got worse. After that, kids would pretend to convulse and then laugh about it. It was horrible."

He took her hand in his. "I'm so sorry, Cassidy. I had no idea . . ."

The way he stared at her made her feel soft inside, like ice cream that had sat in the sun too long.

"I want your program to get more exposure," he said. "What if we had a fundraising gala for your program?"

"What about the bookstore?" If the bookstore closed, she'd no longer have a place to hold her events. What good was her program without a magical place to host it in?

"All the funds would go to your program. I'm even willing to pay for it from my personal account. What do you say?"

Her chest tightened, like someone had knotted a cord around her. When she'd accepted help from Cam in the past, it had always left her feeling indebted to him. She didn't want to repeat that mistake.

"I don't want to borrow anything else from you."

"Can't? Or won't?" he asked, his brow furrowing.

"I can't repay you. Even finishing school right now is impossible."

"You told me you only have one more semester."

"I dropped out yesterday," she said. "I can't pay my upcoming tuition because I'm short this month."

His frown deepened. "I won't let you do that. Call and reapply for the semester. I'll pay for it."

"Absolutely not," she insisted. "Who knows when I'll have the money to pay you back?"

She'd bank everything on her after-school reading program, even if it meant she ended up penniless and couldn't finish her degree. How could she explain that to Liam, who had so much money he didn't even know what to do with it?

"No one has to know about our arrangement." He brushed a strand of hair from her face.

"In case you've forgotten, this isn't real." She pointed between him and her.

"Do you want it to be real?" he asked softly.

Warning bells blared in her head. She crossed the room, trying to put space between them. She'd fallen for Cam before, and look where it had gotten her.

"If you pay for everything, then what happens when we're done?" she asked. "How am I going to make it on my own?"

He circled the couch, moving closer to her. "You'll make it because you're amazing. And I'm not helping you because I expect something in return. I'm giving this to you because I care about you."

She stepped back, bumping the wall behind her. Her apartment wasn't big, which had never been an issue before, but with his presence, the room had shrunk considerably.

"I can't let you do this for me," she said, her resolve fading.

His features had softened and it made every cell in her body want to draw toward him. She pulled at the hem of her sleep shirt. She wished, in hindsight, she'd put on a two-piece flannel set that covered her entire body. Or a suit of armor. Anything to cover up her growing sense of vulnerability, which likely had nothing to do with her clothes.

"Cass, I'm not here to pressure you into anything." He was approaching her slowly, as if at any moment she'd swat him away like a cat. "But whenever you're away from me, I can't stop thinking about you."

Her breath hitched. "Really?"

"You know I wouldn't joke about this." He stopped inches from her. "Do you want me to stay or go? Because if you tell me to go, I'll leave right now."

The last thing she wanted was for him to go. "You can stay."

He was so close now she could almost taste the sweetness of his breath.

"Then would it be okay if I kissed you?"

She couldn't remember if any guy had ever asked her permission to kiss her. Most had sprung it on her like a surprise. A few had given very obvious hints. But nobody, until now, had asked what she wanted.

She nodded, watching his eyes darken and then close as he leaned toward her.

Then his lips swept over hers, not in some passionate display, but as light as silk. His mouth lingered there, as if he were savoring some delicious treat.

Just as she was about to press closer, he pulled away, a satisfied smile on his lips. "If I kiss you longer, I'll never stop." He took a step back, peering at her like she was dangerous territory. "I hope that was okay."

"More than okay." She smiled, wishing he would kiss her more.

"As much as I'd like to continue, we have some planning to do."

How was she supposed to focus on planning for a big event, after he'd kissed her like that? What did it even mean?

He took her hand in his and pulled her to the couch, where he motioned for her to sit down. Then he went over to the stovetop and turned on the kettle.

"I'd let you make the tea, but after the fire, I'm afraid to," he teased. "Besides, it's going to be a long night."

"How long?" She folded her bare legs under her.

"As long as it takes to plan a smashing gala that will raise a ridiculous amount of money."

"Like that's easy," she said.

"It will be," he said, winking at her from across the room. "Trust me."

For once, she wanted to believe it could work. That they could work together.

As he brought over two cups of tea, her doubts still lingered, like a persistent itch under the surface of her skin.

He handed her a cup, the steam curling into the air like unanswered questions. "It might take all night, but we're going to make a plan to save this store."

"And if we can't?" she asked, raising an eyebrow.

"There is no *can't*," he told her. "Don't think about a future that might not happen."

The only problem was she couldn't do that. Her heart hinged on this. On him. On everything that could go wrong.

CHAPTER FOURTEEN

LIAM

Liam yawned as he took another sip of coffee. He'd stayed up too late last night at Cassidy's house, and now, he'd pay for it all day. Despite the tired ache in his body, his heart was floating after that kiss. The softness of her lips. The way her eyelashes fanned over her cheeks. The delicious smell of her hair when he brushed close to her. And that sleep shirt? He couldn't let his mind go there, or else he'd be in trouble.

By accident, he'd shut off his alarm. Only now did he notice that he'd missed a call from his mother.

Her line rang several times before she picked up.

"Mom, what's up?" He stifled another yawn, hoping she didn't ask questions. Not that he had anything to feel guilty about. They'd spent the rest of the night planning the gala before he'd given her one last goodbye kiss that had been so good, he had to wrench himself away before his self-control crumbled completely. After kissing her, he didn't want to kiss anyone else.

"I have some news," his mother said, her voice wobbling.

"Dr. Miller called this morning to share my MRI results." Jane had always been transparent with her feelings, unlike his father, who had stuffed his emotions behind a cement block wall.

"He said the cancer has spread. The new treatment isn't working anymore. He suggested I come in to discuss what to do next."

Liam's chest tightened. "Are you sure that's what he said?" Sometimes his mother's memory failed when she was under stress. He hoped she'd heard wrong.

"Yes, I even took notes."

He ran his fingers through his hair. "Why don't I give Dr. Miller a call and see if he has time for a video consult today?"

"I don't think it's necessary. This was the last option for my cancer. He said if this didn't work, there would be no more options."

Liam's shoulders slumped. *Last option. No treatments left.* In the excitement of his new relationship, he'd nearly forgotten that his mother was fighting cancer. It seemed impossible that as his life was turning around, they'd get a low blow.

"I still need to talk to him instead of thinking the worst. There are new cancer treatments developing all the time." He paced the floor, searching through his notes from the last appointment. Dr. Miller was a world-renown oncologist, and their time with him was always brief but packed with helpful info. He was also the most positive doctor they'd met, always reassuring Jane that she couldn't give up hope.

"I'm calling Dr. Miller's office now." Jane shouldn't shoulder this alone. "I'll be right over."

He sped toward her home, a grand brick Colonial in a gated Chicago suburb. Even after his father's death, Jane refused to move, resolved to hold on to her family memories. For her, living there was the one last tie to her beloved husband and son.

Liam parked outside the garage, right below the room that held painful memories

It had been on a day much like today that his world had changed. He'd just come from the gym and stopped to visit his dad. His mom had been at her weekly book club, which meant he could talk to his dad alone and address some rumors he'd heard about him.

"Dad? Are you here?" he'd called, shutting the door behind him. Only silence greeted him.

"Dad?" he'd called again, taking two stairs at a time.

As he pushed open the door to his home office, he saw a collapsed figure lying on the floor. Liam ran over to the lifeless body and shook his dad's shoulders. "Dad! Wake up!"

No response.

Time slowed as Liam dialed 911.

His father hadn't been sick. He hadn't even retired yet. When the ambulance finally arrived, he accompanied his dad to the hospital. He didn't understand what the EMTs were doing, but he could tell by their tone that it wasn't promising. When the news came, Liam was the first to find out.

As the oldest, it was his responsibility to tell the family, and he was the one who held his mother as she cried.

Only later did they learn that his father had suffered from a rare, undiagnosed heart condition that had caused a massive heart attack. Jane was shattered by her husband's death, reinforcing a lesson that Liam accepted as truth. No matter how wonderful love was, the jagged edge of loss ran deeper.

His mother lounged on a sofa, a rich blue flowered robe draped across her shoulders, looking as lovely as ever. She had aged well, refusing to let the cancer steal one ounce of her beauty.

Her eyes brightened as he entered. "Hello, Liam. I was thinking I should go to Wild Harbor."

"What if Dr. Miller can get you in today? We should start on a new treatment as soon as possible."

She shook her head. "They gave me an appointment next

week. I can wait. Going to the beach is always a wonderful distraction. Sinking my toes in the sand while watching sailboats. Life doesn't get much better than that!"

He pulled his phone out, ignoring her wishes. "I want answers from Dr. Miller first."

Jane stole Liam's phone. "I know what you want is some assurance that Dr. Miller has another trick up his sleeve. But I already know—and you do too—that eventually, there won't be any more treatments. No option B. Unless there's a miracle, my time here . . ." She paused and searched his eyes. ". . .is limited."

He refused to believe it. "You don't know that. You could live another twenty years with the right treatment."

"Liam," she pleaded softly. "Sit next to me." She patted the couch and shifted her body to make room. As a boy, he had always loved cuddling with his mother, smelling her rich perfume as she wrapped an arm around his shoulders.

But this time, her tiny shoulders sank into the safety of his embrace.

"You're just like your father," she murmured, adjusting the hem of her robe so it draped across her legs. "You always know what I need." She rested her head in the crook of his arm.

"I'll always be here for you. You never have to worry about being alone."

"I'm not worried," she said. "Someday, I'll be reunited with both your dad and brother, and it will be the happiest day of my life." She tipped her chin so she could gaze at him.

He glanced away.

"I know what you're thinking, and I want you to stop," she said, poking him in the side.

"You're a mind reader now?" he asked.

"You're as stoic as your father. But underneath, you have a soft spot, just like him. I'm relieved you have a girlfriend. Cassidy has been the answer to my prayers. I even canceled the billboard."

"Mom." He shook his head slowly. "I don't know what will happen between Cassidy and me." He wanted to confess the truth about their initial relationship, but now was possibly the worst time. She'd already gotten bad news once today; the last thing she needed was more.

"I know there aren't guarantees," she gushed. "But Cassidy is the nicest girl you've dated. In some ways, she reminds me of myself at a younger age."

She pulled up her phone messages. "She even promised to take me to Wild Harbor to get my mind off the news. She would make a fabulous daughter-in-law."

"I don't think that's for you to decide," Liam warned. She'd dropped hints before that Cassidy was *the one*, but Liam pushed them out of mind.

Jane patted Liam's knee. "Are you considering the future with her?"

"Of course I haven't," he said, running a hand through his hair. As much as it thrilled him to kiss Cassidy, that was not the same thing as making a lifetime commitment.

"I'm not asking you to make any promises," she said. "But consider it for my sake?"

Before he could answer, the doorbell rang. Liam sprang from his seat, eager to escape this conversation.

"Don't say a word about the future," he warned her. "The last thing I want is for you to scare Cassidy away."

His mother laughed. "I don't think that will be a problem. It's so obvious the girl is in love."

"I'm serious," he said, putting one finger over his lips.

When he opened the door, Cassidy pulled off her sunglasses. "I wondered if you'd be here yet." Her lips curled into a shy smile that made him want to pull her into his arms.

"This is a pleasant surprise," he said.

"I couldn't stay away." She brushed past him and embraced

Jane like an old friend. The fact she'd shown up for his mom made him adore her all the more.

"I'm going to steal you away and take you to the beach," Cassidy promised.

His mom was right. Cass was a lot like her.

"I haven't even packed my bags yet," Jane said. "Let me run upstairs and throw together a few things. By the way, would you like to shop for jewelry first?"

Cassidy shrugged. "Why not?"

"Perfect. You can help me pick out a new diamond bracelet." His mom winked at Liam before leaving.

Liam lowered his voice. "I have a feeling my mom is up to something."

"Like picking out jewelry she thinks you should buy me?"

"Exactly. With these new test results, she's putting pressure on me to commit to a more serious relationship."

Cassidy narrowed her eyes. "What kind of commitment?"

"Hinting at an engagement. She's afraid she's going to leave me alone, even though I told her I'm satisfied with my bachelor status."

Cassidy flinched. "I see."

"She thinks we're more serious than we are," he said.

"And what are we, Liam?" Cassidy asked.

He rubbed the back of his neck and checked the stairs. He hoped his mother wasn't listening. "Do we have to talk about this now?" His whole world had crashed in on him this morning, and she wanted to define the relationship now?

"Liam." Cassidy shifted. "You know I'd do anything for your mom. But it's not fair to let her believe there's a serious relationship when we haven't even talked about what is going on. The way we were behaving last night—well, it was a little more than friendship."

Liam nodded. "I know that. But . . ." He paused, too afraid to get her hopes up yet. "I'm not ready to talk about this."

"Perhaps I read you wrong last night, especially since you're so keen about your *bachelor status.*" She punctuated the last words before starting toward the door.

"Cassidy." His voice was urgent. He was on a tightrope of expectations, trying to keep everything in balance and failing miserably.

"Last night was real," he admitted. "I wasn't pretending."

She rounded toward him. "Are you sure, Liam? Because I'm wondering if any of this is real."

As they walked into the jewelry store in Wild Harbor, Jane's eyes lit up like the glittering gemstones. Jane had always been a fan of "expensive accessories," as she called them. The more sparkle, the better. Ever since his father had died, Liam bought his mom a new piece of jewelry every Christmas. It was the one way he could fill his father's shoes.

"Oh, this is a lovely piece," Jane remarked, studying a diamond bracelet. "Cassidy, what do you think?"

The jeweler pulled the bracelet from the case and cradled it on the counter.

"I'm not a jewelry expert, but that is beautiful," Cassidy said, pressing her hands together, afraid to touch it.

"That would look good on you," he said, moving closer to Cassidy. The scent of her perfume was as distracting as it had been last night when he kissed her.

He sensed she was still annoyed by their conversation from earlier, but she was at least trying to keep the peace in front of his mother.

Jane eyed a few more pieces, sliding one bracelet onto her wrist. "This gold chain bracelet with a single diamond has a simple beauty." She turned her arm in the sunlight, shooting diamond reflections across the walls.

"This is the one." Jane smiled. "Like something Frank would have bought for me."

"It matches your ring," Cassidy noted.

"Frank purchased it before we had any money," she said, a softness flooding her face. "He saved for an entire year, working every job he could. That's when I learned, it's not the size of the diamond that matters, but the size of the person's love." Jane sighed before she changed the subject. "Liam told me about the fundraiser you're planning. If you'll let me, I'd like to give the first donation." Jane fumbled through her purse.

"Oh, no. I can't accept anything from you," Cassidy said.

"I want to." Jane pushed a check into her hands. "Not because you're dating my son. It's for the children."

Cassidy stared at the check. Liam didn't know how much his mother had given her, but he guessed it was generous.

"You don't know how much this means," Cassidy whispered.

"I love seeing my son happy." Jane moved to a display case with engagement rings. "You should look at rings today. For fun, of course."

"Mother," Liam warned.

"It's never too soon," his mother added with a mischievous smile.

A movement outside the shop caught Liam's attention. Cam had pulled up to the shop on his motorcycle and was staring at Cassidy through the window.

Liam held Cassidy's arm so she wouldn't turn around.

"I suppose it can't hurt," he said, hoping that Cam would see them and take the hint.

The door hitched open as he pulled her closer.

"What are you doing?" she muttered to Liam under her breath.

"Don't turn around," he told her. "He's here."

"Who?" she asked, spinning around.

Cam lifted his hand in acknowledgement from across the store, ignoring Liam entirely. This guy had some nerve.

Her eyes widened. "Cam?"

Her ex approached, his hands sunk low in the pockets of his black denim.

"Well, well. Look who's shopping for fancy stuff," he said, his eyes flicking between her and Liam.

"Why are you here?" she asked.

"This saves me a phone call," Cam said. "I have some information for you on the grant. Let me know when you want to meet. Assuming you still want to?" The words hung in the air between them.

She nodded. "For business."

"Great. I'll look forward to it," he said, his eyes sliding back to Liam's. For a moment, there was a tense silence.

"What was that about?" Liam muttered after Cam was gone.

"It's nothing." Cassidy stared at the rings, but he could tell her mind was far away. "He offered to help me secure a grant for the after-school program."

"You're letting him help?" Liam didn't want Cam's involvement. He wanted the guy to stay far away from Cassidy, especially after what he'd done to her.

"He knows how much this program means to me. It's his way of apologizing for the past," she added.

Or worming his way back into her life.

Across the room, Jane's gaze met his with a warning.

"If Cam wants to help, there's more to it than charity," he insisted.

With her ex back in the area, Liam didn't stand a chance with Cassidy unless he could prove he was the better man.

"You don't need his help," Liam added. "I'll make sure of that."

CHAPTER FIFTEEN

CASSIDY

Cassidy picked up a stack of books and slid them into the tent. Hannah had claimed the space as her personal fortress and wasn't interested in reading.

"Did you choose any princess books for me this time?" Hannah glanced over the stack of books. Judging by her frown, she didn't approve.

"You've read all the princess books in the store," Cassidy insisted. "It's time to break out of your rut."

"I like my rut," Hannah said. "But what's a rut?"

"It means you're reading the same things over and over. I'm not reading any more until we try some new books."

"Oh, *great*," Hannah said, closing the tent flap.

Cassidy bent down and peeked in. "May I come in?"

"No grown-ups allowed!"

Cassidy pushed her head through the flap. "If we read these first, I'll let you pick one princess book as a reward."

Hannah considered the compromise. "Why don't you like princess books?"

Cassidy attempted to fold her legs inside the tent, cringing as she twisted them into a pretzel shape. "It's not that I don't like them. They're just not realistic. We don't even have royalty in our country."

"But what about Mr. Liam?"

Cassidy stifled a laugh. "Mr. Liam is not a prince, Hannah."

"But he drives that fancy car and always wears suits."

"That doesn't make him royalty," Cassidy explained. "You're born into the royal family."

Hannah's face fell before she crinkled her nose. "So if the queen didn't give him his money, where did he get it?"

"He's done very well in business. Now he's helping me so I can keep this reading program going."

"You mean by marrying you?" Hannah asked, her eyes gleaming.

"Of course not," Cass said. "Where did you get that idea?"

"I can tell he likes you," she said. "And you like him. It's *so* obvious."

"He doesn't like me. He's just being kind, and we hang out a lot. Like friends do." Cassidy was unsure how to explain the complexities of relationships to a six-year-old.

"My mom said she heard you were dating him."

"We are, I guess." Cassidy opened a book, trying to get out of this conversation.

"She heard he was going to shut down the bookstore, just like his dad."

Cassidy frowned. "What are you talking about?"

"His dad bought businesses and then shut them down. People got mad about it. It was in the paper."

Cassidy rolled her eyes. "I think you've heard things that aren't true. Liam is trying to keep this place alive."

"Maybe." She shrugged. "But you either like each other or you don't."

"He's nice. But dating is complicated," Cassidy said

vaguely, wishing she hadn't involved her feelings. Guys like him didn't date girls like her. And she wasn't going to risk her heart like she had with Cam. Nobody wanted to marry an epileptic who might fall down and have a seizure. They wanted someone safe and healthy. Cassidy had risk written all over her.

"If you like him, it shouldn't matter if it's . . ." Hannah couldn't remember the word. "Whatever you said."

"Complicated," Cassidy finished for Hannah.

"Yeah, that. But you like him, right?" Hannah asked.

"I do, but it's not quite that easy."

"Did you know he stares at you whenever you're not looking at him?"

"No."

"Well, he does. I notice these things because I read *all* the princess books. The prince always gazes at the princess like he's under a magical spell. Just like Mr. Liam looks at you," she said smugly.

"Cass?" a man's voice called. She hadn't even heard the bell on the door. "Are you here?"

Liam sounded like he was standing outside the tent. How much had he overheard?

His head poked through the flap. "I thought someone might be in here."

Hannah squealed. "We were just talking about you!"

"You were? I hope it was good," Liam said.

Cassidy turned toward Hannah with a silent plea. *Don't say a word.*

"It was very good," Hannah affirmed. "You wanna read a princess book with me?"

"Not until you read this stack of books," Cassidy reminded her. "You know the agreement."

Her shoulders slumped as she picked up a book on ancient Egypt.

"Pharaohs are cool too," Liam said, trying to encourage her. "Can I steal Cassidy away for a second?"

Hannah waggled her eyebrows at Cassidy. "What did I tell you?"

Cassidy shook her head. "You're incorrigible."

Liam offered his hand, helping her out of the tent. Even though it was the gentlemanly thing to do, she knew it would only encourage Hannah. She glanced back at the girl, who was smiling like a Cheshire cat.

"Keep reading," she instructed as she stretched her sore legs. "That tent is not made for big people."

"Tell me about it. Next time, get a bigger tent."

"This was all I could afford," she said.

"We need to fix that," he said.

"See? The prince fixes everything!" Hannah called from inside the tent.

"What did she say?" he asked.

"Never mind." Cass pulled him away from the tent. "Let's go to the back room."

How was it possible that Hannah had identified Cassidy's feelings before she could even admit them? Now that Liam was helping her with fundraising, she worried that if their relationship didn't last, then neither would his support. And that meant the end of the program, unless Cam could find her a grant.

Both of her fundraising methods depended on men who might only help her because of their feelings. It made everything as precarious as a stack of wobbly Jenga blocks.

Surrounded by boxes, Liam dug into his pocket and handed her an official-looking letter.

"Since I was coming into town for the wedding shower today, I thought I'd swing by the store to give you this."

She unfolded it and read the first line. "Your tuition is paid in full." She looked at him, frowning. "I told you not to."

A guilty smile stretched across his lips. "I don't listen when it's the best thing for you."

She could feel her stomach clenching.

He put a hand on her arm, sending a loop of energy through her body. "I know what you're thinking, and you don't need to worry about it. I don't expect any repayment for this."

She shook her head and handed him the letter. "Call and cancel this."

"I'm not going to. I can be just as stubborn as you are."

"It's important that I pay for it myself," she insisted.

"Cass, this is no different from a scholarship fund. I could have donated it to you anonymously, but I knew you'd ask me."

"I won't be indebted to you. I'd rather take out a loan."

"You'd take out a loan before you'd accept my money?" He shook his head. "That makes no sense."

"I'll quit if I can't pay."

"I won't let you do that." He moved toward her.

Her body went on high alert, and she bumped against a stack of books.

"I promise. No strings attached," he said. "My gift to you." He lifted his hand to her face and stroked her cheek. "I'd give you all this and more if you'd let me."

How could she resist when he did that to her? It made all her defenses crumble.

He slowly dipped his head and kissed her lips softly. Something began rising in the center of her chest, a deep longing that she'd tried to tuck away for good.

She didn't want to refuse him, but the memory of his comments from the garden still stung.

She pulled away. "Liam, what happens after sixty days when the store closes?"

His gaze flicked from hers to the floor. "Who said the store is closing?"

"That's not answering my question," she asked. "I meant for us?"

He pulled his hands back into his pockets and stepped away. "I've been thinking about that, and I'd still like to date you. If you want to?"

"If?" she laughed. "Like there's a question?"

"No question." He gave her that lopsided smile that made her heart race.

As much as she liked him, this didn't solve her problem. What happened when he realized she was just *a nice girl from a small town?*

Poof. Her Cinderella dreams would disappear. Because the truth was, girls like her weren't princess material. The prince would never pick her.

Her phone rang in her pocket. Cam's name scrolled across the top.

"Excuse me," she said, darting from the room under the weight of his gaze. She had to get away from him before she confessed that she had nagging doubts about their relationship.

But first, she had to deal with her ex.

She returned to the children's department, where the kids were lounging across beanbags, immersed in their books.

"Hey, Cam," she said, trying to act natural, even though her heart was charging like wild horses.

"You sound out of breath," he noted.

She clamped her lips shut and tried to think of an excuse. "A busy day at the store."

"I have some great news on a potential grant, but the deadline is this week. Can you meet me at The French Press?"

"Now?"

Liam lowered himself onto an empty beanbag next to a boy who was reading about superheroes.

"The sooner, the better," he said. "Can you find someone to cover the store?"

She bit at her cuticle, feeling a growing sense of nervousness about hiding this from Liam. "I'll try. Give me a few minutes," she said.

If Liam knew she was meeting Cam today, he'd be livid, but what other choice did she have? If the gala didn't raise enough, she would need a backup plan, and she didn't want to beg Liam. He was already funding the store for two full months and helping her with school. To ask anything more of him felt wrong. At some point, she needed to figure out how to fund her own dreams.

She walked to where Liam was reading a book about pirates.

"Pleasure reading?" she asked with a half-grin. She had to admit, he looked pretty cute.

"Since Landon stole all the superhero books, I'm forced to read about pirates." He gave Landon a pretend look of exasperation. "Seven-year-olds are the hardest to negotiate with."

He closed the book and sat up, his legs sprawled in front of him. "It's fun hanging out with these kids. Abby would love this program. Can I bring her to it?"

"Sure, as long as you can do me a favor and cover the store for a few minutes. Do you mind?"

He gave her a lazy smile and sunk into his beanbag. "Not at all."

As she hurried to the coffee shop, she caught her appearance in one of the shop windows. When had she turned so serious? She needed a break from worrying about the future, but lately, that was all she could think about. That, and Liam.

She took a deep breath before entering the café. It smelled like the rich, nutty notes of coffee alongside the sweetness of cinnamon and vanilla. Her gaze swung across the deserted room

"Hey, Cass." Cam waved from a corner table. "Join me."

Two lattes and a blueberry coffee cake sat on the table.

"For you." He gestured toward the coffee cake. "And a latte with almond milk."

"Thanks," she said without touching the cake. She didn't want to send a message that she was easy to persuade.

She checked her watch. "I'm on borrowed time from the store."

"Is your boss counting down the minutes?" he said, lounging in his chair.

"None of your business," she said.

"It's going to be everyone's business if you're dating." He propped a leg up on a spare chair.

She bristled in her seat. "I thought this meeting was to discuss the grant."

"It is. But I wanna know what's going on between you two." He let the question hang between them uncomfortably.

"Nothing." She shrugged. "A few dates. That's all."

"He's just playing the field?"

His assessment hit her like a punch in the gut. What right did he have making a judgment about Liam?

"Takes one to know one," she shot back. After all, he had played her good. Given her a ring and everything, before taking it all away.

"Yeah, well, I deserve it. I didn't treat you right," he said. "Which is why I'm trying to make up for it now."

She narrowed her eyes. "By cutting down the guys I date?"

"By helping you keep your program."

Maybe Cam wasn't her enemy. After he'd hurt her, she'd pushed him away as far as possible. But desperation was driving her now. She took a sip of her coffee. "Tell me what you know."

"It's a grant from a literacy program in a neighboring county," he said, pulling out a stack of information. "It looks like a perfect fit for your program. Since it's a local grant, you've got a great shot."

"Does it matter that my program isn't in the same county?" she said, fanning out the papers in front of her.

"That's the catch. You would need to offer the program in that county to be eligible. Think of it as an expansion project. You could not only reach kids here, but also in surrounding areas."

The idea of expanding her program thrilled her. Not only would the program offer more visibility, it would expand her donor base. The only question was whether she was ready.

"I need to fund the Wild Harbor program before I can think about expansion. How much are we talking?"

"Fifty grand," he said.

Cassidy's mouth dropped. "Fifty?" That would give her more than enough to work with.

"I can put in a good word for you with the guy who oversees the grant."

"You know him?" She wondered what was in it for Cam. She'd already set a personal rule to not accept any more money from Liam, because it would complicate their relationship.

But this situation was different. Cam wasn't loaning her the money; it was a grant from an outside foundation. Conveniently, it would have no tie to him.

She narrowed her eyes. "Why would you do that for me?"

He shrugged. "I'm trying to make it up to you." Then he held up his hand. "No strings attached."

His boyish smile reminded her of high school, and her heart whirled like a pinwheel.

Even if she suspected there was more to Cam's explanation, it's not like she'd consider dating him. Too much had changed between them, and she wasn't the same person anymore. She'd learned the hard way: trust was earned, not given.

"Well, thank you," she said, straightening the papers into a stack. She still hadn't touched the coffee cake.

"The grant deadline is in three days," Cam said. "We could always get together and pull an all-nighter."

There was no way she was going to spend the night working on a grant with Cam.

"I'll get it done." She avoided his gaze. "Somehow."

"I'm assuming you'll attend the party tomorrow?" he asked.

"I'm throwing the party. Lily is providing the desserts." The party was actually a wedding shower, but Megan had begged not to call it that. So instead, they billed it as a beach engagement party for the couples. "But promise me, you'll get along with Liam, okay?"

"If he's nice. Don't take this the wrong way"—he shifted his elbows onto the table and leaned forward—"but I'd stay away from that guy." He sliced his fork through the coffee cake, spilling blueberries, the juice staining the plate.

"Are you jealous?"

Shoving a forkful of blueberry into his mouth, he thought about her question as he chewed deliberately, the fork midair. "I heard some things about him."

"You heard *things*? Specific facts?" she challenged. She hated when people used vague innuendo. "Otherwise, it's just gossip."

Cam dropped the fork. "Ask him if he fired a guy to cover up a scandal with his father's business. His dad bought businesses and shut them down. But this scandal was something bigger."

"Like what?" she asked.

Not that she could believe anything without checking the facts. But his accusations worried her. Was Liam the type to act ruthlessly? *Like father, like son?* That's what he'd been planning with Books Forever.

To be fair, he'd given the store a second chance, but was this another act? After all, he wasn't afraid to deceive his mother. Would he deceive her, too?

"His father pressured people into doing things his way. When a company owner wouldn't sell, he'd threatened the guy.

Eventually, he got control of the business and it failed because of his dad."

"How do you know the business wasn't already failing? None of this has been proven, right?"

"Not yet, but Liam fired the guy only a few months ago because he had info on Liam's dad about shady investments that brought down the company."

"But why do you hold Liam responsible for something his father did years ago?"

"Because he's still running his dad's business, so he should pay the price. He's withholding information to protect his family." Cam's fork sliced through the cake again, splitting it in two. "He's hiding evidence of his father's wrongdoing."

"You don't know there's wrongdoing."

Cam shook his head. "Not from what I hear. When Frank got involved, it caused the company to tank. Liam had to get rid of this employee because he was going to come out with the news about Frank Henry's unscrupulous leadership. It's suspicious, don't you think? He's trying to cover up a potential scandal and hasn't even mentioned it to you."

He nudged the plate toward Cassidy. The slight curve of his mouth suggested he was planting a seed of doubt.

"I won't believe it until I hear it from Liam," she said, pushing the plate back. Without saying more, she bolted out of her chair and zigzagged around the café, the coffee cake still lingering on the table, an unspoken reminder that she wasn't willing to accept anything from him, no matter how important it seemed.

Someone was lying to her, and she needed to figure out who it was before it was too late.

CHAPTER SIXTEEN

CASSIDY

The sun streamed down in golden ribbons as waves lapped lazily on the shore. The day was hot and sticky, the humidity coating Cassidy's skin like a layer of warm syrup. Occasionally, a weak breeze relieved the heat as Cassidy and Lily arranged pastel macarons on a white cake stand

"Just a pop of color for the brides," Lily proclaimed, circling the distressed wood table. "But not too girly for the grooms. The bacon appetizers are my peace offering, so the men won't complain." She popped a bacon-wrapped date in her mouth while Cassidy tried to cover her yawn.

"Another date with Liam?" Lily asked

"No, I'm working on a grant," Cassidy said.

"I thought Liam was your unofficial patron."

"He wants to pay for it, but I won't let him."

Lily crinkled her nose. "Why not?" Her sister didn't have any problem spending Alex's small fortune on her business.

"He's still my boss. I don't want to use him for his money."

"You're not using him."

"But people don't know that. Besides, I can't rely on people's money every time finances are tight. I need to raise this on my own."

"You're doing that thing again," Lily said.

"What thing?"

"When you bite your lip," Lily noted.

Cassidy put her hand to her mouth, suddenly self-conscious.

"It's your hesitant face," Lily added.

"No, that's my *I'm scared of the future* face." Cassidy flopped onto the porch swing, overwhelmed by the heat and her problems.

"I'm tired of putting my trust in people who disappoint me," she admitted.

"You can't judge all men based on one broken engagement," Lily concluded, her sun-kissed cheeks glistening in the sun.

As long as humanity had existed, so had jerks who'd break your heart. Cassidy leaned her head back onto the wooden seat, letting her body sway with the rhythm of the swing. Cam's information, which was little more than gossip, circled like an unrelenting fly.

How could she bring it up to Liam without prying? *By the way, I heard you might be tied to a cover-up. Care to explain what happened? No? Okay, never mind.*

She couldn't ignore it without getting a serious case of ulcers.

A girl's voice floated through the open screen door right before Abby skipped onto the deck. She wore an adorable flow-ered sundress, and her hair cascaded in flowing waves down her back. Undoubtedly, Jane had helped her granddaughter prepare. If Liam had to advise Abby on clothing, she'd either show up in soccer shorts or leggings. Despite being her guardian, he still had no clue how to raise a girl.

"Are we the first ones here?" Abby asked, admiring their macaron display. "Ooh, I want the pale green one."

"Yes, you're the first, but you can't have dessert yet," Lily said. "The brides and grooms aren't even here yet."

Liam joined Abby on the patio, looking like he'd stepped out of a Tom Ford magazine spread. Even though they'd touted the party as beachwear-casual, Liam sported a perfectly pressed pair of dress pants and collared shirt. His gaze skated over Cassidy's dress with an approving smile.

"You look gorgeous," he said.

"So do you, but Finn is expecting you to play beach volleyball," she warned him. The cedar and musk smell of his cologne made her heart dance.

"I'll take my shirt off," he said.

He most definitely should not remove his shirt. She was already feeling weak at the sight of him with his clothes on.

Lily grabbed Abby by the shoulders. "Hey, Abby, why don't I show you the special chocolates I created for the shower? They're in the freezer so they won't melt in the heat."

Abby followed Lily into the house, giving Cassidy some alone time with Liam.

Liam sank his hands into his pockets. "Is there room for two?"

She scooted over, suddenly feeling like a shy teenager sharing a bus seat with a cute boy.

He wrapped one arm around her, his hand brushing her shoulders, sending a ripple of goose bumps across her arms. "I have secret news that may impact your after-school program in a big way."

"Really?"

His eyes dropped to her mouth, and that's when she realized she was biting her lip again. If he could read her expression like Lily, he'd know everything about her.

He gave her chin a gentle pinch. "I can't tell you yet, but I've got it under control. You need to let it go, like the song Abby has on repeat."

What exactly did he have control of? She was tired of letting the world throw her into a plot where she didn't like the ending.

She attempted a half-hearted smile. "Why bring it up if you can't tell me?" Suddenly she wondered what else he was keeping from her.

"I don't want to get your hopes up. But if it works out, it could change everything."

Doubt coiled in her stomach.

"Don't worry. I'm good at making things go my way." He winked at her before pressing his lips to her forehead.

It was just like Cam had warned her. If he was a player, then she was being played like a guitar.

His lips trailed to her cheek for another kiss before he leaned into her lips for a third. She dodged before he could reach his goal.

"There was something I was going to ask you." She pushed him back, her hands on his chest.

"Ask away, but this might be the only shot we get at being alone . . ." He gave a gentle kiss to her ear, igniting a longing she tried to ignore.

His closeness scraped her desire raw, but if she ran into Cam, she would need to face him armed with the truth.

"It's about your dad's business," she whispered.

"My dad's what?" he said, nuzzling her neck, not paying any attention to the conversation.

The patio door suddenly opened, forcing Cassidy to wrench away from Liam. They looked like kids caught kissing behind their parents' backs.

"Oh, my!" Jane said, backing into Becky Woods, who poked her head out the door.

"Did we interrupt something?" Becky asked, her eyes sparkling.

"Not at all." Cassidy wiped her mouth and gave a warning glance to her mother. *Don't ask.*

"Guests are arriving," Becky said, pointing to the living room.

Laughter erupted behind a curtained window as Cassidy caught her siblings spying. So much for broaching the subject of Liam's dad.

"Excuse me." Cassidy jumped off the swing. "I have guests waiting."

She took a deep breath, trying to find any excuse to get away from Liam. Did she really want a relationship with her boss? And if the store failed, what would happen to their relationship then? They hadn't even addressed how Liam felt about her epilepsy. If he was like Cam, once he realized the risk, it might sour their relationship for good.

Like it or not, her seizures would always end up as the deciding factor in a relationship. Life had dealt her a card she couldn't control, and she needed to accept that, even if it meant losing a guy she loved.

The house was bursting with guests, forcing her to pinwheel across the crowded room. Liam hung back, his gaze scanning the room. His lopsided smile sucked the oxygen from her, making her desperate for some fresh air. She focused on reaching the door, desperately needing some physical space from the crowd. All these boxes she tried to stuff her feelings into were like watercolors mixed into a muddy brown.

She turned away, trying to get space between Liam and her, and almost smacked into Cam. She stumbled forward before he grabbed her shoulders.

"Slow down, girl," he said in that lazy drawl that rubbed like an old wound. "Where are you headed so fast?" His hands slid down her arms, pricking her like thistles. He was the last person she wanted to run into today.

"I need some air," she blurted out, spinning around to gaze at the overcrowded room. "Too many people." Her parents' lake house was modest, but not roomy enough for a crowd this size.

"I can get you out of here," he offered.

"I'm okay." Cass rubbed her forehead. "My head was spinning from this crowd."

"You don't look good," Cam said, worry in his eyes.

Heat and stress were a bad combination for triggering seizures. Years ago, she'd collapsed from a seizure in front of him. After that, he never looked at her the same.

"If you're worried about my epilepsy, I'm fine," she insisted. Head down, Cass swung around and noticed Liam was still across the room, his eyes pinned on her.

Cam sipped something out of a bottle. "Did you think any more about what I told you?" He ignored Liam's glare from across the room. "The grant has a strict timeline."

"I'll get it done," she assured him. Did he think she'd let the money slip through her hands?

"I wouldn't count on your new boss." Cam looked away. "He might have money, but you shouldn't put all your eggs in one basket."

"You've already expressed your concerns," she replied firmly.

"The grant will get you started, and eventually, you'll find other donors. You don't need him." He took another sip from his bottle.

"When all is said and done, you'll see that I'm right," he added. "I still have your best interest in mind."

His smile shimmered with promises.

Was leaving me in my best interest? How about calling off our engagement? All the hurt had piled up in her like dirty snow.

A small cough erupted behind her. "Everything okay here?" Liam jammed his hands in his pockets.

"Yeah, man." Cam's easy drawl couldn't hide the tension that erupted between them. His gaze slid to her. "Right, Cass?"

How nice of him to drag her into the fray, which was Cam's way of deflecting the problem. When he'd broken off their engagement, it had been her issue. *Sorry, but I can't live with the fear of losing you to epilepsy.* It wasn't his fault; she was the problem.

She rubbed her forehead. "My head hurts. I think I'll get some fresh air."

Liam caught her elbow with one hand, while his other slid around her lower back, giving her a zing of energy. She sensed his silent message: *I'll help you if you need me.*

"Why don't we head outside?" Liam said with a decided firmness. There was something invigorating about a man who took control.

She looped her arm through his.

In the almost empty room, Cam called, "I heard what you did."

Liam halted. "Excuse me?" His eyes narrowed into two sharp slits. No more Mr. Nice Guy.

"You can't throw money at your past and expect that people will stay quiet," Cam said, so quietly he might as well be whispering to a sleeping baby. "The truth won't stay buried. Money can't hide what your dad did."

Liam balled his hands into fists. "Is that a threat? Because that's what it sounds like to me."

"Maybe." Cam's laugh was all sharp edges. "It's called the truth."

"Since you're not a lawyer, you'd better stay out of it, if you know what's good for you."

Cam wiped his mouth with the back of his hand. "I could say the same for you."

Liam grabbed Cassidy's arm and tugged her toward the

door. "I'm done here," he muttered under his breath as they walked outside.

Outside, a bouncy pop rock song replaced the tension of their conversation. The sun reflected off the metallic letter balloons that spelled the word LOVE in gold foil, an ever-present reminder to Cassidy of how shiny love could look on the outside when you didn't really know the truth about somebody. Just as everything was falling into place in her love life, a seed of doubt had sprouted alongside it.

Somebody tapped Cassidy's shoulder, forcing her to swing around and separate from Liam's firmly wrapped arm. Edna Long held a paper umbrella-topped cup filled with a frothy red punch in one hand and a Thai peanut chicken skewer in the other. Her lips spread into a giant pink-lipstick grin.

"If it isn't the happy couple!" Edna gushed.

"I'm not the one we're celebrating today." She nodded toward her siblings.

"Soon, you'll join them," Edna said, taking a bite of her glazed chicken.

"Excuse me," Liam apologized. "I'm being summoned by Matt."

"No worries, honey." Edna waved her skewer. "I'll take good care of Cass while you're gone."

Liam's face relaxed into a smile. "Keep the men away, okay?"

Edna looked pleased. "You got it, honey."

As soon as Liam left, Edna leaned close. "How are things going between you two?" Something sparked in her expression.

"Just fine," Cassidy replied.

Edna lowered her brow. "A girl who's in love isn't *just fine*. She's wonderful and glowing, like you are now."

Cassidy rubbed her cheeks. "It's probably the heat."

"You're funny," she cackled. "You don't have to hide it. Jane already told me."

"Told you what?" Cassidy panicked.

"That you went ring shopping, of course!"

The jewelry store visit. Whenever anyone looked at rings in Wild Harbor, they were practically engaged.

Edna threw her arms around her neck, squeezing so hard Cassidy's breath caught. "Sounds like wedding bells!" Several people swiveled toward them.

Thelma hustled over to Cassidy. "Did Edna say you went ring shopping?" She pulled out Cassidy's hand and searched her fingers.

"I'm *not* engaged." Cassidy pulled her hand away. The last thing she needed was for Edna and Thelma to spread something that wasn't true.

"Yet," Thelma corrected. "Not engaged *yet.*"

"You don't understand," Cassidy tried to correct her, but it was too late. Guests were descending on her like vultures to roadkill.

The florist shop owner approached next, chomping on a piece of gum. "Did I hear you're engaged?"

"No!" Cassidy insisted as the party music swelled.

Nobody could hear her now.

Edna interrupted. "But she will be soon! They went ring shopping!"

"Oh, my!" the woman replied, her jaw working the gum harder.

Cassidy needed to squelch the gossip before anyone else heard.

"There's no engagement!" she yelled, but between the music and the noise, nobody heard her.

Pushing through the crowd, she searched for Liam, but he'd gone off with Finn and Matt toward the beach.

"No, no, no . . ." she whispered, apologizing as she bumped into people like a game of pinball. "So sorry. Excuse me, can I get by?"

As she made her way toward Liam, two men in uniform

approached from the side of the house. Their faces were hard, their body positions tight, like someone who was about to share awful news.

As they approached the group of men, one cop pointed to Liam.

Every muscle in her body tensed as they surrounded him. The policeman shouted something, while his partner grabbed Liam's arm and pulled him forward.

The music from the deejay quieted as the crowd turned to witness what looked like an arrest.

Cassidy stumbled forward. "Where are you taking him? What's going on?" she asked, tagging after the officers.

"Down to the station for questioning," one man responded gruffly. He didn't even bother looking at her.

"Right now?" she asked. "Is that really necessary?"

"Cassidy," Liam warned, giving her a side eye. "Don't ask questions."

Cassidy stepped in front of the officers.

"Ma'am, you need to stay out of the way," the policeman barked at her.

Suddenly, someone grabbed her arm and yanked her back as they loaded Liam into the back of the police car.

She spun around, anger rising in her belly like a pot ready to boil over. Cam held her wrist and gave her a warning glare. "Leave him be."

"I want to know what's going on," she said, resisting his grip and lunging toward the car.

"Cassidy, you need to keep out of it," Cam warned, tightening his hold on her arm.

"Why won't you let me go?" she pleaded, trying to twist free.

He spun her around so she could look him in the face. "I'm doing this for your own good," he said. "Do you know those officers could arrest you?"

"I have done nothing wrong."

"Stick with him, and you're going to end up in trouble," Cam said, letting his words sink in.

Cassidy shook her head in disbelief. "What are you talking about? They must have mistaken him for someone else."

Cam's mouth curved into a hard edge before he dropped the truth on her. "Liam's in deep. The guy he fired? He's now missing."

CHAPTER SEVENTEEN

LIAM

I t's like one of those cop shows. *One second, I'm joking with the guys, and the next, I'm facing an interrogator in a drab white room while he fires questions at me.*

Liam rubbed his hands over his face and prayed his answers satisfied the investigator. Other than getting out as soon as possible, he was consumed by one thought. *Would Cassidy believe him?* She'd witnessed him carted off like a criminal and had insisted on trying to intervene.

But would she think differently of him when she found out the truth?

If only his dad hadn't left him in charge of his company, this whole mess would have quickly faded in the wake of his father's death. He just wished Stephens hadn't gone missing so soon after he'd fired the guy.

"Mr. Henry." A cop with a husky voice roused him from his thoughts. "You're free to leave now. Mrs. Jane Henry is waiting for you."

The door swung open before they escorted him through a

narrow hallway into an entry area. His mother's furrowed brow reeled him back to when he was a kid. He could take his dad's disapproval, but never his mom's.

He squared his shoulders and met his mother's steely gaze. "Thank you for coming," he whispered.

"You've got a lot of explaining to do," she muttered, the frown lines deepening in the harsh florescent light.

Boy, did he ever.

As he held the phone to his ear, his finger traced the circled lip of his coffee mug, catching on the smallest chip, pricking him.

"Can we talk?" Liam asked Cassidy, rubbing the sore spot on his fingertip.

As soon as he'd returned to Chicago, he'd called her, determined to defend his innocence.

"Jane hinted at a few details," she said.

"Like what?"

Even his mother didn't know everything. He'd purposely glossed over the parts that tarnished his dad's reputation and brushed it off as a problem between him and Stephens. He didn't want to place any more stress on her during cancer treatments. He was willing to risk his reputation to protect her.

"She told me a guy you fired is now missing. And because things ended on bad terms, the police questioned you about his whereabouts." She paused. "Liam, is everything okay?"

"It is," he replied. "Don't worry. I've got it under control."

Like my dad's unscrupulous business dealings that left a giant mess for me to clean up.

"I stayed with Abby while you were gone." Her voice sounded tired. "She was mortified that you'd been carted off by the police. I told her she didn't have to tell anyone, but she's worried someone from her boarding school will find out."

"It won't be on the news," he said. "Not if I can help it."

He'd already talked to Megan and Finn about it. Finn promised he'd bury it in the back of the paper.

"How was she when you left?"

"Better," Cassidy sighed. "That's the nice thing about children. Unlike adults, they accept whatever you say is truth."

"And you?" he asked with a nervous flinch of his fingers. This time, he caught the chipped edge of the cup again, slicing open the tiniest of cuts. He put his finger to his lips as a heavy pause hung between them.

Cass finally broke the silence. "So it's true you're not involved?"

He grabbed a tissue off his desk and wrapped it around the nick. "Of course I'm not," he said. Maybe it was the stabbing pain in his finger that was making him irritable, but he couldn't believe she didn't trust him fully.

"I wanted to hear it from you," she said, her voice catching.

It's not totally her fault she doesn't trust you. She's probably fielding questions left and right. The gossip had the potential to hurt the fundraiser.

"What can I do to help?" he asked, trying to change the mood. "I can come over—"

"I think it's best to stay away," she interrupted. "For the time being."

"I can't just leave this on your shoulders," he insisted. *Otherwise, Cam will take over and steal you back.*

"You're not leaving anything on me," she said quickly. "But if things aren't settled with this missing person case, it could reflect negatively on the program."

Her words slammed into him. She didn't want him involved because of his father's past.

"Can I still visit you? At your place? No one would have to know." An urgent desire to be with her pulsed through him.

"I think it would be best if we didn't for a while," she said, her voice heavy. "With the rumors flying around, I need to clear things up first."

"You mean the missing person case? Or our so-called engagement?" He'd heard about the rumors at the wedding shower.

"Both," she said. "Even though I'm not wearing a ring, everyone is expecting we'll get engaged soon. It enrages me."

"I tried to explain to my mother that we weren't getting engaged."

"She was already asking me when I was going to look at wedding dresses and invited herself along. You need to explain everything." Cassidy's voice grew insistent. "Or I will."

"She refuses to hear the truth." He circled the mug with the opposite hand, stopping on the chipped rim as he pressed down on the jagged edge. A perfectly good mug ruined by one small chip, kind of like his whole life. One mistake ruining everything.

"Liam, you can't blame your mother for this. We're the ones who made the deal. I never should have agreed to this. Especially dating you."

Her words pinched. "What do you mean by that? The agreement was mutual. I thought our feelings were too." He'd kept the store open for her. All those kids still had a program because of *him*. If he'd had his way, he would have killed the bookstore immediately and opened a gym.

"Dating me was a convenient way of keeping your mom from putting up any more billboards." An edge of hurt lined her tone. "It made perfect business sense, like all your decisions."

Was that what she thought? That she was *only* a business transaction? He thought he'd made his feelings clear when they kissed, but her opinion of their relationship was a low blow. How much of a jerk did she think he was?

"Keeping the store open was a financial risk. I honored your request," he said, trying to keep his voice firm and businesslike. "Even though you were my employee."

He sounded like he was addressing a subordinate, which was ironic, since she *technically* was his employee. He just had never treated her like one.

In the background, she stacked books, each hardback slamming onto a table.

"I thought . . ." Her voice cracked under the weight of the tension between them.

Why was she taking so long?

"I was more than an employee to you and this store meant something more to you than just"—her voice crumbled as she fought for words—"another way to use people for money. I guess I was wrong."

"That's not what I meant." His voice rumbled like distant thunder.

After everything he'd sacrificed for her, he thought she knew him better. Couldn't she see he had a weak spot only for her? He'd never let anyone into his heart the way he'd let her in. But after all this time, she still believed he was using her for his own gain.

He pushed harder on the crack, and the nerves in his finger shot painfully through him.

His feelings were clear: he loved her like no one else. But now she threw his feelings back in his face. No wonder he'd avoided dating relationships. No matter how hard he tried, love always destroyed him in return. If this was all she thought of him, how could he change her opinion?

"I need to go." Her voice wobbled, overcome with too much emotion.

"If you think the only reason I'm dating you is for business gain, then why did I keep the store open, even though it was bleeding money? I could have shut it down a long time ago, but I didn't because of *you*." His voice hitched. "If things have changed, then maybe I should close the store at the end of our agreement."

"Maybe you should," she repeated.

He could hear the stubbornness in her voice.

"Just let me find a space for my program," she said. "That is, if you'll let me keep the program."

"I would never take that from you," he said. "Whether we're together . . . or not."

He might as well lay it out now and let her decide the outcome of their relationship.

"I see," she whispered.

He wished she would yell at him, come over and swing her fists, or give him a good slap on the face. That would hurt less than this.

"I need to go." Her voice turned rigid, like she was his employee again and not someone who had wrecked his heart.

"Me too," he said, wishing he could say so much more, dying to apologize to her, instead of dropping into free fall and hoping he survived the crash.

It wasn't supposed to end this way. Not when he'd give anything for her.

If everything was falling apart, this was the one thing he wanted to save.

A WEEK WENT by before he drove to Wild Harbor, despite her request for him to stay away. He needed to see her, to brush his hand across the curve of her jaw, to let his fingers trail down the soft silk of her arm.

Pushing the gas pedal harder, he sped around curves in the pouring rain, the droplets catching his headlights, shimmering like silver bullets in the darkness. Rain splattered the glass before his wipers swept them away, clearing his view for a few seconds. His knuckles tightened around the wheel, whitening under his grip.

He'd always been in control. But as he held on tighter to the wheel, it felt like control was slipping from his grasp, both personally and professionally.

Even if he couldn't convince her that their relationship was real, he didn't want to stay away. The bookstore was *still* his business, and she was *still* his girlfriend.

The last thing he wanted was for Cam to come slinking around like a tomcat. Even at the engagement party, the guy had been giving off some serious vibes for her. No matter how things went down with the store, he wouldn't let some jerk steal his girlfriend.

As his car hugged the edge of the dark road, a man suddenly appeared, walking along the shoulder in the darkness. Liam swerved to avoid him, but hit a huge puddle that fanned out from his car. As the man dodged Liam's speeding vehicle, the spray from the puddle drenched the poor guy.

Liam slammed on the brakes and checked his rearview mirror. He immediately recognized the man. "Joshua?" he called out the window.

The man squinted at Liam's car, unable to see him.

"It's Liam Henry. What are you doing walking the highway on a dark, rainy night?"

"Oh, hello." Joshua was soaked. "My truck broke down some ways back," he said, still mopping his thinning hair. "Wasn't really my choice."

"Hop in. I'll give you a ride."

Joshua climbed into the seat next to him. Liam pulled out a sports towel and offered it to Joshua.

"If you're wondering what jerk splashed you, it was me. I saw you at the last minute. When I swerved, I hit the puddle instead."

Joshua chuckled. "Honestly, I couldn't tell. My eyes were full of water."

If it had happened to Liam, he would have been livid, but all Joshua could do was shake his head.

Joshua wrapped the towel around him like a blanket. "Look at it this way. If I'm going to get hit by something, I'm glad it was water."

"You're a legend around here. Hitting you would make me the town villain."

"Believe me, you probably couldn't do worse than any others. When it's my turn to go, well, I won't be sad about it." Joshua laced his fingers together, and the sleeve of his shirt rose just enough that Liam caught the deep scar on his wrist.

He'd seen it before, but had never felt comfortable asking Joshua about it. They didn't really know each other that well, but to be fair, he had nothing to lose. He was Joshua's captive audience.

"Where did you get that scar, if you don't mind my asking?"

Joshua lifted his wrist and rolled his sleeve back, revealing an arm that was all sinews and bones. The cut was deep, etched halfway across the inside of his forearm, like a road cut into a mountain.

"Not a pretty story," Joshua admitted.

"I never liked pretty stories anyway," Liam replied, his gaze glued to the road. He believed hard stories made him a better man. After the week he'd had, he needed to get his mind off Cassidy.

"It started as a disagreement with a friend."

"A friend?" Liam choked out. "Some friend he was."

"When Pete and I graduated, we went into business together. Learned my lesson the hard way. Our friendship didn't survive. But we made our peace."

Liam nodded in the dark. "My father said you could never be great friends and business partners. It was one or the other. He had a lot of enemies, actually."

"Money complicates things. So do love interests. Pete fell for Lizzie even though she had no interest in him. When we started dating, the jealousy ate him alive."

"He tried to harm you?"

"It never came to that," Joshua said. "He might have been foolish, but he wasn't vengeful. I tried to stop his suicide attempt. Ended up getting hurt."

"Because of Lizzie?" Liam asked.

"Not just that. He made several poor decisions. At some point, he stole money from the business to pay off some gambling loans." Joshua shook his head. "But that was how he self-destructed. Falling for a woman he couldn't love and money that wasn't his. The weakness of every man."

"How did you know?"

Joshua folded the damp towel into a square. "I was the one who kept the books. Money was draining from our account for no reason, so I confronted him. At first, he denied it. Then Lizzie told me about his feelings for her. He'd betrayed two people he cared about, and the guilt ate him alive. I found the note he left at the office and tracked him down at his house. He'd been drinking too much and attempted to threaten me if I stopped him. There was a fight, and he accidentally struck me with a knife."

Liam shook his head. "You could have died."

Joshua's eyes grew distant. "He didn't take anything that wasn't mine to begin with."

Liam rolled those words around in his head and wasn't satisfied. A man had to protect what was rightfully his. His business, his woman, himself. "But he had no right to what was yours."

"That may be so. But he meant more to me than any business." He turned to Liam. "Ironically, Lizzie and I broke up a few months later. One stupid argument caused more harm than Pete ever did."

Liam didn't know how to respond. Too much loss will sour a man, but Joshua didn't seem bitter at all.

He focused on the wet pavement where he could only see as far as his headlights. Beyond that, the road was a dark abyss.

"Cassidy knows the story about Lizzie," he said, turning his head to the side window where Liam couldn't see his face. If Joshua was sad, he couldn't tell. He was as much of a closed book as Cassidy was.

"What happened to Pete?" Liam asked.

"Pete's still around. Decided business wasn't his thing. Stopped drinking and cleaned up his life, then became a teacher. Now that he's retired, he lends a hand with Cassidy's reading program."

"Nice of you to forgive him."

"Nice has nothing to do with it," Joshua insisted. "That's grace, my friend. The older you get, the more you realize how much you don't deserve it."

Liam turned the car onto Main Street. They were nearing Joshua's salvage shop, and Liam knew that his time with Joshua was running out.

"Not sure why I told you all this. Just a hunch that you needed to hear it."

As the tires crunched gravel in the parking lot, Liam slowed to a stop. "Are you sure you don't want me to take you home?"

"This is my home." Joshua nodded at the salvage shop. "Other than my cabin, which I don't use much. I suppose I should sell it, but I just can't bring myself to let it go." Joshua tilted his head toward Liam, as if he were thinking.

"If you ever decide to sell, let me know."

"I'll keep that in mind." Joshua climbed out of the car. Turning, he leaned in one last time.

"Cassidy's a wonderful girl," Joshua said. "Don't lose her."

Liam nodded, unsure whether to admit the truth.

I'm afraid I already have.

CHAPTER EIGHTEEN

LIAM

L iam parked his car on Main Street and stared at Cassidy's window. Ever since they'd had that awful conversation over the phone, he'd kept his distance. But Cassidy continued to consume his thoughts like an intense addiction, and he couldn't take her silence anymore.

I'm doing this for her.

Exhausted and grumpy, he'd packed up in the middle of the night and drove to Wild Harbor without telling her. To be fair, he wanted it to be a surprise in the morning and catch a sleepy-eyed beauty opening the door, a tangle of hair framing her face.

For now, a single light burned behind a curtained window, and he imagined her curled up on the couch in that same men's button-up shirt that had tempted him. All he wanted was to watch her sleep, the half-moon of lashes shadowing her face, the way her lips softened when she relaxed. In his dreams, she was close enough to touch. *Almost.*

But in his car, he grappled with his terrible longing for her, not knowing if he'd ever get the chance to touch her again. And that was the worst part. Wanting something you could not have.

Don't lose her, Joshua had warned. And yet, she'd slipped through his fingers like crumbling sand. For once, all his business skills meant nothing. His money was useless. The only thing that might save their relationship was laying it all on the line for her. Every messy truth.

But that would require humility, and there were no guarantees she'd stay with him.

As chairman of the board for his dad's company, people usually came groveling to him. Apologizing was a foreign concept. It was the equivalent of eating a mouthful of dirt, and frankly, he didn't like bending down with his face in the muck to gain someone's favor.

But Joshua had reminded him that you can't demand grace, it was a gift. And maybe that's what he'd been fighting against all along.

To earn trust back, you had to let go of any pride you had.

That was his plan for the fundraiser tonight: To win back Cassidy before Cam stole her away.

A few hours later, he caught her opening the curtains at daybreak, her shirt askew on her shoulders, her face reflecting the morning sun. He ran toward her apartment, taking two stairs at a time and pounded on her door.

For a split second, hesitation tore through him. He should have brought a gift. Some token of apology. A coffee, at least. *Idiot.*

The door cracked open, and a sliver of her bare legs caught his attention. He'd been right. She wore that nightshirt again, the one that made him feel like all his muscles were temporarily paralyzed.

"Liam? What are you doing here?" She hid behind the door, tugging at the hem of that shirt.

"Can I come in?" he asked.

"Now?" she asked. "I'm not"—she glanced down at her bare legs—"dressed yet."

"I've seen you in that nightshirt before," he reminded her, like it was a neutral subject. Her legs were anything *but* neutral to him. But if she knew that, she'd never let him in.

"Only for a few minutes," she said, trying to smooth the knots out of her messy hair. In the past, he'd always dated women who prided themselves on their perfectly coifed hair, but only now did he realize how much he loved her disheveled look, like she'd just rolled out of bed.

"I have a lot to do for the fundraiser tonight," she added, opening the door.

"How can I help? I want to do whatever it takes to make tonight a success."

"I can't let you help. Not with what happened," she said.

So the investigation was still on her mind.

"I had nothing to do with that man's disappearance. You've got to believe me."

"I do," she said, turning away from him and reaching for her coffee. "But if people see me with you, they're going to assume things."

"Cass," he said. "My whole family is attending. What will my mother think?"

She swiveled to face him. "I can't pretend anymore. It's not fair to your mom. Especially since her treatments aren't working anymore."

"I'm not letting her give up. We'll find another doctor, a different cancer center, whatever it takes—"

"Liam," Cassidy interrupted. "She doesn't want a new treatment. She wants to spend less time in oncology centers and enjoy the time she has left. I refuse to lead her on." She folded both hands around the cup, pressing so hard her fingertips were white. "You know what she told me? The one thing keeping her going was the hope of our engagement. All I wanted to do was throw up, because I'm lying to a dying woman."

Liam stepped toward her, but she immediately backed away, afraid of his closeness.

"Cassidy," he murmured, brushing his fingers across her cheek.

"Don't," she said, closing her eyes. "You need to confess the truth."

"I'm going to tell you first." He swallowed hard. Eating dirt wouldn't feel good. But he was willing to grovel at her feet if she'd give him a second chance.

"I know our relationship started out as little more than a contract," he began.

"That's an interesting way of putting it," she told him. "As my boss, you forced me into an awkward situation."

"I kept the store open for you," he reminded her. If this was a battle of wills, he was not going down without a fight.

"You kissed me," she said, crossing her arms.

"There was no forcing. I asked first, and you more than willingly kissed me back."

She considered her response. "I had to save the store," she insisted, but the slight blush on her cheeks gave her away.

"By kissing the boss?" he said. "Admit it, you liked it."

"I did not!" she shot back. Her lips curved into a wicked grin. "Okay, maybe I did."

Her smile tempted him to kiss her again, but he couldn't. Not until he finished his confession first.

"You weren't the only one. The more time we spent together, the more I realized I wasn't pretending. I wanted to do everything for you." He held her gaze to see if she understood.

"You liked the benefits of having a pretend girlfriend," she told him.

"Nope." He shook his head.

She gave him a pointed look. *Liar, liar, pants on fire.*

"Fine," he admitted. "I loved the benefits. Kissing you. Touching you. But there was so much more to it. I realized I liked *you*. I wanted to make you happy. Give you your wildest dreams. Take care of you so that you didn't have to work so hard."

"You . . . liked . . . me?" She tripped over her words.

"Yes." Maybe he was getting through. "More than liked, actually."

"Like a sister?"

"Definitely not," he admitted.

"Then a friend?"

"No," he said, cutting the distance between them so that he could pull her closer. "Like a woman I can't stand being away from. I don't ever want to let you go, Cass."

Her mouth dropped, like she wanted to say something, but was speechless.

All he wanted was to kiss her until she believed him, but he couldn't do that now. Not unless she kissed him first.

He'd wait forever for her.

"But you don't go for women like me," she said, not believing him. "You confessed that."

"I was stupid. Dead wrong. An idiot."

She crossed her arms. "I don't know, Liam. How do I know you're not using me again? For your own gain?"

"Trust me," he insisted, running his hands through his hair. "I'm trying to make things right between us. I'll do whatever it takes to win you back."

She tilted her head. "That's funny. Because I haven't heard you apologize once."

"What?" Fear rose under his rib cage. He wasn't good at this. "I'm sorry, okay?" he mumbled.

She shook her head, crossing to the sink to dump the hard sludge of coffee that had settled at the bottom of her cup. "That didn't sound like much of an apology."

"What do you want me to do? Just tell me."

"That's the problem." She slowly turned from the sink, her face weary. "I don't know what the truth is anymore."

"But I told you the truth . . . I want to take care of you."

"What if I don't know if I can trust you anymore?"

He frowned. "I don't believe you."

"Maybe you should," she said before crossing to the door and opening it, an obvious invitation for him to go. "I'm sorry, Liam, but I can't deal with this today. Not until you're ready to tell your mother and me everything."

"When can I see you next?" he asked desperately, refusing to leave until she gave him an answer.

She leaned her body against the side of the door, as if the weight of their conversation had wiped her out. "When I can learn to trust you again."

HE WAITED OUTSIDE THE BALLROOM, the sun bleeding orange and red as it set across the lake. Couples walked arm in arm into the fundraising gala, dressed in sleek black tuxes and expensive dresses, reminding him of what he didn't have. *Cassidy.* Until recently, he had been like a puppeteer orchestrating all his marionettes, and it had worked for years. But this time, he wanted to let go of his need for control and secrets between them. If that's what it took, he'd do it. He only hoped it wasn't too late.

He strode into the ballroom and scanned the perimeter for Cassidy, who wore an off-the-shoulder black silk dress that hugged her curves. *Goodness, she looked stunning.*

She was shaking hands with the mayor as her eyes flicked over to him and held his gaze for a few seconds before returning to her conversation.

As the mayor walked away, Liam crossed the room. It was

now or never. He placed a hand on her shoulder and she startled. "Liam, I thought I made things clear between us."

"There's no way I would miss this. I don't care how you feel about me. I'm here to support your program." He held out an envelope.

"I can't take your money," she said, glancing around the room to check if anyone was looking. "Not with your situation."

"Then I'll slide it under your apartment door later. Even sleep outside if you want me to."

She cracked a smile. "I'd rather you bother me than stalk me."

"Can I bother you now?" He laid a hand on her arm, and her gaze slid to his touch. "If you'll give me a chance, I want to tell you everything."

Could she feel the effect she was having on him, the endless connection that looped between them?

"Right now?"

He nodded and led her to a deserted corridor. "There will be fewer eyes on us out here." He checked to see that no one was around. "My dad made some bad choices. Things I've had to fix since his death."

"Like what?" Hesitation flitted across her gaze.

"He looked for opportunities to buy failing business and close them down, but other times he made those businesses fail a little faster. It wasn't exactly illegal, just unscrupulous. That's what happened the year before he died. Mitch Stephens was an employee in that company and threatened to expose him. My dad bribed him to keep quiet, but after he died, I refused to continue. A year ago, he gave me an ultimatum. Pay him or he'd ruin my father's reputation. So I fired the guy."

"But if he blackmailed you, why did the police question you?"

"Stephens went missing, and they're looking for someone

who might have reason to harm him. Someone tipped them off about my dad's business dealings."

"But who would do that?"

He shrugged. "I'm not sure. My dad had several enemies. He was ruthless in his business dealings, and unfortunately, I've had to iron out several problems since his death. My guess is someone wanted to get back at the family. That's part of the reason Abby is in boarding school and I'm at my mother's house frequently. It's safer."

He was the only one who knew that danger threatened their placid life, and he would do anything to protect his family. It was the reason he couldn't let people into their lives easily. Cassidy was the first woman he'd allowed to get close, the one person to witness the jagged cracks and gaping holes in their family life.

"So that's why you didn't tell me," she said, her face softening. "To protect Jane and Abby."

"And you," he added. "That's why keeping the bookstore open was a tough decision. My dad's past makes it a target for someone who wants to take me down. I just don't want to see you get hurt."

"Liam, why didn't you tell me this before?"

"Because it was complicated," he admitted. "And I don't like being vulnerable. But for you, I'm willing to do anything."

He reached into his pocket and pulled out a small blue box. "Something to celebrate your success tonight."

Her eyes flicked over the box before she put a hand up to stop him. "I told you no gifts."

"But you don't have the right jewelry for tonight. And I can fix that."

She opened the lid and discovered a simple gold necklace with a diamond pendant inside.

"How did you know this was the one I liked?"

"I saw the way you looked at it in the store."

"You were watching me?"

"Always," he told her with a smirk. "It's hard not to watch you when we're in the same room."

She closed the box. "It's too much."

"It's *not* too much." He took the necklace and dropped it around her neck, feeling the brush of her skin as his fingers worked the clasp.

She turned around and adjusted the diamond, her eyes bright. "How does it look?"

"Perfect," he whispered, giving an approving smile. "Now, go get some massive donations for your kids."

She squeezed his hand before disappearing into the crowd.

He watched her cross the room, mesmerized by her beauty and wanting to protect her from his past. He'd trained himself to stay alert, always watching out for Jane and Abby. But now he insisted on doing the same for Cassidy. Even if she rejected him, he'd still protect her.

If only his father had been a different sort of man. And if only Liam could determine what sort of man he wanted to become.

Like father, like son? Not if he could help it.

From a distance, the outline of a man's face made him stop. *Cam.*

As much as he'd like to escort him out, he needed to let Cassidy handle it. She wasn't his to boss around. No more marionette strings. Instead, he pinwheeled through the crowd and found Jane and Abby, but kept his eyes on Cassidy.

Her shoulders tensed as they talked, and her face grew rigid as he touched her shoulder. She left him then, but Cam's glare lingered for another minute before spotting Liam. Cam's mouth quirked with a slightly wicked grin that warned, *you're going down.*

Liam gently grabbed Abby's arm and nudged her toward

Jane. "Would you stay with your grandmother tonight? No matter what happens?"

Abby frowned. "Are you leaving?"

"I may need to," he muttered. "If something comes up."

"It looks like the program is getting a lot of excitement," Jane said, plucking a shrimp cocktail from a server's tray. "You must be so proud of how things are going for you and Cassidy."

"I am," he said. "But I had nothing to do with it. Cassidy gets all the credit."

"Ladies and gentlemen," Cam's voice came over the speaker as he held a paper in his hands. "I'd like to make an exciting announcement tonight. On behalf of the Greater Foundation of Kent County, we'd like to award the Wild Harbor children's reading program with a fifty-thousand-dollar grant. This means that the program will expand into other communities across the state."

Cassidy looked elated as he handed her the official document and led her backstage. Was this part of Cam's scheme to win Cassidy back?

Jane leaned close to her son. "Did you know about this grant?"

"She mentioned it," he said vaguely.

"Cassidy told me all about it," Abby said, eating an enormous slice of white cake with colorful frosting. "She told me she hoped she didn't win because the grant would force her to move her program."

"What?" Liam looked over at her. "Are you sure?"

"Yeah," Abby said, her mouth lined in frosting. "I think that's what she said."

Liam glanced around for Cass, who was mysteriously missing from the ballroom since she'd received the grant. He wanted to look over the details before she signed anything.

He slipped into a vacant back hall and crossed to the other end of the building before turning into a darkened corridor. He squeezed past stacked chairs and found an exit door propped open with a chair leg. Where had Cassidy run off to with Cameron?

Outside, overgrown bushes lined the property. No one would exit from here unless they knew of a shortcut. Before he shut the door, he noticed a dirt path that led to the lake. Two people stood on the dock. In the darkness, Liam couldn't make out their distinct features, but when he heard a muffled cry, something nudged him forward into a sprint.

Cassidy.

She wrestled away from Cam's arms as he pulled her toward him.

"What are you doing to her?" he asked as he yanked Cam off of her.

"Nothing," Cam yelled as he fell backwards onto the wood planks.

Cassidy pulled at the fallen strap on her dress, relief flooding her features.

"It's none of your business if I want to have a conversation," Cam said, slowly rising.

"Everything about Cassidy is my business." Liam nodded. "And it didn't look like a conversation."

"We'll see if she stays," Cam hissed. "After your dad's news is exposed."

"How do you know about it?" Liam asked, trying not to lose control.

"I did a little research on your family. Seems like you've had to cover up his business deceptions," Cam sneered.

Liam suddenly wondered whether Cam was the one who'd tipped off the police.

"You don't know what you're talking about," Liam threatened.

"You act tough, but it's all pretend," Cam warned, backing

away, his eyes glittering like diamonds. "I already know about your convenient *arrangement*."

Liam's gaze slid to Cass. Her face told him everything. She had revealed their fake dating agreement.

"I'm so sorry," she mouthed to Liam.

Of all the people to confess to, he wished it hadn't been Cam.

He turned back to Cam. "It may have been an arrangement at the beginning, but not anymore. I've fallen in love with Cass, and I'm willing to fight for her."

Cam laughed in disbelief. "After that fake dating stunt, there's no way she'd ever go back to you."

"She might not," he shot back. "But at least I didn't call off a *real* engagement."

Before Liam finished the last word, Cam flung himself toward his opponent. Liam dodged before he got hit with a full-body blow, knocking both men to the dock. Cam tried to strike Liam with his fist, but Liam rolled out of the way at the last second. Stumbling to his feet, he pushed Cam so that he lost his balance and crashed into the lake.

Liam rushed over to Cass, his breath ragged. "We should go."

"But Cam can't swim," she cried. "The water is too deep."

Liam spun around, searching for him under the surface. He didn't have time to think. He jumped into the water and began sweeping his arms under the shadowy surface. Night swimming was like being plunged into ink.

He surfaced for a second to grab a mouthful of air and then sank under the water again, his arms pumping through the murky lake. Liam pushed forward, his lungs screaming for breath, his right arm bumping into something. In the gloomy darkness, he grabbed what felt like Cam's arm. Liam wrapped his other arm around his chest and swam to the surface.

Liam tried to help Cam climb onto the dock, but he resisted.

"I don't want your help," Cam spat.

"Suit yourself," Liam said. "But don't touch her again."

Cam slowly pulled himself out before turning to Cassidy. "Are you choosing him or me?"

"What are you talking about?" she asked.

"I'm giving you a second chance to make the right decision. This is your future. You know what they say about families. Like father, like son," he sneered, jutting his chin at Liam.

Liam balled his hands into fists. He had tried for so long to be a better man than his father. But right now, the anger pummeled through his chest like a freight train.

Cassidy grabbed Liam's fist and intertwined her fingers through his, melting the raging fire in his bones.

"Say what you want about his family, but I've never met more generous and kind people than Liam, Jane, and Abby. Given your track record, I don't think I could ever trust you again. If that means giving up the grant, I'll do it. Whatever it takes to end things between us."

A harsh sound escaped Cam's throat. "You'd do something stupid like lose the grant? After all I did for you?" Cam shook his head in disgust. "Don't come crawling back to me saying I didn't warn you."

"The warning I should have listened to was the one telling me to stay away from you," she shot back.

"If you think I'm the only one disappointed about your decision tonight, you're wrong."

"What are you talking about?" she asked.

"You'll see," he said, a wicked curl forming on his lips before he stalked away from them.

Cassidy glanced at Liam. "What should we do now?"

"Let's get through tonight first," Liam said.

She hurried back to the fundraiser while Liam went to change into a spare outfit. After the mud-splattered suit incident, he always carried an extra set of clothes in his trunk. *Just in case.*

When he returned to the ballroom, Jane was sliding on a light jacket, her face twisted and pinched.

"Why are you leaving early?" Liam said, hurrying after them. He caught up to them in the foyer, as Abby glumly stood by Jane's side. "Is everything all right?"

Jane spun slowly around, her expression tight. "Is it true?" she asked.

Abby stared silently at the floor, unable to look at him.

"Is what true?" he asked.

Her frown deepened as the light in her eyes disappeared. "This whole thing between you and Cassidy? Was it a hoax from the beginning?"

He swallowed hard. The heavy weight of disappointment punctured the air. He didn't dare look at Abby.

"Who told you?" he muttered.

"It doesn't matter who," Jane said. "All that matters is whether it's true."

If he was trying to become a different man than his father, now was his chance to make things right.

"It was my idea," he admitted. "A terrible one. I roped Cassidy into agreeing to it. But let me explain—"

His mother put up a hand to stop him, her face weary. "I don't want your explanation. I want the truth."

"This is the truth. I'm a different man than Dad was."

She tilted her head, questioning his statement with a sharp look. "Are you? Because I'm wondering if you know what the truth is."

"I'm sorry," he said. "I shouldn't have deceived you and Abby."

Jane's lips tightened. "There's only one girl you should apologize to. I don't know if she will ever forgive you for the embarrassment you've caused her family."

Jane's gaze slid to an invisible figure behind him. As he spun around, Cassidy stood in the doorway, her face crumpling.

She'd heard every word of their conversation, all their secrets exposed.

"Cass, I'm sorry," he said as she turned and ran toward the exit.

He needed to reach her before she shut him out. "Cassidy!" he called, but she didn't stop. After everything that had happened between them, she was gone for good.

CHAPTER NINETEEN

CASSIDY

"Why do I feel like a horribly lousy person right now?" Cassidy said. "Like I stole a dying woman's last hope?" The sisters rocked on her parents' porch swing, glasses of lemonade sweating in their hands. It had been a week since the truth about her and Liam had come out, and everyone from her family had been disappointed, although no one as much as Jane.

Letting down a dying woman and her practically orphaned granddaughter had to be the worst thing she'd ever done.

"It wasn't her last hope," Megan reminded her.

"It was the only thing she wanted!" Cassidy pitched her head back onto the wooden swing.

"Look at it this way," Megan said. "You're the infamous superhero of Books Forever. We always knew you'd sacrifice your life for that place. We just didn't know the lengths you'd go to do it."

Cassidy gave her a sharp look. "You mean lying to everyone?" She covered her face with her hands. "To think I fell for my boss. If I could do things over, I would have walked out of Books Forever and never returned."

"By staying, you saved the after-school program," Lily reminded her gently.

"The fundraiser gave the program a huge windfall. But I can't afford to keep the bookstore open on my own. Especially now that I'm turning down the grant and Liam's two-month contract is over."

She hadn't talked to Liam since the fundraiser when the news came out about their fake relationship. After her broken engagement with Cam, she'd vowed not to trust another man. Then she'd stupidly fallen for Liam. Hadn't she learned anything?

"Wait, you're not taking the grant?" Lily asked, her eyes wide.

Cassidy shook her head. "Not after the move Cam pulled on me at the fundraiser. He called the next day and tried to get me to reconsider the award, but I told him no. I need to do things on my own terms now, without Cam or Liam's help. That's why I'm moving my program to another location in Wild Harbor. I can't work with Liam while I have feelings for him."

"How does Liam feel about that?" Megan asked.

Cassidy shrugged. "I told him I'm finally doing what's best for him and me. And he didn't say anything to stop me."

Now that things were over, Liam was free to turn the bookstore into a fancy gym and date whomever he wanted.

"Maybe he wants you to decide," Megan said. "He's giving you the one thing you've always wanted. The freedom to choose your own path."

"Then why did he confess his love for me in front of Cam? Why hasn't he brought that up?"

Lily sighed. "He's still technically your boss. It's an awkward situation for him."

Megan squeezed her sister's hand, then glanced at Aspen.

"No matter what happens, we still want Abby and Jane to attend the wedding."

Cassidy let out a breath. "I don't even know if Jane will want to, honestly. She probably hates me for deceiving her. The worst part is that I really care for her and Abby. But now she thinks it was all an act."

"It wasn't your idea," Lily said.

"But I went along with his plan. What kind of person does that? I ruined her dream." She rubbed her aching forehead, wishing she could rub the pain away. "I will not throw Liam under the bus. Jane and Abby feel like family. I wish things could have ended differently."

"Then make them," Megan urged.

"But how? If I go to her and she shuts me out, I'll only feel worse." She bit her lip. Seeing Liam and Jane would take more of her than she could give. Any time she was within a few feet of Liam, her heart was kicked over like a bucket of water. Running into him would only reawaken everything she was trying to smother.

"I will not see Liam. Not if I can help it." Her hand brushed the necklace he'd given her, and a sharp pang twisted inside her. She couldn't keep his gift, not when so much of him had already become part of her.

"Can you make sure he comes to the wedding? And Jane too?" Megan asked.

"I'll try. I just can't promise it won't be awkward."

Who was she kidding? Life had become one awkward mess ever since she'd fallen for Liam. She thought she knew better, warning herself not to fall for a man who could never be hers. But warnings were as flimsy as wet paper.

Megan squeezed her hand one last time. "That's what family is for. Getting through the awkward parts together."

~

As Cassidy waited on the stoop of Jane's colonial home, her feet felt like lead. It had taken her days to work up the courage to face Jane.

Afraid of chickening out, she hadn't told Liam or Jane she was coming, but decided on a spontaneous trip to face Jane in person. Liam's work schedule usually involved Wednesdays in his Chicago office, which meant she could avoid a potentially awkward encounter with him.

As she rang the doorbell, her chest tightened with an overwhelming crush of anxiety, causing her to bolt toward the car with a swift one-hundred-and-eighty-degree turn.

"Cassidy?" a woman's voice called.

Too late.

She swiveled toward Jane, her voice faltering. "Oh, hello," she squeaked out.

Jane looked her over with a mix of curiosity and reluctance. "This is a surprise."

"Do you have a minute?" Cassidy continued. "I won't keep you long."

Without saying a word, Jane pushed the door open wider, inviting her to enter.

To calm her frazzled nerves, Cassidy focused on a bookcase stacked with family pictures, a carefully curated image of happiness even though grief had cloaked the Henry home.

Everywhere she went, she faced reminders of Liam, like he'd woven himself into the fabric of her life. Seeing his photographs stripped her of what little confidence she had.

Jane gestured toward a stiff wingback chair. Cassidy lowered herself onto the edge, like a cat ready to dart out the door if danger approached. She knew Jane wouldn't harm her, but the act of confession wasn't neutral. She'd hurt Jane, and that sliced her like a thousand tiny cuts, each memory haunting her with a stinging ache.

When you're fully aware of your guilt, it feels as dangerous as a brandished switchblade.

Jane sat across from her in a matching chair, her lips pursed. "I take it you're here to see Liam?"

Cassidy shook her head. "I'm here to chat with you." *Chat* wasn't exactly what she'd wanted to say, but her grip of the English language seemed to be failing her. *Chatting* implied a friendly, no-agenda conversation between friends. She'd rehearsed a checklist while driving, hoping they could resolve things on a friendly note. Her apology might bring closure, the best Cassidy could hope for in this situation, but it didn't always mend the extreme pain caused when the seam of a relationship ripped apart.

"I came to apologize," she stammered, pushing her hands under her thighs to avoid showing her shaking. "My behavior was inexcusable, and I should never have agreed to anything more than a friendship with Liam."

"Which was questionable," Jane cut in with bold certainty.

The heat in Cassidy's neck rose with Jane's accusation. His mother had already drawn her conclusions about Cassidy. Toppling them would be like trying to strike down the Eiffel Tower.

She balled her hands into fists under her thighs. "I can't speak for your son," she said in a controlled voice. "But I considered him and you my friends, no matter what you think of me now. I'm deeply sorry for the decision I made. When I first agreed to it, I never thought our relationship could be anything more than an agreement between an employer and employee. I was so dedicated to my program and the store that I was willing to do anything to save it. It was only when I realized I cared about you that I regretted what I'd done. By then, it was too late. Everyone was invested, and the only way out was the truth."

Jane's eyes sparked, like a tiny, lit flame. "What *is* the truth, exactly? Because you put on a good act. I believed you were in love with my son."

Cassidy's eyes slid to the floor. How could she confess she'd tried to tamp down her feelings for Liam? Everything in her had fought to squelch these emotions, and yet something kept rising back up, fighting for space in her heart.

"I fell for him," she said weakly, embarrassed to admit it. "Completely. I tried not to. But when you pretend you're a couple, it's only natural to grow closer."

Even though she didn't want to give Jane false hope, a glimmer of hope blossomed in her expression.

Cassidy shifted uneasily. "I don't know how Liam feels about me after everything that's happened. Now that we've had some space apart, I realize it was all a ridiculous dream. He even admitted at the garden party he could never fall for someone like me."

"Liam won't talk to me about it," Jane admitted. "Abby is devastated by the news, and I can't make any promises that she'll forget it. That girl has been hurt by so much at such a young age."

Cassidy shivered. She knew what it was like to carry scars into adulthood, the pain of your past looping on repeat.

"That's part of the reason I'm here," Cassidy said. "Our family still wants you to come to the wedding. If you'll allow me to see her, I promise I'll do whatever it takes to prove my friendship with her is real."

Jane glanced toward the hallway, distracted by a noise. "That will be up to Liam. He's her guardian."

"Could you at least ask him?"

"Why don't you ask him yourself?"

Her gaze darted to the hallway, and a realization sent a flush of heat through Cassidy's body.

"He goes into the office on Wednesdays, right?" Cassidy asked.

Please don't let him be here.

"Most of the time, but today, he decided to work from my house since I wasn't feeling well."

An invisible urge to flee rocked Cassidy. She needed to leave before Liam discovered her.

"I had no idea . . ." Cassidy mumbled, fighting to regain her composure.

Normally, she kept her emotions under lock and key, but she could sense the furious rush across her flaming cheeks.

"You don't have to go," Jane insisted.

"I'm sorry. I didn't know." Cassidy was dizzy from panic, like she'd spun on the merry-go-round too many times. She stumbled toward the door, then remembered the bulging envelope in her pocket. She pulled out the donation check Jane had given her for the after-school program.

Jane frowned. "I didn't want this back."

"It was generous of you, but you donated this money before you knew the truth. And I don't feel right keeping it."

"But it's for the kids," she said. "Your bookstore needs it. *You* need it."

Cassidy couldn't believe that Jane didn't know. "I'm not staying at the bookstore. I have no choice."

"But I thought the bookstore meant everything to you? That's why Liam kept it open. For *you.*"

The words were like bricks stacked on her chest, pressing all the air out.

"His funding was only for two months. Our agreement is complete." This conversation was ripping open the seam of everything she was trying to stitch back together.

A man appeared from the hallway. "That's not entirely true," Liam stated, interrupting their conversation.

Even from across the room, his presence stirred something in her, pulling her toward him like a magnet.

Rooting her feet to the floor, she refused to give in to her body's pull. "You told me so yourself," she said, trying to rein in the bucking horse of her emotions.

He moved closer to her, and her skin prickled with a flood of conflicting emotions. Wanting him. Wanting to flee. She couldn't even think straight anymore.

"Mother, if you'll excuse us. I think we need to clear up a few things." He grasped her elbow and gently tugged her onto the porch, shutting the door behind them.

In the daylight, his gray eyes looked like stone. "Is this what you want? To break all ties with me and the store?" he said. "You didn't even attempt to ask for another solution."

She didn't think there were other options. Or maybe in her hurt, she'd only interpreted it that way. Doing business with him seemed risky to her heart. And risk was the one thing she couldn't tolerate.

"I didn't know if anything was still an option between us," she said weakly.

"What if it was? Would it change anything?" His voice chipped away at the wall she was trying to put up between them.

Liam waited for her answer, drawing an imaginary line in the sand. *Stay or go. Be his partner or not.*

Deep down, she wanted another chance with the bookstore and with him. But what if he closed the store in a few months? If she wasn't in control of the store, then the program would remain in jeopardy. And so would her heart.

If she worked alongside him, she would always love him, whether or not he loved her.

After her broken engagement with Cam, her heart was too bruised to take more disappointment. Her ex had given her a humiliating blow, but Liam had crushed it in a different way, obliterating it into a thousand tiny shards that, when pieced back together, only resembled a poor imitation of the original.

What would she lose if she took a risk on Liam now? *Everything.*

Any contact with him would only foster an intense desire that would never be satisfied. Her resolve to stay away had been shredded where only one tiny thread remained. When that thread broke, she wouldn't be able to keep her distance any longer. It was all too risky.

"I'm sorry, but any sort of partnership is a distraction," she said.

"A distraction," he repeated flatly, his jaw muscle flinching. "How is this a distraction?"

She avoided the question, her emotions funneling so deep she turned hard as stone. "It's a possible risk to the program. I need one hundred percent control, otherwise any decision you make could adversely affect the program."

"You know I wouldn't do that," he muttered under his breath.

"I don't know what you're capable of," she admitted. "But I can't afford the risk. We both know it would never work between us." She turned to go.

"Cass," he growled, willing her to stop.

But she couldn't glance back and allow him to tug at her tattered emotions.

One thread was all that kept her from him.

"I'll move my stuff out of the bookstore this week," she tossed over her shoulder. "Don't bother stopping by."

CHAPTER TWENTY

LIAM

L iam waited inside the darkened bookshop, staring at the single box he'd brought with him. He tossed a book from the shelf, the pages flapping as it landed with a thud in the hollow box.

The happy couple on the cover mocked him before he realized he'd seen this book before. *The Successful Man's Guide to Dating and Love.* He let out a bitter laugh. The book his mother had given him. He'd forgotten that he'd donated it to the store. Maybe if he read it, he could learn what *not* to do to ruin a relationship.

Who was he kidding? When you make a train wreck of your own life, even a good book can't fix your self-destruction.

The irony struck him like the clear note of a tuning fork. He'd sought out a safe, calculated life, focusing more on outcomes than people, a perfect duplicate of his father's reputation, even if it wasn't true. *Like father, like son.*

He grabbed a dozen self-help books and tossed them all in

the box with a loud thud. "Might as well start with these," he said to himself.

If he needed to work on his relationship skills, then this was the first step. He'd never be perfect, but he could become a better man, even if it was too late for him and Cassidy.

When Abby had asked whether Cass was going to visit again, he'd tried to let her down gently. "I'm not sure if she's ever coming back," he said, feeling as heartbroken as Abby looked.

"Then why don't you go to her?" Abby pleaded. "Say you're sorry."

"Sometimes sorry isn't enough," he explained. "It's not like a fairy tale. Problems don't disappear because of love."

"Do you know what Cass told me once?" Abby said with a flash of excitement. "When she was my age, she had a dream about a magical land hidden in the bookstore. She was the only person who knew about it because it was a secret place. But one night, there was a prince there. When she asked him what he was doing, he told her, *Waiting for you.* That's why she created a magical place in the bookshop."

Liam tilted his head, unsure why she was bringing up this story now. "Are you suggesting I crawl into the tent to escape from my problems?" His lips twisted into a semi-serious smile.

Abby shrugged. "I don't know."

Like most kids, she was great at recording information, but terrible at interpreting it.

"Just don't take her magic place away," Abby said. "Keep the tent and lights for Cass. She'll know what to do with it."

He squeezed her hand. "I promise."

He walked over to the children's section where the tent and lights sat untouched. She had to come get them before the bookstore closed for good.

Flicking the switch, the warm glow of lights illuminated the space, drenching everything in a shimmery golden hue.

He lowered himself onto a children's bench, his knees

propped up like a giant's as he took one last look at the shelves. This was the last time he'd probably ever step foot in here, and a gloomy sadness washed over him. He didn't want it to end this way.

"What are you doing there?" A woman's voice nearly jolted him off the bench.

Cassidy stood in the doorway of the children's section, her auburn hair cascading around her bare shoulders. A white gem flashed across her neck. The necklace he'd given her.

"Taking one last look at the store," he said, trying to hide his emotion.

"I thought you were gone," she said, looking like a cat on the defensive, eyes wide, protective stance, circling around the shelves to avoid moving closer to him.

"I'm glad I wasn't."

"I'm packing this up tonight, taking it to my new place." She motioned toward the lights and tent. "My new store is pretty plain. No books or decorations. But I can create it again with the tent and lights. It doesn't have to be in this place. It doesn't have to be *here*."

He drew up behind her, the white twinkle lights reflecting off the smooth skin of her shoulders. She was so close he could smell her soft vanilla scent, the one that made him dizzy with want.

"Cass," he whispered. "This doesn't have to be goodbye."

If only he could touch her, stroke the soft flesh of her neck, drag his fingers across the hollow of her collarbone, run ragged shivers down her arms. He could hardly hold himself back.

"Why did you come tonight?" she said, an undercurrent of tension pulsating between them.

"I was waiting for you," he murmured.

"What did you say?" Cassidy shifted, like the words knocked her off-kilter.

"I was waiting for *you*," he repeated.

She turned suddenly, her breath catching when she realized how close he was. "Don't," she said in a low voice. "I didn't come here to play games."

As his eyes slid to hers, she blinked back tears, trying to stem the rising emotion.

"Cass," he whispered, his voice softening into a gentle plea. "This isn't goodbye unless you want it to be." He slowly took his hands and cupped the sides of her face. Then he rubbed his thumbs across each place where the tears held, wiping them away.

"But I need it to be. I need closure," she pleaded, her voice echoing with a hollow sadness. "Not just from the store, but from you."

Her words pinched hard, like a knife twist to his gut.

He still held her face in his palms, his thumbs rubbing over the high planes of her cheekbones. If he regretted telling her this later, he didn't care. He was already burning for her.

"I've hidden my feelings for you for so long, afraid of getting hurt the same way my father's death devastated my mother. I thought if I didn't fall for anyone, then I could never experience that level of pain. But then we met, and everything in me wanted you. When you drove away after our argument, my life fell apart. You were mine for two months, and I was never brave enough to tell you how much you completed me."

His hands drifted to her jaw, then slid down the gentle curve of her neck. "Falling for you was the best thing that ever happened to me."

He pulled out the store key and dropped it into her palm, wrapping her fingers around it.

She stared at her fist. "Why are you giving me this?" she whispered, her voice trembling.

"It's yours now," he said.

"A key to your gym?" she asked hesitantly.

"I'm not turning this into a gym. I'm giving you a place for your reading program."

She shook her head and tried to shove the key back into his hands, but he quickly pulled away.

"This place is yours," she pleaded. "I can't afford it." She held the key out for him.

He backed away, afraid of igniting any more desire. He wanted so badly to take her in his arms.

"You're set as long as you want it. I'm transferring everything to your name," he concluded, like it was a done deal. All he needed was her approval, and he'd get the paperwork completed. "You can use it as the headquarters for your new expanded reading program." He gave her a melancholy smile remembering how much joy helping kids brought her.

"I don't understand." She shook her head. "I'll never be able to keep up with the bills."

He raised a hand, stopping her. "I talked to the grant foundation, and they agreed to award you the money anyway, as well as some leniency on where you're located."

"You reinstated the grant? But how?"

"Doesn't matter how. All you need to know is that your headquarters can remain in Wild Harbor as long as you open an additional program in their county. That will be more than enough to keep things running."

Her mouth opened, then closed, and he could see the questions whirling in her head.

"Why are you doing this?" she asked.

He threw up his hands. "Isn't it obvious?"

She propped a hand on her hip. "Not to me."

Her look of frustration made him want to kiss her hard, melting all the needless tension between them. He rubbed the back of his neck, trying to rein in his desire. He couldn't kiss her. It would break what little trust was left between them, if any still existed. But he had to make her understand how much she meant to him.

"Cassidy, I love you. Even when I'm gone, I'll think of you *here*, under the lights with that sexy look of intense concentration. And I'll know I gave you the one gift that no one else could." He put out his arms, sweeping the space with the length of his arms. "*This*."

Maybe it was because she was standing directly under the twinkle lights, wrapped in the glow of a golden blanket, but the way she looked at him was different now, like something was blossoming.

"But you wanted this place," she whispered.

"No." He shook his head. "I wanted you."

With a few steps, she closed the distance between them, her hands grabbing the back of his neck and pulling him toward her. Her lips met his with intense desire, and he soaked in the sweet softness of them, drinking in more of her with every kiss.

His hands lodged in her hair, carefully dropping to her neck, then dragging across the softness of her shoulders. He tried to form a clear thought, but his mind spun like a swing wound tight.

He kissed her cheek before dropping his mouth across the smooth line of her jaw, following a path to the soft curve of her ear. Instead of pulling away, she leaned into him, as if she wanted this as much as he did.

What does this mean? His desire for her swept away his ability to answer. He kept trying to circle back to all the reasons he shouldn't be doing this, but his longing highjacked the switch in his brain. Bracing his hands against her shoulders, he tore himself from her, his breath ragged. If she was trying to keep him from leaving, she was doing a good job.

"I need to stop," he admitted, letting out a long breath. "Because you're making it hard to say goodbye."

She locked on to his gaze. "I don't want you to go." She

shifted inside his arms, stepping back, trying to get her footing. "I know this doesn't fix everything, especially with your pending investigation."

With their recent breakup, he wondered whether he should even tell her. "They dropped the investigation. Stephens faked his disappearance to get back at my family and blackmail us. Cam found out about the scheme and tried to use it against me."

Her eyes widened. "Cam was involved?"

"When he found out we were dating, he started digging around on the internet for information on my family. He landed on the news of Stephens's firing, and he contacted the guy. They hatched a plan to try and ruin my family's reputation."

"How did you find this out?"

"Somebody tipped off the police about Stephens's location. He agreed to meet with me, and I decided to resolve this situation once and for all. Fortunately, my father left detailed records about his businesses, including information on Stephens. Apparently, the guy once stole money from the company. When my dad discovered it, he forgave him the full amount if he returned the money. He agreed, and my father never said another word. When I brought this up, I told him I'd forgive his mistake as long as he never targeted my family again."

"What about your dad's investments?"

"According to his records, he was trying to save the company with a last-ditch attempt at a risky investment that ultimately failed. To everyone else, it looked like he was taking down the business on purpose, but I don't think he was. He took calculated risks—ones that usually failed, but a risk nonetheless."

"Does your mom know about this?"

"She'd stayed out of Dad's business affairs, but the news didn't surprise her. To the rest of the world, he looked ruthless. But Dad was the only one brave enough to try to save a dying company."

"Kind of like you," Cassidy said, something shifting in her eyes.

"Not really." He rubbed his forehead. "What I did—buying the building—was not an attempt to save the bookstore. Until I made that deal with you, I had no intention of keeping it open. That's why I'm trying to make things right. Even if that means taking a loss."

"What about buying a home?"

He took her hand, his body lighting up under her touch. "If I lived here and couldn't have you, it would drive me crazy." He rubbed his hand down her arm. Her skin slipped like silk; it begged to be touched.

Something swirled in her eyes, an intensity rippling beneath the surface that made him want to pull her into his arms and melt into her. But until she gave him permission, he wouldn't touch her.

"What if I told you not to go?" she asked. "My program needs you."

"So, it's about your program?" For a moment, he hoped there was another reason. "I have full faith in you, Cass."

"Liam." Her voice dropped. "I don't want this place if you're leaving too."

He rubbed his palm across her cheek, tracing the contours of her face so he could etch it into his memory. "You'll make the place a success. Your program, everything you've created—it's magic."

"That's not what I meant," she said, her eyes flaring, like fire was rising in them. "I want you to stay with me."

He dropped his hand from her face, narrowing his eyes. He couldn't get his hopes up. "A business partnership?"

She shook her head. "A real partnership. No contracts. No agreements. Just us." She slid her hands onto his chest, right over his heart, which was racing uncontrollably now, every beat pulsating beneath her fingertips.

"When you gave me the store, that wasn't a business decision. It wasn't even you feeling sorry for me. It was a gift. And that realization broke me. I'd been holding everything back from you, scared you'd leave me the way Cam did, afraid that I was a risky game of Russian roulette because of so many things—my epilepsy, this store—all of it a dangerous gamble."

He took her hands in his and rubbed his thumbs over them. Memorizing every part of her had become second nature to him.

She gazed down at their entwined fingers. "You saw your mom's grief, and you distanced yourself from the risk of love. I was a reckless move, a wild card. The *nice, normal girl* you'd never take a chance on because I didn't meet your criteria. When I realized that, I couldn't live with the weight of any more disappointment, of trying to stamp out all my feelings when it was impossible. I'm a risk. The dark horse with the five-hundred-to-one odds. And nobody wants that."

"I want that." He blurted out before he could think twice. "I want the nice, normal girl now. I want us. And I'd gamble everything on you, Cassidy Woods, even if the odds were a million to one."

She shook her head. "You don't know what you're gambling on. My seizures are under control now, but what if that changes? What if I can't make this program work? What if it all goes wrong?"

"I'm willing to take the risk." He tugged at her arm, pulling her into him, her body melting into his, like a candle to a wick.

"If I get you," he said, his voice low and coarse. "Then I win."

"But what if you lose everything? This business is a risk. I'm a risk. You said you don't take risks and you don't fall in love. They're your life principles."

"That's where you're wrong," he said, cupping her chin. "I only take *calculated* risks. There's a difference. It means I'm fully aware of the consequences. If your seizures come back, we'll try

GRACE WORTHINGTON

a new medication. If the program fails, we'll fix it. I've weighed everything, and I'm willing to take a chance on us."

His forehead met hers, their eyes so close, he was falling into the dark pool of her pupils, swimming in gold flecks and the soft swirling sea of her irises. He kissed the tip of her nose, then moved to her lips. "This time, I'll risk everything. Even if I lose it all, if I still have you, then I win."

He kissed her so gently, savoring every touch, that he could feel her racing heart against his own, their bodies puzzle-pieced into an embrace where neither could see where one ended and the other began.

"Liam," she whispered as he caught her bottom lip with his kiss. "Does this mean we're dating? Like for real?"

"Let's just skip dating," he whispered between kisses. "Go straight to engagement."

"Isn't this a little soon?" she said as he trailed kisses down her neck. Even though he'd made a crazy request, she didn't pull away.

"Not in my book," he whispered, his breath warming the curve of her neck. "We've been dating for months." He circled her neck with kisses, following the diamond necklace like a trail.

"Fake dating," she reminded him.

"Not for me, it wasn't," he admitted, finding his way back to her mouth. "You complete me in every way. I'm a reformed grump because of you."

She tossed her head back, laughing. "It wasn't me," she said. "It was love. And your mother finally gets her happy ending."

He pulled away, a wry smile crossing his lips. "You had to bring up my mother at a moment like this?"

Cass cringed. "Did I ruin the moment?"

"Not really," he laughed before circling one arm around her waist. "But you're right. She'd be ecstatic." He pulled back, searching her face. "But would you? Is this the ending you want?"

The question hung between them, shimmering with tension. He knew she hated when her favorite stories ended or an unresolved storyline wasn't wrapped up. But he was determined to give her the storybook ending she wanted. It wouldn't be perfect. But they would be together, and somehow, it would be enough.

She folded both arms around his neck and leveled her gaze at him.

"This is everything I want," she whispered before leaning into him, her eyes heavy with longing, the lights reflecting like fireflies, fanning everything into flame.

"I love you," she whispered.

"I love you too."

This time, there was no hesitation. His love was like breath, like the warm breeze in the morning, a strong wind that pushed the current toward an unknown sea, the depths of his love tumbling farther and faster, on course toward a future that stretched like the horizon, wider and longer and deeper, just like their love.

CHAPTER TWENTY-ONE

CASSIDY

A s Cassidy zipped the ivory gown with gold flecks, she turned in the three-way mirror, the silk shimmering in the light. Even though it was only a bridesmaid's dress, it was the most elegant gown she'd ever owned, draping every curve and pooling around her feet. No wonder Liam hadn't been able to keep his eyes off her when he'd seen her try it on in the store a few months ago.

"Oh, Cass. You're a princess!" Abby exclaimed. "Just like in the books!"

"Not a princess. Just a bridesmaid. But this dress would make a lovely wedding gown." Neither Megan nor Aspen was very conventional when it came to traditions. Even Edna had clucked her tongue in disapproval when she'd found out they weren't having separate ceremonies in a church.

"You look perfect," Jane noted, giving an approving nod. "My son will be speechless, I'm sure."

"I hope so," Cassidy said, fidgeting with the diamond ring on her finger. Her wedding day couldn't come soon enough now that she and Liam were engaged.

Jane took her hand and looked at the diamond. "I'm so glad he gave you the ring that Frank gave me."

"I still feel bad you gave up your ring, though. It really should stay with you."

"I don't." Jane patted her hand. "What good is the ring to me now? When Liam asked me about giving it to you, I was thrilled. I knew it was the right choice, and I was never so happy to pass it along."

"Are you sure?" Cassidy asked.

"Positive." Jane smiled.

Cassidy looked at Abby who was curled up on a chair in the corner reading another fairy-tale adventure. With Abby soon to join the family, the brides had asked her to be the flower girl for the double wedding on the beach.

"I hope that someday I can pass it along to Abby," Cassidy added.

"You will," Jane said. "Even if more children come along."

"Abby will always be my first daughter, even if we're not blood-related." Cassidy had been relieved when Abby had forgiven her after finding out about her and Liam's fake dating arrangement.

As soon as Liam had told them the news that they were dating again—this time, for real—Abby and Jane had welcomed her back into their family without reserve.

A knock sounded on the oak door. "Who is it?"

"The brides," Megan's voice said.

Jane turned to Abby. "We should leave so thee ladies can prepare for the wedding."

"But I'm part of the wedding!" Abby complained, jumping out of her chair and trying to smooth her rumpled flower girl dress.

"I know, but I have a job for you. A secret mission!" Jane looked over at Cassidy and winked.

She had no idea what secret mission Jane was referring to, but if it was a way of getting Abby to leave, it was working.

As Jane and Abby left, Megan and Aspen entered, looking as stunning as ever, with Lily trying to fix their wedding trains from behind.

Cassidy peeked out the door, making sure no dawdling grooms were standing outside.

"The coast is clear," she whispered over her shoulder to her sisters. "No one is here to watch us sneak out."

"Do you think we should do this?" Aspen whispered back, stepping onto the creaky wood floor, holding up her wedding dress so she wouldn't trip on the lace train. "Everybody is waiting for us down by the beach. We'll be late to our own wedding."

Megan boldly strutted into the hallway in her form-fitting lace gown, which clung to every curve, not worried about how little time they had. "They'll wait. We're the brides. The show will not go on without us," she said, propping one hand on her hip.

"This is crazy," Lily said, adjusting the strap of her bridesmaid dress. "My stomach is sick with nerves. I feel like I'm going to throw up."

"Why are you nervous? You're not the one getting married today," Megan said.

"I know." She ran her hands over her stomach, trying to squelch the nausea. "Can you pull over if I get sick?"

Megan squinted as she looked over Lily. "Didn't you complain about your stomach yesterday when we were finishing up the party favors?"

"I was tired," she said. "I needed a nap."

Megan appraised her more closely. "You're never *that* tired. I've watched you pull all-nighters for chocolate-making blitzes."

Lily's gaze swung from one sister to the other, her eyes growing watery. "If I tell you, Alex will kill me. He wanted to wait until next week. He said we'd look like we were spoiling your big day."

Aspen gave Megan a look before the question spilled out. "Are you—"

Lily nodded fast, her tears spilling down her cheeks. "I'm due in April. Please don't think I'm ruining your wedding day," she begged.

The three girls wrapped their arms around Lily, like a pep session for a sports team.

"We would *never* think that," Megan said.

"We're so happy for you!" Aspen added.

"How could this news spoil anyone's day?" Cassidy rested her head on Lily's shoulder. "You're my sister and I couldn't be more excited for you and Alex. But as much as I'd like to get all the baby details, we have to hurry if we want to sneak out of here."

"That's right," Megan said, hurrying past Cassidy. "We need to hurry."

Megan and Aspen hurried out the door with Lily following closely behind. Considering Lily was nauseous and tired, she hadn't lost her ability to run.

Cassidy pulled up the hem of her long silk bridesmaid dress, chasing her sisters through the back door of the church. Outside in the parking lot, Megan's red convertible Mustang waited.

Megan stopped, forcing everyone else to halt behind her. "Oh no. They already decorated my car. That wasn't supposed to happen yet!" Silver cans hung off the bumper. Someone had written, "Just married!" in bar soap.

"How are we going to sneak through town now?" Aspen asked. "All those cans are a dead giveaway that we're running out of here before our wedding."

"Maybe." Megan's red lips twisted into a mischievous smile. "But they'll be the perfect entrance when we return. Like a big marching band announcing our arrival."

"Are you sure we'll get back in time?" Lily asked as she crawled into the backseat next to Cassidy.

"He said to come now. I don't argue with instructions." Megan pulled onto the road, her veil flapping in the wind like a sail.

Megan turned on the car radio, blaring fifties love songs as she sped through town, the clattering cans drawing attention.

"What will the guys think?" Aspen bit her bottom lip as she waved to a child who jumped up and down as they passed. "Somebody is going to report us."

"We'll be back in time," Megan promised. "We're not leaving for good. Just for one last trip."

As they escaped Main Street and raced toward the countryside, the day was as perfect as a framed beach painting, all blue-sky glory and fragrant wildflower fields lining the untended edges of the road. Just beyond, Cassidy could see the shimmering lake in the distance, an idyllic wedding backdrop. The only question was why Joshua would call them to his cabin before the wedding.

As the car turned onto the long gravel drive toward Joshua's cabin, the wheel caught a pothole, bumping Cass into Lily.

"Sorry!" Megan cried, gripping the steering wheel as the car swerved. She slammed on the brakes, giving everyone whiplash.

"What's wrong?" Lily cried, rubbing her belly. This wasn't helping her nausea.

Megan hopped out, her eyes sliding over her car's exterior and landing on the back tire. "Just what I thought. When I hit that pothole, it caused a flat tire."

Aspen's face fell as she examined the tire. "How are we going to get back to the wedding in time?"

"Walk?" Megan shrugged.

"What?" Aspen's mouth dropped open. "I've got three-inch heels on."

"So do I," Megan said, starting up the hill toward Joshua's cabin. "Race you to the top," she tossed over her shoulder as the two brides hitched their skirts and attempted to run in their heels the rest of the way.

When they reached the cabin, Joshua rested on the steps, a paper clenched in his hands. As he glanced up, his eyes danced. "I've never seen such a pretty sight as all these brides." A warm smile stretched across his face as he opened his arms and hugged each girl.

"When you sent this cryptic note, we had to come," Megan said.

Joshua twisted his mouth. "Something secret. Everyone is waiting beyond the trees."

Cassidy looped her arm through his. "What do you mean?"

He glanced at her, his eyes twinkling. "You'll see."

He escorted Cassidy through the woods until they came to a clearing overlooking the lake. Five people stood waiting, including her parents with Liam, Jane, and Abby.

"What's going on?" she whispered, confused how they knew to meet here. Jane and Abby hadn't mentioned they were coming.

Joshua handed Cassidy over to Liam, who took her hands in his and gave her a smile that made her dizzy.

"Liam?" she asked, her eyes narrowing. "What is happening?"

Liam's gaze locked on to hers. "You told me you didn't want a fancy wedding. That you'd be happy exchanging vows with family surrounding us. But I don't want to wait until next summer. My mom might not have that long. And I've waited long enough for you. So what would you think if I asked you to marry me today?"

"Today?" Cassidy blinked, her heart hammering in her chest. "But Aspen and Megan are getting married today."

"Right now," he said, tightening his grip around hers. "Joshua will do the ceremony. And all the people we love are here."

She glanced at her sisters, as if she needed their support before she could say yes. They pressed in close, the force of their love spilling over onto them, like an unspoken blessing for this moment.

"Is it okay?" she asked.

"Of course it is," Megan said.

"One hundred percent," Aspen agreed.

Cassidy turned back to Liam. As he took her hands in his, she knew she'd never forget what it felt like to be surrounded by love, to know that the ending of her story was worth waiting for and that everything had been leading up to this.

As Joshua led them in reciting their vows, they weren't repeating words, but the promise of a lifetime, a family story passed down for generations, a love story that would never end.

AFTERWARDS, the story became Wild Harbor legend. Cass and Liam holding their own secret ceremony next to Joshua's cabin. The couple hadn't known that some years ago, Joshua had gotten his license to marry Cassidy's parents. When Liam had hatched the plan for the secret ceremony, Joshua had offered to do it at his cabin.

"It only seems fitting, given I married her parents," he'd remarked.

When the first wedding was finished, the group raced back to the beach for wedding number two of the day. Liam squeezed everyone into his car, even if they had an illegal number of people. When a cop stopped them on the way back, he told him how they'd been stranded with a flat and were now late for their own wedding. Since it was a small town and the cop knew the Woods family like his own, he took the two brides in his police car and turned on his sirens, racing toward the ceremony with Liam and Cassidy following behind.

It wasn't the entrance they'd imagined, but it was one that no one would forget, least of all their grooms, who were stunned to witness the beautiful brides hightailing it out of a police car in three-inch heels. All the guests turned to gawk as the women raced to the altar, their veils whipping in the wind, stopping to catch their breath as the harpist plucked out "Canon in D" for the second time. Even though they were fifteen minutes late, it was perfect timing with the sunset, like a glorious display of spilled paint across the horizon, bruised purples rolling into flamingo pinks and burnt orange.

The two couples were silhouetted against the setting sun, reciting vows that would become the thread of promise woven through their years.

Whatever happened down the road, they'd remember this day, how it had all unraveled like a giant spool of thread, their stories intertwined like a centuries-old quilt, separate pieces sewn into a blanket representing their family story.

Afterward, all the guests piled into cars and headed to the reception at DeSoto's, where laughter soared across the room, and couples linked arms on the dance floor, swaying to a melody all their own.

When the night faded into the collective town memory, all four siblings escaped to the now dark beach, where the girls ran into the surf holding their skirts in one hand and the hands of their husbands in the other, their voices floating through the darkness. There was a chill in the air that hadn't been present before, a hint of the next season to come, when they'd need their spouses more than ever. This wasn't their last evening together, but it reminded them that things would never look the same again. A family of four becoming four new families, expanding and changing like the seasons around them. When they went their separate ways, they left behind footprints lit by moonlight, the only evidence of their presence. By morning, the prints would be gone, but the memory would still burn in their minds.

Cassidy and Liam returned to Joshua's cabin that night, settling into the porch swing, listening to the rustling of the leaves. He'd offered it to them for their wedding night, and told them there was one more surprise before handing them an envelope.

"Don't open it until you get to the cabin," he said, giving them a mischievous wink.

Cassidy rested her head on Liam's shoulder as they nestled together on the swing, her gown swishing against her ankles while he unbuttoned his collar and wound his arm around her shoulders. She could hear his heartbeat thrumming in her ear as she settled against him.

He was hers forever.

"I don't know how we can top today," Cassidy reflected, as she intertwined her fingers with his.

He kissed the clasped fingers of her hand. "I hope we don't. And it's not over yet."

She sat up straighter. "Have you looked at Joshua's surprise?"

Liam pulled out the unopened envelope and dangled it in front of her.

She slid her finger under the seal and found a letter from Joshua.

Liam and Cassidy,
For years I've mulled over what I should do with this cabin as my time here on this earth is coming to a close. I don't have any children to give it to, and your family has been the closest thing to family that I have known. I always intended to pass it along to your parents, but then they bought their own place and all your siblings have settled in to their homes. Liam mentioned he wanted a place for his mother to spend her last years, and that

was when the idea occurred to me. It's a nice place to spend your final years, and I hope this cabin will suffice.

Eventually, when I'm long gone, bring your children here and tell them stories about old Joshua, who knew what family was, thanks to your family.

Joshua's scrawling signature filled the blank space at the bottom, the shaky cursive like a final goodbye, a tribute to a man who always gave more than he took.

She carefully folded the letter as she pulled away from Liam's arms.

"This is his cottage. His home. I can't believe he'd give it away."

"But that's just it," Liam remarked. "He always knew he'd let it go, and he was looking for the right person."

"And your mom gets her peaceful closing chapter," she murmured, turning the letter over in her hands.

Liam brushed Cassidy's hair from her face. "Now he wants us to write our own story and continue what he began here."

She leaned into him, finally understanding. "Our stories are never just ours alone."

She turned toward him, all the joy and pain from their past and future settling deep into her heart. As she kissed his lips, she'd never forget this moment, the way everything swelled and blossomed inside her, the horizon stretching out like unwritten chapters, its pages never ending.

EPILOGUE

ONE YEAR LATER

"Why do you think my parents want to have us over today? They know it's our anniversary," Cassidy said, packing the last of the towels for their outdoor beach party at her parents' home. Not that she didn't want to see them, but she'd been hoping to get away with Liam for a celebration, and she had a strange feeling her parents had an ulterior motive.

"It's practically everyone's anniversary," Liam said. "That's why they dubbed this date *three weddings and a baby.*"

"So you don't think they know something about our news?" she asked.

"Nope," he said, kissing her nose. "They're celebrating with us."

Her logical husband, no longer *Mr. Grumpy Pants,* was keeping her from jumping to conclusions. For the last year, life had been good for Cassidy and Liam. She'd finished school and her thriving after-school program was expanding into several counties. Even the bookstore was earning a small sum of money now, a delightful surprise after the community had rallied around it.

Liam's mother was still doing well, thanks to a new experimental treatment that had extended her life, and Cassidy's seizures remained under control. All in all, their little family had much to be thankful for.

"By the way, happy anniversary, my love." Cassidy leaned into her husband, wrapping her arms behind his neck. She kissed his lips softly, but when she attempted to pull away, he strengthened his grip around her waist and held her firm. If they weren't careful, she could forget all about the party.

"*Ew*, are you kissing again?" Abby interrupted with a disgusted look.

Cassidy reluctantly pulled away from Liam's kiss. "That's what married couples do." Then she gave Liam an apologetic look. "I'm sorry, but if we don't go, we'll be late."

"Rain check, later?" he murmured in her ear.

"You don't have to ask," she replied with a grin.

When Cassidy, Liam, and Abby arrived at their parents' lake house, a mouthwatering picnic was already waiting on a picnic table. Fried chicken, alongside an enormous bowl of fresh potato salad, anchored the feast with wedges of juicy watermelon piled Jenga-style on a platter. Two warm cherry pies cooled on the other end, dotted with a sprinkling of sanding sugar, made just for Bill. Her dad had always boasted about his wicked sweet tooth, especially for fresh fruit pies, and Becky was more than willing to spoil Bill.

As Abby and Liam ran over to join Megan and Finn in the lake, Cassidy spied a row of beach chairs where Lily perched, a chubby baby on her knee. As she bounced the baby up and down, he cooed and kicked, belting out a high-pitched squeal. The baby had entered the world rosy-cheeked and plump, and

Lily and Alex had chosen the name William, after their father, Bill. Lily was making faces to delight William, and he responded by giving her big toothless grins.

"Who wants to be held by your favorite aunt?" Cassidy held out her arms while Lily passed the squirming baby to her.

"Just don't let Megan hear you say that. She'll go ballistic and make it a favorite aunt competition."

"You're right," Cassidy said, addressing William in a singsong voice. "We can't let Aunt Megan know who your favorite aunt is." William agreed by blowing raspberries with his lips.

Cassidy's gaze followed Megan as she tossed a ball toward Abby, playing a game of keep away from Finn in the water. There were shouts of laughter and then a splash as everyone dove toward the beach ball.

"Megan is fabulous with kids," Cassidy remarked. "She'll make a great mom someday."

"I was thrilled when they announced they're starting the adoption process. I was afraid that she'd given up on her dream of motherhood."

Cassidy turned to see Becky make her way to the beach with a platter of barbecue ribs.

"Where's Dad?" Cassidy asked.

"Oh, he's coming. He can hardly tear himself away from his baseball game." Becky wedged the sweet glazed ribs next to the fried chicken. It looked like she was feeding the entire neighborhood.

"Are Matt and Aspen here yet?" Becky asked, shading her eyes as she scanned the beach.

"Not yet," Lily remarked, handing the baby a colorful teething ring. The baby kicked as he gnawed on the squishy toy.

"As soon as he gets here, will you tell me? I don't want the food to get cold."

"Better yet, let me eat now, and you won't have to worry about it," Matt replied as he rounded the house, his arms loaded with beach bags. He and Aspen had recently returned from a backpacking trip in the Rocky Mountains, and they looked sun-kissed and refreshed from the time away.

"I'll tell your father we're ready," Becky said. "Matt, can you call the rest of the family to the table? We've got some news to share, and I want us all together."

As she walked away, Cassidy and Lily glanced at each other.

"I knew it," Cassidy said in a low voice.

"Has Mom given you any hints?" Lily asked. "I'm worried."

"Do you think it's something bad?" Cassidy said. "Why else would they want us all together?"

As the rest of the family gathered, Bill and Becky made their way to the circle of chairs.

"Why don't you go ahead?" Becky gave Bill's hand a squeeze in silent solidarity.

Everyone grew quiet.

"We want to tell you about Joshua before you heard it in town," Bill said.

"Is everything okay?" Lily asked. "He's not dying, is he?"

"Do I look like I'm dying?" A voice said behind them. Joshua sunk his hands in his pockets, the sun reflecting off his face brilliantly, his eyes sparkling with life.

"Well, no," Lily replied. "It just seemed like . . ."

"I might be old, but I'm not dead yet," he interrupted with a wry smile.

"We didn't know you were coming," Becky said. "I thought you wanted us to tell them the news."

"I couldn't stay away. It seemed wrong to leave without saying goodbye."

"Wait," Cassidy said. "You're leaving? For how long?"

"Don't know."

"Where are you going? You've never left Wild Harbor before," Megan said.

"It's been a long time. *Too* long," he said. "It's time to fulfill a promise I made a long time ago."

"A promise?" Aspen asked.

"To your great-aunt Lizzie. When we were engaged, I promised her I'd see the world someday. We thought we'd travel after we were married, but then we broke things off, and I never fulfilled my end of the deal."

"She went without you," Aspen said. "She traveled a lot as a single woman."

"And I never did. Every time she returned from one of her trips, she'd tell me about it. It felt like salt in an old wound, even though she didn't mean it that way. She saw how I was stuck in my shop, always fixing these broken trinkets, never moving on. She wanted me to go. To never stop living."

"So why now?" Matt asked.

"It doesn't make sense, I know." Joshua rubbed the back of his neck. "I'm old. My world has become very small. Truth is, I don't know how much time I have left. But it's time to fulfill the promise to myself."

"But when will you return?" Lily asked. "You're like a grandpa to us."

He ruffled the baby's hair. "Don't know when I'll be back. But someday, when you least expect it, you'll see me in town, and it will be like I was never gone. Until then, your dad has the key to the shop, which I'm closing indefinitely. Who knows what might happen while I'm away? Maybe I'll meet some new friends. Or even fall in love again." He gave the girls a mischievous grin.

"If you fall in love," Becky instructed, "don't get hitched without us. I won't believe it otherwise."

"I wouldn't dare." Joshua winked.

"Not to change the subject," Bill interrupted, "but I'm hungry for that pie. Would you stay for dinner?"

Joshua nodded. "I'd be honored."

Cassidy held up her hand. "I'd like to share something," she said. "Liam and I weren't planning on making this announcement today, but with Joshua leaving, I want him to know." She looked at Liam, who nodded in agreement. "We're expecting a baby."

"What?" Abby exclaimed as she jumped out of her chair. "A baby?"

"Yep," Liam said, beaming.

"It's about time," Abby said. "I've been waiting *forever*."

"Oh, Cassidy," Becky gasped, taking her daughter in her arms. "I'm so happy!"

"William will have a cousin!" Lily exclaimed as all the siblings gathered around her.

"When are you due?" Aspen asked. "I need the details."

"In six months."

"Listen, you girls can talk all you want about babies, but there's some fried chicken calling my name," Matt said, pointing at the food table.

As the girls circled round her, Cassidy had the sense that this was a moment she'd always remember. Her whole family together with Joshua, laughing and crying, sharing food and stories that would live on in their memories for years.

She knew life wouldn't always be rosy. In the future, they would face hard things, but they'd always have each other to lean on. No matter what they faced, as long as they did it together, it would be more than enough.

Through a thousand sunsets and sunrises and a dozen generations.

Theirs was a story of a love that would never end, and a future where there were no goodbyes.

THE END

∾

Want a free sweet romcom novella?
The Dating Hypothesis is available when you sign up for Grace
Worthington's newsletter!
Go to graceworthington.com

The next series is coming soon on Amazon!
Renovation Romance:
A Sweet Romcom Series

RENOVATION ROMANCE SERIES

She never met a DIY project she couldn't tackle. Until she met him.

Their families have been enemies ever since they bought neighboring vacation homes. Over a decade later, she returns to the beach and discovers her childhood neighbor is not only a handsome hunk...but also the grumpiest neighbor ever.

Now she's trying to turn his life upside down and convince him that his home—and his heart—needs a renovation. What could possibly go wrong? *Everything.*

The Renovation Romance Series follows three different friends who make a pact to return every summer to their family vacation homes where they're involved in a renovation project and find love along the way.

THIS IS FOR YOU!

The end of a series and the beginning of another!
Get a free book at graceworthington.com

I love bookstores. You know the kind: small, quaint, smelling of newly printed paperbacks and old hardwood. They often have big windows in the front, displaying the latest releases. I'm like one of Pavlov's dogs when I walk by these storefronts, salivating over stories that promise me something: an escape to a never visited place, insight into the human condition, or experiencing that falling in love feeling all over again.

It's no surprise that I've included an adorable bookstore in this series. For those who are curious, my inspiration was Forever Books in St. Joseph, Michigan. Because I loved their name so much, but didn't want to duplicate it *exactly*, I switched the name of my fictitious store to Books Forever. (I know! So original!)

I'm thankful to say that it's still around and it's the type of place I could spend all day in. And that's a reason to celebrate. We still love stories. Books survive no matter what else changes.

I'm going to miss writing about the Woods family and their

THIS IS FOR YOU!

quirky neighbors and friends. But they'll continue to live on in Wild Harbor, especially old Joshua, who feels like a grandfather to all of us. I wanted his character to have some mystery and interesting quirks, but always be the guy you count on to steer the characters back to truth.

Sometimes my heart needs a little of his encouragement, and I'm sure yours does, too. Who knows? Maybe your own Joshua will show up when you least expect it with just the right thing to say.

My hope is that these books will provide something that is life-giving to you. Faith to press on. A reminder that you're loved unconditionally.

∿

Get my free romcom novella, *The Dating Hypothesis* at graceworthington.com

You can also join me on Instagram or Facebook @graceworthingtonauthor.

ACKNOWLEDGMENTS

To my readers: I can't thank you enough for your support. You make writing fun and I can't wait to give you more stories with love and laughter.

Thank you to my ARC team and those on social media who rallied around these stories in a big way. You are the best readers a new writer could ask for. I'm so grateful.

Thanks to my team: my editor, Emily Poole, and my wonderful beta readers who give me such valuable feedback, Leigh Ann, Joy, and Heidi. You help me see things I can't on my own. Thank you to Judy Zweifel for giving this story a final proofread and Kristen Ingebretson for the beautiful cover design.

Thanks to all my writing friends, including my friends online and in person. You keep me inspired.

My family, you are dear to me. Thank you for all the ways you love and support me.

To my husband: These books wouldn't exist without your constant encouragement. Thank you for being my first reader and for all the coffee.

ALSO BY GRACE WORTHINGTON

Love at Wild Harbor

Summer Nights in Wild Harbor

Christmas Wishes in Wild Harbor

The Inn at Wild Harbor

A Wedding in Wild Harbor

ABOUT THE AUTHOR

Grace Worthington writes sweet romance and romcom novels. She loves quaint small towns, and the beach is her happy place, which is why you'll find both in her books. She has a degree in English and lives with her husband and two children in Indiana.

A new sweet romcom is here! Get *The Dating Hypothesis* **at graceworthington.com.**

Made in United States
North Haven, CT
20 September 2022

24369775R00157